UNDER WATER

UNDER WATER

Casey Barrett

KENSINGTON BOOKS
http://www.kensingtonbooks.com

KENSINGTON BOOKS are published by

Kensington Publishing Corp.
119 West 40th Street
New York, NY 10018

All Kensington titles, imprints, and distributed lines are available at special quantity discounts for bulk purchases for sales promotion, premiums, fund-raising, educational, or institutional use.

Special book excerpts or customized printings can also be created to fit specific needs. For details, write or phone the office of the Kensington Special Sales Manager: Attn. Special Sales Department. Kensington Publishing Corp., 119 West 40th Street, New York, NY 10018. Phone: 1-800-221-2647.

Kensington and the K logo Reg. U.S. Pat. & TM Off.

Library of Congress Card Catalogue Number: 2017951247

ISBN-13: 978-1-4967-0968-4
ISBN-10: 1-4967-0968-3
First Kensington Hardcover Edition: December 2017

eISBN-13: 978-1-4967-0970-7
eISBN-10: 1-4967-0970-5
First Kensington Electronic Edition: December 2017

10 9 8 7 6 5 4 3 2 1

Printed in the United States of America

To the Linus

"That's why I like it better underwater," David said. "You don't have to worry about breathing."

Ernest Hemingway, *Islands in the Stream*

She's already taken her last breath. It was inhaled in one great hyperventilating gulp that will extend this final plunge for a few reflective minutes. She recognizes the irony in wanting to extend her life at the same moment she's decided to end it. As she settles onto the pool's bottom, she exhales. Bubbles burst from her mouth and float away like last words.

She looks up. The surface above her is shimmering and clear. She feels as if she's already crossed over, or under, into another world. It's quiet down here, not like the dryland world. Her body feels weightless and, finally, free.

She remembers the story of dolphin suicide. Depressed in captivity, certain tortured Flippers will close their blowholes and sink to the bottom of the tank, drowning in desperation. A noble decision, she thinks.

Her throat is starting to constrict, her diaphragm starting to spasm, her lungs deflating. Carbon dioxide is building like a rising red tide through her blood. The urge to breathe is overwhelming. She could swim up at anytime, but she won't. She can feel herself beginning to lose consciousness, her brain deprived and demanding oxygen, or else.

Not much time left.

Chapter 1

She looked determined to stop time. Tall, maybe sixty, though she'd never admit it. Her face was feline; pulled and ironed and injected until the mask bore little resemblance to the original product. *Aging* and *gracefully* were two words that she had never paired. Below a long neck was a chest that stood too high, framed for admiration like fine art. She stood above me in bare feet, looking down with distaste. Pale, pedicured toes curled over the edge of the pool.

"Lady says she has some business with you, Duck," called the lifeguard from across the deck.

She crossed her arms and waited, and did not remove her oversized sunglasses. A sleeveless ivory dress covered a body denied indulgence; an excess of gold jewelry matched the color of her dyed, chin-length hair. The chlorine hung heavy in the uncirculated air. Whatever it was she wanted to talk about, it couldn't wait.

I climbed out and extended a wet hand. She offered a dry one.

"Duck Darley," I said. "What can I do for you?"

"You don't remember me," she said. "Do you, Lawrence?"

"I'm sorry, you are . . ."

She took off her sunglasses, and I took a closer look. Beneath all that work was a woman I couldn't forget. The memory floated up like a dead fish from the bottom of a dark lake. Her name was Margaret McKay, the mother of an old friend, an old teammate who went all the way. Charlie McKay: he won Olympic gold some Games ago, days after the death of his father. Appeared on a Wheaties box a few weeks later. We hadn't stayed in touch.

"Mrs. McKay, wow, how have you been?"

"It must be twenty years," she said. "You look well. I'm glad to see you've stayed in the water."

"Only way I stay sane," I said. "How's Charlie?"

"He's fine, gone into finance like his father. Long hours, lots of stress, but he seems to enjoy it."

She spoke with a crisp cluck of permanent annoyance. Looking at her cosmetic re-creation, I mourned the beauty that had been there as I remembered. She was the mom crush of every boy on the team back then, a source of endless innuendo for her son. I went off to grab my towel from a bench, began to dry off as I let her gather her thoughts.

"Lawrence, my apologies for meeting you so early," she said. "But I could use your immediate assistance with something."

The name on my birth certificate reads: Lawrence James Darley, Jr. The Senior version of that name achieved enduring shame after it turned out my father's fortune was built on a far-reaching fraud. I was twelve years old when the story broke, a scandal made to order for the *New York Post*: the wretched excess of a crooked king. Things went bad after that. Everything in my once-privileged life was stripped away, except the nickname. I'd become Duck in grade school, due to a waddling walk and a natural affinity for the water. Someday I'll have my given name officially changed and shed the disgrace of it for good, but it always feels like too much work.

"Who told you I'd be here?" I asked.

"Lorraine Hart? She said you did some work for her last year. When I heard the last name, I was very surprised to make the connection."

"Did Lorraine also mention that I have a phone number and can be reached during normal business hours?"

She gave a slight smile that didn't move her cheeks. "Lorraine informed me that you weren't the easiest person to reach, that you have no email and seldom return calls. She suggested that this might be the best place to find you. She's a dear friend; I trust you remember the work you did for her."

One side of her mouth twitched, enough to say she knew details. I had done some divorce work for the lovely Lorraine a few months back. It ended in a not unusual way: proved husband was cheating; evidence secured her an eight-figure settlement. She paid me with a generous check and a grateful blow job on her ex-husband's former oceanfront deck in East Hampton. We'd stayed friendly. I hadn't worked since, but now that check was long spent. I make it a policy never to seek work. It has to find me. I've seen where ambition can get you.

"How is your father?" she asked. "Do you see him often?"

"Still incarcerated. And no," I said.

"I'm sorry, I didn't mean to pry."

"So, how immediate is this problem of yours? I'm hungry, and you're sweating. Let's not catch up on the bad old days."

Margaret McKay gave me a look, then turned and headed toward the exit. She said, "Then go dress and take me somewhere where we can speak in private."

I followed her out like the scolded oversize brat she remembered. Two decades go by, and some impressions never change.

Out on the sidewalk, it was a brilliant blue September

day, the sort of too perfect morning that makes you look out toward the Hudson and search for low-flying planes headed for tall buildings. Margaret had slipped back into high heels that capped a pair of long yoga-toned legs. She dropped her phone into a reptile-skin handbag and waited for me to lead the way.

I guided her to my local diner, Joe's, on the corner of 16th and Third. There was an open table toward the back by the bathrooms. The rest of the seats were claimed by self-segregated groups of NYPD cadets. Fresh-faced Irish boys, thick Latina women, and stern black guys, all huddled in packs of three or four over their eggs and coffee. They had that itching insecure energy of almost authority. A year from now their chests would be puffed out with cop pride as they busted kids for scoring blow outside East Village bars.

Manuel the waiter brought over a coffee and a Beck's and no menu. He looked at Margaret and waited for some instruction. She told him water would be fine, and he called over for Joe to start on my western omelet, nothing for the *puta*.

"How long have you been doing this sort of work?" she asked, eyeing the morning beer.

I took a searing gulp of the coffee, chased it with a long pull. "What sort of work is that?"

"The sort that involves helping those in need," she said. "For a price."

"Like a superhero for hire?"

"Don't be assy, Lawrence. You're an investigator, correct?"

"Listen, if you're looking for some former cop with a tragic tale and an obsession for justice, you should probably look elsewhere. I'm a finder. Private eyes are passé. Besides, the state of New York won't grant me a license to practice."

"And why is that?"

"Youthful indiscretions."

She considered that. Some demand specifics, and depending on my sense of the client, sometimes I share them. Sometimes I leave it at two words open to interpretation. If they get up and leave, seek out someone with a gold plate on a door and a team of snoops with all the latest spyware, so be it.

Margaret McKay didn't ask for details. Maybe she already knew them. They're not hard to find. I used to deal a little weed. A little became a lot when I wasn't looking. One rainy day when I was twenty, getting off the 4 train at 59th Street, I got stopped with a backpack full of the stuff—two pounds, to be exact. Part of which was separated into two-gram plastic canisters, meaning intent to distribute—meaning, a Class C felony, punishable by up to five years. If my family still had any money, an expensive lawyer would have been hired, and I would have been freed with a dismissal to "Drug Court" and a bit of community service. Instead, the judge, a righteous fat woman named Susan Duvel, relished the shame of my name. She gave me two years. I served thirteen months. Enough time for a formerly rich white kid to find out that his fears about prison were well founded.

"Well, license or not, it appears you've earned a fine reputation," she said. "Lorraine said you were excellent."

"Guess I know where to look for things."

She liked that. Her cheeks tried to lift with her smile.

"So, I do divorce work, mostly. Find the occasional fuck-up. Which one is it for you?"

She took off her sunglasses and set them on the table. I doubted she removed them often. That's where the years hid. No amount of work around the edges could erase the worry and the decades of mean wisdom. Her eyes were the darkest brown, almost black, like the tinted windows of a celebrity's car. They could see out, but you could never peer in without pressing your nose to the glass. And no one would ever let you get that close. Those eyes narrowed, and I lost the staring contest.

"It's the latter, I'm afraid. The fuck-up in question is my eighteen-year-old daughter. She's been missing for the last week."

"I didn't know Charlie had a sister," I said.

"No reason you should. Madeline was much younger. You quit the team before she was born. I didn't think I was able to have children any longer. Steven and I were content being the parents of an only child. But somehow I became pregnant again in my forties. It was not an easy pregnancy, and Madeline has not been any easier since the day she was born. Then, of course, Steven died when she was very young . . ."

Her shoulders sagged, but she recovered quickly. I remembered the whole sad story. The media had lapped it up when Charlie McKay was the golden boy Olympic swimming champion du jour. He dedicated his gold medals to his recently deceased father and his rock of a mother. *The strongest woman on earth*, he told the cameras. Madeline would have been about six at the time. I didn't remember her in a single shot.

"A week isn't very long," I told her. "Maybe she's just . . ."

"It is for her," she said. "My daughter maintains frequent contact with me. It is often troubled and unpleasant, but we speak or exchange text messages almost daily. That is, until seven days ago."

"Have you considered notifying the police, filing a missing persons report?"

She gave a quick snort. "Please. I have no faith in those dim little blue men. And I certainly don't want them sniffing around in my life."

Two cadets stiffened behind her and glanced back. They

were a pair of big-backed Irish guys with buzz cuts and emerging neck fat. A silence stretched over their table, their eggs frozen on forks in mid-bite.

"When was your last contact?" I asked.

"It was last Monday, Labor Day. She sent a text that said 'I'm so sorry.' Nothing else. It is not like Madeline to apologize—for anything. I've no idea what she was referring to. It could have been any number of things. She was last seen, by her brother, the day before at our country house in Rhinebeck. It seems she left in a state soon after he arrived. Things have not been . . . easy for her. I wrote back, left voice mails, notes at her apartment. No response. I'm worried."

"How have things not been easy?"

"Madeline has always struggled," she said. "She came out angry, as some children do, I suppose. It was mostly manageable when she was younger, and she was so talented as a swimmer, just like her brother. For a time, that seemed like the outlet that would save her. But soon after she turned twelve, it got bad. Her temper became uncontrollable, her grades awful. I found cocaine in her bedroom when she was thirteen."

I let her relive the memory and waited as the silence stretched. She put her sunglasses back on; then almost immediately she took them off again. Manuel brought over a fresh Beck's, my western omelet, and an unopened bottle of Tabasco. I shook it and unsealed it and drenched my eggs while Margaret continued the tale of her problem child:

"We tried therapy, of course. She refused to speak. We tried putting her on medication, but she stopped taking it after a short time, and went back to her self-medicating. She was almost expelled from Miss Hewitt's when they caught her high on several occasions. But Madeline kept swimming, in her uncommitted way, coming and going whenever she felt like it. We wanted to make it the one constant in her life, the one place where she would always be special. She really is so talented. Even as she's spiraled downward she remains nationally ranked in the butterfly. We keep praying that at some point she'll embrace her gift and get through all that anger and self-destruction."

"I'm sorry, Mrs. McKay, I know your husband passed away; who is *we*?"

"Myself and Coach Marks," she said. "You must remember him."

Sure I did. The guy had tried to save me too. Like her daughter, I had proven to be a lost cause. Blame it on a broken family at an impressionable age, on too much temptation for a teenager in the big city. Old story. Happy families are all the same; the unhappy ones only think they carve out original issues.

Teddy Marks was a legend in the swimming world. Charlie McKay wasn't the first Olympian he'd coached, and he wouldn't be the last. He started Marks Aquatics, fresh from the Navy SEALs, back in the mid-eighties out of a narrow dungeon pool on East 26th Street. Now it was a national powerhouse, an Olympian factory. He was a long, angular man, a menace of motivated energy, with a whistle through his teeth that I still hear in my sleep. He had that coach's magic; he believed in you more than you believed in yourself. I understood why Madeline kept coming back. Quitting had been easy, but disappointing Coach Marks had left years of guilt.

"He's a good man," I said.

She nodded, took a sip of water. "He's been a saint."

"How has Madeline's relationship been with Marks?"

"Much like my own, I suppose. One filled with bottomless patience and diminishing hope."

"And you've reached out to her friends, to anyone in

her life who might have heard from her? Does Madeline have a boyfriend?"

Margaret McKay reached down and opened her bag. She removed a folded brown envelope and placed it on the table. She said, "Maddie has had her own apartment since graduating from Hewitt last spring. I pay for it, of course. It's my name on the lease and all the bills come to me, but she insisted that she needed her own space. It's on Barrow Street in the West Village. She's enrolled nearby at the New School, but we'll see."

She reached inside the envelope and took out two pictures. I wiped my hands and picked one up. Madeline's yearbook shot from her senior year. She wasn't smiling. She had unwashed brown hair that fell from her head like a moldy shower curtain. The prim Hewitt's uniform looked like a Halloween costume on her. There was a stud in her nose, but no other jewelry and no makeup. All that effort to look unattractive wasn't working. Her cheekbones were model high; her eyes were dark and dull, ready for the runway. She had the wide, fishy mouth of a Hollywood starlet. Her lips looked like a dirty Internet search.

The other picture was of Madeline at a concert, her arm around a tall, skinny kid in a tank top and torn jeans. She was dressed in a short vintage plaid skirt; a ripped Runaways T-shirt showed off a flat stomach with another piercing in her belly button. The couple gave the camera a smiling scowl. Behind them were a packed floor and a stage, Bowery Ballroom from the looks of it.

"I took that one off of her bedroom mirror at her apartment," said Margaret. "That's her boyfriend, or was. His name is James Fealy, a film student at NYU. He claims they broke up three weeks ago, and he hasn't spoken to her since."

"When you went by her place, did you take anything

else? Any journals, other photos, anything else that might give you some indication of her day-to-day life?"

"No, there was nothing else of note. The apartment was filthy, but otherwise in order. There was ten days of mail."

"Okay," I said. "So, you talked to the ex-boyfriend. What about other friends?"

"I wish I knew. Maddie never had many close girl-friends growing up. There was one, Lucy Townes, a girl on the team. She was the only girl who ever came by our home that I can recall."

"Have you spoken to her?"

Margaret McKay's eyes began to swell. Tears dampened the edges of her mascara. She grabbed at her sunglasses and pushed them back over her face. "I just don't know," she said. "I know so little of my daughter's life. I feel like we communicated every day, and I never learned a thing about her. It was always dealing with her anger, about her allowance, about missing practice, that sort of thing. I don't know how to reach Lucy, or anyone else that she might be close to. The only way I was able to reach James was through his father. Charlie works with him. I called him the day after I received her text. Such an unpleasant boy; he was of no help."

She sighed the way a woman sighs when she knows a relationship is over, after all the fighting's been done and there's just the mess to clean up off the floor. She said, "Tell me your rate, and then please go find my daughter."

I told her. She didn't flinch, just went back into the envelope and produced a wrapped stack of crisp bills about half an inch thick. "To get you started," she said. "There's five thousand, for expenses. I hope it goes without saying that price is not a concern."

"Of course," I said. I waited a respectful five seconds before reaching for the bills. Didn't count them.

She pushed over the rest of the envelope. "Inside you'll

find Madeline's personal information: her address; apartment keys; cell phone records; email accounts; bank statements. Madeline receives a generous allowance of twenty thousand dollars each month. Somehow she manages to spend every dime by the end of the fourth week. On the first of September, as usual, the funds were direct deposited. She removed three thousand dollars over the first few days of the month, but has not withdrawn anything since Labor Day. If there is any activity on her account, I'll let you know right away. Her latest wireless statement indicates a large number of calls and texts to James Fealy. She also tried to reach Coach Marks the same day she sent me that text. He missed her call, and she left no message. After that, nothing."

I peered into the envelope, flipped through the documents, searched for anything she might have missed.

"You'll also find all of my contact information, and Charlie's, as well. You should call him. He'll like hearing from you. Please let me know of anything else you might need. Like I said, everything comes to me."

"Did you see Madeline's passport at her place?" I asked.

"I didn't, no," she said. "But I must admit, I didn't give it the most thorough of searches. I try to respect my daughter's privacy," she said with a note of defense.

"Is it possible that Madeline could have left—"

"Left the country? No. My daughter has a phobia of travel. She is very particular. She's only comfortable in her own bed—in the city or sometimes upstate. It makes swim meets very difficult, I can assure you. Leaving the country is out of the question. She has not traveled abroad since she was eleven years old."

"I assume she's on Facebook, Twitter, Instagram? Have you checked her social media for any updates since you last heard from her?"

"She is the rare teenage girl who isn't, I'm afraid. Madeline has always valued her privacy. And friends, well, they never seemed to be a priority."

Margaret McKay looked down at her daughter's file. The mystery of her life seemed to bring physical discomfort. She shifted in her seat, waited for the waves of pain to pass.

We'd reached the point in the conversation that no parent of a missing child wants to hear. I waved to Manuel for another Beck's. "Mrs. McKay, do you think your daughter could have hurt herself . . ."

"My daughter is alive," she said. "A mother would know."

"I'm sure she is. But your daughter hasn't used her cell phone in over a week. She hasn't touched her bank account either. And you think it's unlikely she could be staying anywhere but her apartment or your country house, where she was last seen. With all this in mind, we have to consider the worst."

Margaret stiffened but did not speak.

"Consider it only to eliminate that first," I said without much punch. "You mentioned finding cocaine in her room when she was young. To your knowledge, is Madeline still using?"

"I don't know. Probably. Most likely."

She stood up on unsteady legs and looked down at my half-finished omelet and empty beer. The hem of her ivory dress ended just above the knee. Her toned legs vibrated with distress signals as she gathered her bag and pushed at her glasses. "I need to go. Please find her, Lawrence. It was very nice seeing you."

Manuel came by with another Beck's, and together we watched her go through the window of the diner. The two pictures of Madeline stared up at me, an angry little girl lost. Her mouth, that wide, fishy swath, was her most striking feature. She wasn't a girl forgotten in a crowd. Like her brother and her mother, she radiated a presence that people would remember. I sat there sipping my beer, looking into Margaret McKay's water glass. It was marked with lipstick like a dried circle of blood.

Chapter 2

I walked the block back to my apartment, back to Elvis passed out on my side of the bed. I opened the back garden door and waited for the hound to rouse himself from his slumber. He eyed me without moving, then stretched and jumped off the bed and ambled past my knees outside. He lifted his leg over the first withered plant he saw. Some best friend. He spent some time snorting and sniffing around the perimeter of the garden and then collapsed in a sliver of sun.

Home. A rent-controlled subterranean garden apartment on East 17th Street, 219A. Affordable thanks to a sympathetic lifelong bachelor who once worked with my father and lives in the four-story brownstone above. It has low ceilings, a bedroom without closets, a galley kitchen, and a small front room stuffed with books and little else of value. And the garden—you can't beat the private outdoor space.

I grabbed another beer from the fridge and joined Elvis on the patio. Then I called Cassandra Kimball.

A hard woman's voice answered, "The Chamber."

"Is Cass available?"

"I think she's just finishing a session; let me check."

I waited on hold, sat back and relished my sunken little

slice of the city. I heard my landlord, old Mr. Petit, puttering in the kitchen a floor above. I knew he liked to watch me out here, with thoughts I didn't care to consider. It was a small price to pay for this below-market patch of shade and hints of sun.

"This is Cass."

"An early morning session?" I asked. "Sounds like they're beating the door down for you."

"I'm the one who does the beating, darlin'. What's going on?"

"We have a new client. You have any time to spare?"

"For you, always. My last session finishes at six today. I'll come by after. Think you can stay sober that long?"

I told her I'd try. She hung up. I looked at my beer. Number four, not yet nine a.m. Might want to slow the pace a bit.

When she isn't torturing kinky, pain-loving men at her day job, Cass is my sometime partner. At the Chamber, she's known as Mistress Justine, a nod to the namesake of her profession, the Marquis de Sade. *Justine* was an early work by the eponymous sadist; its original title was *The Misfortunes of Virtue*.

She was private about her work there and lighthearted about its requirements, but we both knew too well the dangers that could lurk behind those whips and role play. That's how we met. Cass was one of my first clients. She was being stalked by one of her slaves. I was informed that the occasional stalking came with the territory. The owner of the dungeon, Mistress Rebecca, said it happened all the time. There were always slaves who developed obsessions for the ones that administered the pain they required. This one was an ineffectual little man named Clifford. Scaring off a whimpering masochist, I figured, how hard could it be? But I failed to remember that every man is effective when holding a handgun.

Back then, I was a clean-living wannabe badass filled with righteousness. I'd taken my parole seriously, vowed never to go back, and wasn't touching anything stronger than coffee. I'd devoured every piece of pulp in the prison library, envisioned myself a real life Jack Reacher. I knew what I was going to do when I got out. Who needed a licensed firearm? I got into aikido instead. Went to the dojo every day until I earned a few degrees on my black belt. Started working the fringes, finding different things for different folks, built up some nice word of mouth. Then Cass called.

One cold winter night, it was January twelfth, just after two a.m., I approached Clifford on a Lower East Side sidewalk across from the old Motor City bar. Cass was inside partying. Cliff had been lurking outside, smoking and swearing to himself, waiting to follow his mistress wherever she went next. He would never approach, never speak to her, but he continued to move in closer. He was more nuisance than threat. A few days earlier, Cass had informed him that she wouldn't see Clifford for sessions any longer if she caught sight of him outside the dungeon again. But he couldn't resist. I approached, too casual, too confident in my aikido-honed instincts, a cocky character from a bad action movie. I asked him for a light, then ground out my cigarette as soon as it was sparked. Told him that I'd like to speak to him about Mistress Justine. I often consider the ways I failed in my training. This is the moment that aikido prepares you for. An attacker unveils a weapon, and he is disarmed and neutralized before his violent thought can become action. I failed. Clifford slipped a .38 from his coat pocket and fired off a shot into my side before I could reach his wrist. I turned left and took it through the spleen, which I learned later was better than turning right. That would have meant the liver and greater harm. I was able to disarm him and break his arm, but too late. I was unconscious for the rest of it.

It was during my recovery that my living became a little less clean. I developed a taste for painkillers. The drinking became a bit of a lifestyle. On the upside, the incident increased my profile. My caseload increased, and so did my rates. Cass became a friend, fueled by that inevitable guilt. When I tried to become more than that, her denial came cruel and clean. But somewhere in there she became fascinated with my trade, and she knew I could use her help. You might think it comes with a sense of charity, but that would miss Cass's true nature. Truth is, the woman is addicted to secrets. That's what fuels her work at the dungeon, and that's what thrills her about helping with my cases.

Secrets. I wish I knew hers. She keeps them hidden better than anyone I've ever met.

Time to get to work. How long had it been, five, six months? Two seasons of swimming and drinking and occasional visits to the dojo had left me feeling like the idle rich I might have been. It's hard work to avoid making a living. I never wanted to. When I was the young, proud son of loaded Lawrence Darley, the concept never occurred to me.

I opened the envelope and shuffled through the cell phone bills and the bank statements, the contact list and the pictures. Madeline was hiding somewhere amidst all that paperwork. But this was no way to ease into my first case off a layoff. Better to hit the pavement, poke around the quarry's natural habitat. I grabbed Madeline's apartment keys, slipped the contact list into the back pocket of my jeans, and splashed some water into Elvis's bowl. The ungrateful hound ignored me on my way out.

I found a cab heading south down Third Avenue, gave

the address and told the cabbie to take 9th Street, always one of the only dependable streets to beat the crosstown traffic. We passed by NYU buildings, the dorms full of new arrivals. Young girls wearing tight purple T-shirts, young guys clad in baseball caps and flip-flops. My window was down, and at a stoplight I found myself staring at two young blondes in skirts that barely covered their tan thighs. One of them stared back; the other looked uncomfortable. The light turned green as I calculated that I was almost twice their age. They were Madeline's peers, though the girl in those pictures looked far older.

Between Fifth and Sixth Avenues, I admired the rows of perfect brownstones. There's one on the south side of the street closer to Sixth that has always stirred my New Yorker's real estate lust. The house is a classic redbrick half covered in ivy with Victorian-style double front doors of glazed glass. Through the parlor windows, floor-to-ceiling bookshelves are visible along one wall; a grand piano sits in the opposite corner. The thought of lying on a couch in that room, pulling a book at random from the shelves, and reading while a beautiful woman plays that piano . . . Goddamn, I wish I were still rich. I like to think someone brilliant and worthy lives there. A man of medicine, perhaps, a man busy curing disease, with a poet wife, and three perfect children who study history and want to work in education. But it's probably just a finance jerk on his third marriage with four other homes in other cities that are just as beautiful. He'll never appreciate any of them.

Madeline lived in a seven-story, turn-of-the-century co-op at the corner of Barrow and West 4th. Apartment 7M. It was the sort of Village residence stocked with single girls living in studios and one-bedrooms, still receiving plenty of help from home. Five grand a month for six hundred square feet—but hey, it was all about the location. The doorman glanced up as I crossed the marble lobby. I gave him her name, and he took his time scanning a list beneath the desk.

"ID," he grunted.

I handed it over, waited some more. A game of Texas Hold 'Em was paused on his phone next to his list. He didn't appreciate being interrupted.

"Good cards?" I asked.

"Seventh floor," he said, handing back my license. He waved me to the elevators in the back.

I stood there watching the numbers descend above the elevator door. As the elevator reached 3, a door opened off to the right. A small sign by the buzzer read SUPER. A round Latino man wearing cargo shorts and a Hawaiian shirt stepped out and stopped in front of me.

"Help you?"

"Going up to a friend's apartment," I said. "In seven M. Name is McKay."

"She's not there," he told me.

"I know that," I said. "I have her keys. Her mother asked me to stop by."

"She hasn't been there for a week or so. I have her mail, inside." He motioned to his apartment behind him. "The mother, she stop by a few days ago, asked me to collect mail and to call her when she come home."

"That's nice of you."

He shrugged, looked over at the doorman back playing poker on his phone. "Lot of ladies live here," he said. "Lot of men stopping by. My job to keep an eye out."

"Any men stop by her place?"

"Just one. Boyfriend, I think. Tall, skinny guy."

The elevator door opened, and I moved to get in. I said, "You want to join me?"

He thought about it for a second, decided to trust me. He shook his head and said, "Hope everything's okay."

"Me too," I replied as the doors closed.

The apartment was ready for an open house. Through the foyer, a bright living and dining room with high-beamed ceilings and exposed brick. The furniture was modern and comfortable, everything matching just so, from curtains to coffee table: the work of a well-paid decorator. A framed Rothko print was over the couch, another by Jasper Johns in the dining room area. A long casement window at the end of the room offered postcard views of the Empire State Building. Issues of *Interview* and *EW* and *New York* magazine were stacked in piles next to the couch. In the open kitchen, a single wineglass sat upside down on a drying rack next to the sink. The fridge was empty except for a Brita water filter and a few Coronas in the side door. There was a frosted bottle of Ketel One in the freezer, along with full ice trays, and little else.

I walked into a bedroom done in tasteful earth tones. A queen bed was made crisp and plump, the work of a cleaning lady, not any teenage girl. All that was missing was the chocolate on the pillow. A print by Gauguin, Tahitian period, hung over the bed. Another by Klimt was over a bare desk in the corner. Her nightstand was devoid of any personal touches; the diary inside the drawer was full of empty pages. Along the edge of a standing full-length mirror, there was an outline in the side where Mrs. McKay must have removed the picture of Madeline with her boyfriend.

The bathroom was freshly scrubbed and equally sparse. A toothbrush and toothpaste, a black brush tangled with black hairs, but no cosmetics or moisturizers or any of the accessories one might expect from a rich city girl. There was nothing interesting in the medicine cabinet, no orange prescription bottles to be found, only a stick of Secret deodorant. Dry swimming suits, cut for racing, were draped over the towel rack. A pair of smoked Swedish goggles hung from the doorknob. I tried the walk-in closet. More tidying by the cleaning lady, but not much to tidy: racks less than half full, with what appeared to be thrift store finds. Tattered T-shirts, moth-eaten sweaters, a beaten black leather jacket. Black combat boots and flip-flops were her only choices in footwear. Whatever it was she spent her twenty grand a month on, it wasn't beauty or fashion.

I patted around the upper shelves of the closet, looking under stacks of sweaters and jeans. Felt around inside every jean, skirt, and jacket pocket. Went back out to her room and dug through her dresser. I felt like a pervert as I sifted through her lingerie drawer. Mostly unsexy cottons and utilitarian bras, but at the bottom, I found a few pieces from Kiki de Montparnasse. Black lace numbers made for pleasure viewing; and wrapped in black tissue paper in the back corner, a pair of gold handcuffs. Lucky Mr. Fealy.

I checked under her bed. A few swim bags, a large empty suitcase, a box of art supplies. I went back out to the living room and had a seat on the sofa, flipped through the top issue of *Interview* in the basket. Lady Gaga talks to Madonna. I gazed out the window at the Empire State crowing in the center of the skyline. Then I crossed the room to the flat-screen standing on a long, low cabinet. The center doors hid the electronics and the remote controls; the side drawers were empty except for a Twilight Saga box set. It was the "Ultimate Collector's Edition," complete with movie stills and special features. On top of the box, the inscription read: *And so the lion fell in love with the lamb* . . .

I opened the box and sifted through the stills. Beneath the last one I found what her mother had missed: Madeline's stash. I counted eight small plastic bags, three mostly empty with white coke residue. Maybe enough to scrape together a line or two if the dealer wasn't calling you back. There were a few nuggets of nice looking weed in another bag. Six mollies sealed in another. A colorful collection of pills: light blue Xanax, yellow Vicodin, pink Oxy, the usual rainbow. None of this really worried me, a pretty standard party girl collection, but the last bit did. It was a bundle of tiny unwrapped paper squares, some light brown remnants left behind. Heroin. Not exactly performance enhancers for a nationally ranked athlete. I helped myself to a sampling of the pills and returned the rest to the bottom of the box set.

Then I went into the kitchen, poured myself a wineglass of water, and washed down a couple Vicodin. I took another pass around her apartment. A slow search around all the same soulless spaces, and any I might have missed. No passport to be found, no framed pictures of friends or family, nothing that might reveal the person who lived here. The drugs were the only personal remains left behind.

Down in the lobby, the round super was waiting for me in his cargo shorts, along with a trio of yelping dachshunds pulling at a three-headed leash. "Find anything?" he asked over the noise.

I ignored the question. "Has anyone else been by her apartment in the past week?"

"Only the mother," he said. "And the housekeeper. She come every Friday."

"No sign of the boyfriend lately?"

He gave it a second's thought. "No. Maybe two, three weeks?" he said. "He used to be here all the time. Many nights a week."

"Maybe they broke up," I offered.

"Maybe." He shrugged. "After the mother leave, I check the security tapes. I not here to see everything all the time, you know? We have cameras in the lobby, in elevator, and in the halls on every floor. No one come here for her, only the mother. Last time I see girl on the security is

Labor Day weekend, on Saturday night. She leave around midnight and not come back."

"Was she carrying anything? A bag, a suitcase?"

"Don't think so. Would have to check again."

"Could I see them?"

"Not now," he said. He motioned across the vacant lobby and down at his whining dogs. "Too busy, maybe if you come back later."

I thanked him and produced a business card. "Name's Duck," I told him, extending a hand. "Anyone else comes around, think you can give me a call?"

"I'm Angel." He shook my hand and examined my card. "I knew you were no friend."

"No," I said. "But it looks like our girl could use one."

Chapter 3

I found an empty bench in Christopher Park across from an aging drag queen. He wore a scarlet dress and ripped stockings and stilettos and had a day's stubble coming through last night's makeup. He gave me a tight smile and went back to his *Post*. It was just the two of us, along with four frozen ghosts: a gay rights sculpture of two couples painted white as death—the men were standing, the women seated on a bench next to them. They seemed to sense I was there. The small park was haunted by distant city spirits, their melancholy lingering for another age.

I sat still for a few minutes enjoying the cloudless blue morning. A light bite of wind carried the coming colors of fall. A warm sun offered its last best kiss of summer. It was too beautiful to trust. The city in September . . . So easy to be fooled.

I reached in my back pocket for the contact list. I considered calling Mrs. McKay, telling her about the drugs, but figured it was too soon for a check-in. Charlie McKay's number was the first one she'd listed. May as well start at the top.

Broken memories from another lifetime . . . Charlie fucking McKay. I was better than him, once. Back when we were ten years old, I was a top-ranked, record-breaking little stud. I used to smoke him in every stroke. Coach Marks had pulled my father aside and whispered about my Olympic potential when Charlie was still a slow-lane chump who could barely swim a lap of butterfly. And so much for that. Top young athletes are like child stars—poor bets for long-term gains. The day Charlie won his first Olympic gold, I was dealing with a coke hangover on Avenue D.

I called his office line at Soto Capital. He picked up on the first note of the first ring.

"McKay here," he said.

"Charlie, it's Duck Darley. Long damn time."

"Who?" There were urgent voices in the background. I had that instant guilt you feel anytime you call a trading floor. What could you possibly want that could be more important?

"It's Duck Darley," I said, louder. "From Marks Aquatics. Your old—"

"Oh shit! Duck. Yeah, man, I was expecting—wait, hold on a second." I heard hard typing, and then he snapped, "Yes, I already fucking told you.

"Sorry, man, I can't really talk," he said. "But I'm psyched you're helping us out with Madeline."

"Is there a time we can meet up? Maybe grab a drink after—"

"Goddamn it, I already told you! Wait, hang on, Duck." In the background, muttered apologies from some sad-sack junior associate. Then he was back. "Look, I'm really sorry, Duck, but I gotta go. I'll be honest—I think Mom's overreacting. Maddie'll turn up, I know it. But we should catch up soon, okay?"

The line was dead before I could ask when. Nice to hear big brother's concern. Then I remembered the all-consuming urgency of the markets, the way my father would scream and hang up if you dared call him at work without an emergency. It was the nature of certain beasts.

The White Horse Tavern was a few blocks up. It's a tourist trap thanks to dead poet's lore, but not before noon on Tuesdays. Then it will always be a professional place for professional drinkers. A fine refuge.

There were two old sentries seated at the end of the bar with a stool between them. I remembered them from past daytime trips; they'd shared their sad story with me a while back. They were both retired New York City firemen. As fate would have it, they retired from the FDNY in the summer of 2001. That September they lost damn near every friend they ever had in the Trade Center. Now they drank away their survivor's guilt and wished they'd died a fast, heroic death rather than this slow, wet march. They sipped at their whiskeys and didn't recognize me.

I didn't recognize the bartender. She was a big-chested redhead with watery eyes and lipstick smeared on her teeth. She poured me a Stella, and I took a seat at a small table in the corner.

I knew where I had to go next, but I didn't know how I would face him. I would need some fortifying. He would smell it on me, but I didn't care. The roots of disappointment were planted plenty of years ago. How long had it been? More than two decades since I was one of them. There had been some calls through the early years, always answered. *Just calling to catch up, see how the team's doing*, I'd say. *You can always come back*, he'd say. *You laid the base. We'll get you back in shape in no time . . .* I'd tell him maybe, that I was thinking about it, but I'd never show. He stopped saying it after a while and then I stopped calling. It had been at least a decade since we'd had any contact at all.

For a moment I thought about calling Margaret McKay and telling her that I was the wrong man for the job. Once a quitter . . . Too many painful memories.

Beneath the contact numbers and the email for Coach

Marks, Mrs. McKay had included the team's practice schedule. Same as it ever was. Still at Cooper College, every morning from five a.m. to seven; every afternoon from three thirty p.m. to six; every Saturday morning from eight a.m. to noon. Hell of a way to spend your teenage years. And for what, the long-shot Olympic dream? A college scholarship, where you'd pass your college years with more of the same? Just looking at that schedule made me tired. With the stash I'd found in her apartment, it was unlikely that Madeline had seen a morning workout in some time.

Who could blame her for the rebellion? Forced to spend most of your waking life under water, a champion older brother you could never live up to, a father who died when you were barely old enough to remember . . . A toast to self-destruction, my dear. When I find you at the rocky bottom, I just may join you. I drained the rest of the pint and returned to the redhead for a refill.

On my way back, I felt the Vicodin veil descending. A killer of pain indeed. Like a bride or a widow, the veil protects you in its comforting cover. I clicked my jaw and rubbed my nose and settled back into that warm, gauzy state. The second beer went down easy, and the bourbon that followed did not need ice.

I arrived a little before three thirty p.m. You could smell the pool a block away. The sense memory sobered me up like the scent of violent death does for a veteran. The nostrils burn with recognition, and your body adjusts. I became aware of my footsteps, straighter than before. I popped a piece of gum and congratulated myself on the quick cleanup.

Marks Aquatics had been operating out of the Cooper College pool for at least thirty years. After an All-American career at USC, Teddy Marks joined the SEALs and saw action in some serious hot spots. He witnessed a friend, a fellow swimmer-turned-SEAL, die in front of him. Then he settled in the city and started his swim team at twenty-eight. By thirty he'd produced his first Olympian; he'd placed at least one swimmer on the U.S. Team at every Games since. He'd been profiled during Olympic broadcasts as an authentic American hero. Marks ran his program with the values he'd learned in the service: honor, accountability, and complete devotion to the mission. Other teams called us the Marks Navy.

The man had spent most of his life on deck inside the same windowless basement pool, arriving before dawn every morning and not leaving until after dark. He'd surface sometimes for lunch. Like the mole people of the subways, his New York was one beneath the sidewalks, surrounded by chemical water and clanging pipes and tired faces.

I signed in at the security desk and pointed in the direction of the pool. The guard shrugged and waved me past without checking ID. The pool stench was heavy now, thicker with every step down the stairs. At the bottom, there was a small lobby with two red doors to the locker rooms. Between the doors, a narrow window looked out at the pool. There was a big man with a crew cut slumped forward on a bench beneath it. Seeing me, he stood and put his hand in his jacket. Upright, he looked like a ruined offensive lineman, six-five at least, and well past three hundred pounds. He stepped toward me and blocked the entrance to the men's room.

"Help you?" he asked.

"Going to see Coach Marks," I told him.

"And you are?"

"Brad Pitt. And you?" I moved to go around him, and he shifted his bulk with an eager aggression. He moved like a man who missed violent physical contact with other men.

We regarded each other from close range. His hand stayed in his jacket. I went through my aikido progressions, felt the rush of confrontation. I was sober enough to be presentable, but still drunk enough to look for trouble.

"Tell Coach Marks that it's Duck Darley," I said. "He knows who I am."

He gave me a hard look and a good long ten count before responding. I could tell he was disappointed; so few chances for action anymore. "Stay here," he said.

I stepped up to the glass and looked out at the old pool. *Abandon all hope, ye who enter*, we used to say. It was a place of sanctioned torture, a dungeon full of paddles and surgical tubing and boards and buckets. The tools of the trade. The ceiling was low, with flickering fluorescent lights hanging above each lane. The cinder block walls were painted red; the chipped deck tiles were black. At the far end of the still pool around twenty mostly naked bodies stretched and yawned behind their lanes. Their faded nylon suits concealed little.

Marks was in the center of the group behind lane four. He was dressed in standard coach's wear: wet New Balance tennis shoes, khaki shorts, navy USA Swimming polo, and mustache. He twirled his stopwatch like a weapon in his right hand; in his left he held a folded notebook. His body was straight and slim and still fit, but it was startling to see how much he'd aged. The mustache had gone gray, and there wasn't much hair left on top. It had receded halfway up his scalp, a thin, fading afterthought. But he had that same presence about him: the posture of a president, the compassionate eyes of a priest.

He called out a series of commands that his swimmers absorbed without reaction. Then they shuffled behind their lanes and peeled on their caps and goggles. When the lap clock reached sixty, one by one, they fell into the pool and swam off.

The big man had waited from a respectful distance until the last swimmer was in the pool. When Marks was alone behind lane four, he approached like a scolded soldier. He leaned into his ear as Marks listened and nodded and then smirked. He looked up toward the window and shook his head in amusement. The big man shuffled back my way.

"Told you," I said when he emerged from the men's room.

"He said to go on in," he grunted. Then he slumped back onto the bench and stared at his phone.

It was like walking back in time, to a place where the pain was prouder, or at least more pure. There were ghosts in the cramped locker room, by the showers, in the stalls, and they all recognized me. Out on deck, the ceiling was lower and the pool was darker than I remembered. It felt smaller, as places from your youth often do. We made eye contact across the pool as I walked toward him.

"I'll be damned," he said. "The prodigal swimmer returns."

"Hey Coach, long time."

He gave me a fierce hug and then forced me back and held me by the shoulders. His eyes burned right through to the back of my skull, and I looked away.

"You've stayed fit, Duck. What you been doing?"

"Still swim a few days a week over at the Palladium," I told him. "Just a few grand with a masters' group, nothing much."

"Gotta do something to flush out the booze, huh?" He winked. "Smells like you had a nice liquid lunch."

"Nah, just a beer with a burger," I said.

"Right."

"What was that about?" I asked, motioning toward the entrance. "Team needs a bouncer these days?"

"Don't ask," he said.

"I'm asking."

"It's nothing. We just need to be careful. That's Fred Wright, an ex-SEAL. We served in Yugoslavia together, in another lifetime. A good man." He paused, looked out toward his old friend. "There's been a few . . . incidents. Some stuff getting stolen from the lockers, that sort of thing."

A former SEAL turned pool security guard; I decided not to mention his over-qualifications. We looked out to the pool and watched the kids warm up. Neither of us spoke for a hundred yards or so. This was the Elite group, the kids with national cuts and Olympic goals, not dreams. They ranged in age from thirteen to twenty, mostly high schoolers, a few college kids who'd decided to attend school in the city so they could continue training with Marks.

"Got some good ones in there," he said. He pointed to a boy with a long, loping stroke over in the end lane. "That's Ian King, tough bastard. I think we can get him under fifteen minutes in the mile this year."

"Not bad," I said. "Where's Coach Kosta? You still got him leading the D group?"

Marks shook his head, gave a pained frown. "Parted ways, I'm afraid."

"Sorry to hear. I always liked the little Greek."

"Me too," he said. "John was one hell of a distance coach."

"Where's he coaching now?" I asked.

"He's not. Decided to become a civilian, it seems." Marks put his hand on my shoulder. "Goddamn, Duck, it's good to see you. You haven't changed a bit." I appreciated the lie.

A girl flipped hard at our feet over lane three and drenched our shoes. "That one's Trina Harp" he said. "Nasty piece of work. Two hundred flyer, four hundred IM. Won Pan Pacs last summer. Mean as can be." We watched her streamline and swim off. Her stroke lacked any fluid grace, but she pulled at the water with bad intentions, like a boxer hitting the heavy bag.

"So, Coach, I'm here . . ."

"I know, been expecting you. Margaret told me you'd be coming 'round."

"When's the last time Madeline was at practice?"

He thought about it for a lap, looked off at the clock. "Little over a month," he said. "August third. She showed up at a Wednesday afternoon workout. Stayed for warm-up and half a pull set. Then got out and said her shoulder hurt." His mouth got tight as if hurt by the memory.

"And before that? Had she been making practices regularly?"

Marks shook his head. "Not as tough as I once was," he said. "Back in your day, a girl like that? She would have been gone long ago. Got no time for it. She wants to throw away her talent, that's up to her, but I got kids in here . . ." He swept his arm across the lanes. "I got kids in here who *want* it, who are willing to put in the work. Athlete like that, all that talent and no commitment, she's bad energy for the entire group."

"But since she's Charlie's sister . . ."

"Yeah, I know, she gets a pass." He sighed. "Like I said, I've gone soft in my old age. That family has been so good to me. I need to do right by them. By Charlie, and by Margaret too. Their girl's in a bad way, and I need to be there if she wants to get her act back together."

"Mrs. McKay is worried. She hasn't been able to reach her in the last week. Says Charlie saw her, briefly, leaving their place upstate last Sunday. Then she says she got a text that was out of character, apologizing for something. And there was a missed call to your number that same day?"

Marks nodded. "She didn't leave a message."

"That sounds like her last attempted contact with anyone. Any idea what she could have been calling about?"

"Not a clue," he said.

"She call you often?"

"She's barely a part of this team," said Marks. "If I had to guess, I'd say she was calling to tell me she'd finally decided to quit, for good."

"You try calling back?"

He took a step closer to the edge of the pool. "The girl needs rehab, not swim practice," he said. "I know she's using, just like I know you've been drinking. You folks think you can pretend to straighten up and fool people, but you can't. Or at least you don't fool me."

Called out, I felt a wave of intoxication wash over me. His words stripped away my false sobriety and I was drunk again. I realized I was sweating heavily; I felt the whiskey seeping through my cheeks.

"Does she have any friends on the team?" I asked.

"Not a one," he said. "When she's here, which is rarely, Madeline keeps to herself. She's older than most of this group now. She's got no interest in 'em. We've got a few her age in there, maybe she talks to them, but I've never seen it."

"You mind if I ask them about her?"

"Right now? Yeah, I do mind. We're getting ready to do a three thousand for time this afternoon. I'm not getting anyone out for any interrogations. You come back in a few hours, at six, sober, and you can talk to whomever you like after practice."

In here the world operated on his terms, every second under his control. It was pointless to object. I understood why he rarely surfaced. A shaky hand found a business card in my pocket, and I offered it to him.

"Be back in a few hours then," I said. "If you hear from her, would you mind giving me a call?"

Marks looked at the card with amusement. "Duck Darley," he read. " 'Finder and Consultant.' What does that even mean?"

"Don't ask," I said.

On the way out I met two of his lieutenants, assistant coaches who looked like they stepped from a Speedo catalog. Both were blond, late twenties, unsmiling. The boy had close-cropped spiked hair and the wide shoulders of a butterflyer. The girl had a hard air and harder blue eyes. They walked together with the self-conscious closeness of a couple pretending they weren't. I stopped them and introduced myself. They weren't impressed. They told me their names were Nicholas and Anna. Anna had a thick Eastern Euro accent.

"You're late for practice," I said. "Warm-up's almost done."

"We coach the younger group," said Nick. "Their practice doesn't start till six."

"We come early to help with Elite," said Anna.

"Very industrious. How long you been working for Marks?"

"Few years," said Nick. Anna said nothing, just stared back at me like a leopard trying to decide if she was hungry.

"You guys know Madeline McKay?" I asked.

They exchanged a look. "Uh huh," said Nick.

"Seen her lately?"

"No," said Anna. "I believe she has quit. Is that right, Nicholas?"

"Yeah, she hasn't been here in, like, a month," he said.

"Well, if you see her, or hear anything about her, maybe you can let me know?" I offered Nick a card. Anna took it from him and examined it. She frowned and slid it in the back pocket of her jeans. She had slim hips and thick thighs that could crush little Nicky and leave him patting the mat in submission.

They slipped by me and nodded their hellos to Fred. He scampered up and held the women's room door for Anna. I climbed the stairs into the daylight, out of the chlorine, trying to stop the sweating. I needed to lie down, to clear my head. Clouds had rolled in and the temperature had dropped, the seasons turning like the caravans of cabs changing shifts along Third Avenue. I looked up at the sky as the sun was swept behind a dark, moving mass.

It looked like rain, and I wanted to get drenched.

Chapter 4

It was after seven when I felt her foot in my face. I was passed out on the couch with Elvis curled at my feet. There was a dull ache behind my temples, and my tongue was as dry as cured meat, but at least the sweating had stopped. A leather toe pressed into my nose and I heard her laugh above me.

"So much for staying sober," she said.

I opened my eyes. All six-plus feet of Cassandra Kimball stood above me. She set down her foot and put her hands on her hips. Black heeled boots, black leather pants, long-sleeved black crocheted shirt, a cross around her neck that fell into C-cups held by black lace. Above a long, pale neck, a porcelain face of runway model proportions. Her black hair was pulled back into a severe ponytail. Her brown eyes were still heavily mascaraed and her crimson lipstick looked like a violent gash of premeditated passion.

"Will you marry me?" I asked.

"Get up, you drunkard," she said.

She reached out and grabbed both hands and helped me to my feet. Elvis grumbled and jumped down from the couch and rubbed himself against her boots.

"See you've been hard at work." She walked off to the

kitchen, poured a glass of water from the sink, and removed an ashtray from a cabinet.

"It's been a rough one," I said. "Turns out memory lane is full of potholes."

Cass set the water and ashtray on the coffee table and settled into my recliner and lit a Parliament. She released a dragon plume of smoke between us. We watched each other until she sucked it down to the filter. Then she stubbed it out on her boot and tossed the butt in the tray.

Not for the first time, I wished I liked what Cass liked. Vanilla sex doesn't interest her, and being tied up and beaten and berated doesn't do much for me. Alas, it appears I'm doomed forever to lust over my incompatible partner. There are worse problems to have.

"How was work?" I asked, ever the good wannabe husband.

"Crazy," she said. "Had a new client this afternoon. Hasidic rabbi. Those guys are insanely kinky, even for me."

"What did he want you to do?"

"Confidential, Duck, you know that."

"C'mon, just a hint, you know how much I love to hear about your day, dear."

She giggled, reached into her pack and lit another cigarette. "Let's just say he needed diapers. And a few, um, shocks to the system."

"And that turned him on?" I asked.

"Oh, yes, most definitely. He'll be back. I suspect he'll be a regular."

"Different strokes," I said. "Go figure."

She shrugged, puffed away. "So, are you gonna tell me about *your* day? I thought we had a new case. Or have you just been getting shit-faced with Elvis on the couch all day?"

"I put in a hard day on the pavement," I said. "Admittedly between a few drinks. Although it appears I've missed my last appointment this evening."

Cass leaned forward and began to scroll through the artists on my iPod. She tapped at the screen with an approving smile. The speakers at the corners of the room crackled, and then Jimmie Dale Gilmore began to croon.

While I told her about Margaret McKay and Charlie and the fuck-up kid sister, Madeline, old Smokey sang to us about heading for a fall. I told Cass about the girl's West Village pad, the drugs, her twenty grand a month allowance, and my visit to see my old coach. Cass knew all about him; she's heard about my aborted glory days. She listened in her intense, nonjudgmental way, watching me like a shrink from her chair.

When I finished, she asked for the envelope from Mrs. McKay and got to work. She examined the two pictures of our missing girl first, took out her phone and snapped pics of the hard copies and set it aside. I got up, went to the kitchen, and dropped a cube in a glass and poured myself four fingers of Bulleit. The sweet bourbon burn washed away my grogginess, and the tension behind my temples evaporated. I watched Cass through the counter space of the kitchen. She was hunched forward on the couch with her back to me. Her shirt crept up to reveal the tattoo at the small of her back. In Gothic type, it read KNEEL. Call it a tramp stamp at your own peril. Next to Cass's laptop, Madeline's phone records and bank statements were spread out in a blizzard of white paper across the table.

"What are we finding?" I asked.

"Well, according to her latest AT&T statement, it seems this Madeline really likes the person at 646-555-4414. Over six hundred texts to that number; some nights she was sending more than fifty." Cass cross-referenced the statement with Mrs. McKay's contact list. "And that number would belong to one Mr. James Fealy."

"The boyfriend," I said. "When's the last one she sent?"

"According to this, her last text to Mr. Fealy was sent, let's see, seven days ago. Storm texting him every day, then it stops entirely."

"The mother claims they broke up."

"Maybe you can ask him why."

"What's the number again?"

She read it off, and I dialed James Fealy. Voice mail, of course. No one answers an unrecognized number anymore. I put on my best could-be-a-cop voice when it was time to leave a message. *Yes, good evening, Mr. Fealy, I'm calling in reference to a Miss Madeline McKay. I am investigating her disappearance, and I'm told you may be of some assistance* . . . I left my number and stressed that a prompt call back was appreciated and expected.

"Poor little rich girl," said Cass. "Broken-hearted, into the hard stuff . . ."

"I know. I'll check in with Dr. Burke. See about any Jane Does at the morgue."

"No missing persons report filed by the mother?"

"Appears she has an aversion to cops," I said.

"Fair enough." She went back to studying the paper trail. "Last withdrawal was two grand cash, on Saturday, September third. Then the texts a few days later, and nothing since. Are we looking for an OD?"

"Her mother is sure she's alive. Says a mother would know."

"Don't they all."

"There's no sign of her passport," I said. "It's not at her place, and her mother doesn't have it."

"If she really wanted to get away, I suppose that last couple grand could have gotten her somewhere."

"Except Mrs. McKay claims her daughter has a phobia of travel. Hasn't left the country in years."

"Lovely. What about friends in the city?"

"Mother only remembers one. Girl named Lucy Townes, fellow swimmer, only friend her mother could recall."

Cass was scanning search results on her laptop, half listening. "Google 'Madeline McKay' plus 'swimming' gets you a bunch of meet results, with her name next to times, but not much else."

"The mother says she has no presence on any social media, that she closely guards her privacy."

"Eighteen-year-old girl who's unplugged from all that stuff?"

"Bizarre, I know."

"What did you say that friend's name was again?"

"Lucy Townes. See what you can find on her."

Cass typed a few strokes and leaned in. "Okay, this is more like it," she said. "Looks like a cute blond girl, seventeen, a breaststroker. Usual presence on Facebook and Twitter. I'll reach out."

"What can you find about the ex-boyfriend? Mother says he's a film student at NYU."

"Let's see. James Fealy, was it?" Her sharp nails clicked over the keys. "A senior, in the Tisch School of the Arts. Founder of Scion Productions, how obnoxious. Lists himself as a director, producer, impresario. Search also places him as the son of one Max Fealy, some hotshot hedge funder. Hence the name of the production company."

"Does Scion list an address?" I asked.

Cass clicked back, scrolled down. "It does. 259 East 7th Street, suite 3W."

"Presumably his apartment. If I don't hear back from the punk, I'll stop by."

My four fingers of bourbon were down to a fingernail. I drained the rest and returned to the kitchen. I decided to be responsible and grabbed a Beck's instead of an amber refill. "What else are you finding over there, Ms. Watson?" I asked.

She glanced at the papers splayed before her and opened a new tab on her browser. Cass clicked on something, and her eyes widened as she read. "Wow, Madeline's brother was Sportsman of the Year?" It was an old story from *Sports Illustrated*, a hero's feature on Charlie post-Olympics. "You knew this guy?" she asked. "He sounds remarkable. Hot too."

"A regular Greek god," I said.

"It's so sad—their father died just four days before the Olympics. Then his son goes out and wins four gold medals in his honor. Can you imagine?"

"A tale for the ages. Did wonders for the TV ratings too."

Cass read the piece in silence. I sat there brooding, filled with those coulda-been-a-contender memories that never fade. I remembered Charlie's father from meets when we were kids. Slick Stevie, my father used to call him. He was an overcaffeinated, hairless man who talked too fast and knew the best times to the hundredth of every swimmer on the team. He worked in finance like all the other dads, but far from my father's growling testosterone orbit. Steve McKay's considerable fortune was a product of his proximity to wealth; a rich boy who learned how to rub elbows with the old boys and funnel billions into his funds, where he grabbed the usual two percent for doing nothing at all. Big Larry Darley disdained pretty much everyone, but he left special contempt for those born-to-it country club clowns who compounded their trust funds while risking little of their own. Dad built his false fortune from the bootstraps up. He was the son of a degenerate gambler from Queens, a public high school teacher who pissed away his paycheck on the ponies at Aqueduct. Maybe bad bets are in the Darley blood.

In any case, Slick Stevie died and Big Larry went off to prison, and their sons went off in different directions too.

Cass stopped reading and held up the yearbook picture of Madeline. She looked into her face and smiled softly. Some kind of female empathy passed between them. "She's a beautiful girl," she said. "Even when she's trying to look ugly."

Chapter 5

The bar at Zum's was full, but I found a seat in the corner and sipped on a half liter of Hofbrau. I'd popped a few more of Madeline's vikes, and all was feeling fine and free with the world. I was back at work, with a bundle of cash in my pocket, and something to find. These were the best times, the first steps on a trail, when the romance burned brightest.

It was a cool, clear night with the moon almost full and little darkness down Avenue C. It used to be junkie land, but now it was just another conquered stretch of bars and boutiques. Some people lament the lost edge of certain once dangerous neighborhoods, but not me. Get mugged a few times, feel the tip of a blade on your belly as you fumble for your wallet, then tell me you miss the broken window days. Now there were clean, safe bars of a half dozen ethnic varieties—German, Aussie, Serbian, Austrian, Irish, and Brazilian—on this block alone. An urban Epcot for the thirsty man.

The bar at Zum's was a tall redbrick wall that jutted out around a semicircle of good German beers on tap. A portrait of a Prussian kaiser was framed above my head to my left, and three tipsy girls pressed into my space on my right. They held big empty liter glasses and were searching without success for refills. The barmaid saw them and was avoiding eye contact. The girls were shameless and clueless and jovial. They called for drinks and chattered about their jobs and the guys who were screwing them over. They looked like they wanted to keep getting screwed.

The noise in the bar was full of laughter and loud talk that drowned out the bad German music. There was a speaker positioned nearby; I think I was the only one to hear the Scorpions above the din. Then someone behind me bellowed: "The Duck man!"

Roy Perry stood there, shit-faced and swaying and wiping a runny nose. I gave him a knowing grin. Roy was trouble, a coke buddy from way back; I could see by his reddened nostrils that he was already into the stuff tonight. Thanks to his profession, he also served as my all-access pass into every celeb haunt and hipster lair in the city. I figured Madeline might have been seen in those parts.

"Thanks for meeting me," I said.

Roy muscled between the girls and called out to the barmaid by name. Sylvia turned and, seeing him, shook her head in amusement. She came over and leaned across the bar and kissed both his cheeks. She began pouring him a liter without asking and told him it had been too long. "Too many bars in this town!" shouted Roy. "Too many beautiful bartenders to keep up with!" Sylvia gave him an indulgent smile and pushed his liter in front him. Foam sloshed down its sides and Roy hungrily slurped off the overflow. "Three more for these ladies," he called. "I do believe they were waiting before me." He turned to them and offered a rogue's bow. "On me, girls," he said with a wink.

When it comes to drugs and drink, I have just one rule when on a case: no blow. I can function just fine, better than fine, in fact, with a steady stream of booze to keep me loose and fearless. But the moment I have a bump, all is lost. The night unravels, and I'm useless to remember a single detail when I'm into that rotten stuff. Can't deal with the vicious hangover either. I was trying to remind myself of these things as Roy tried to press his palm into mine without discretion. "Care for a pick-me-up?" he asked.

There had been so many mad nights that started just the same. A steady buzz exploded by the contents of my friend's ultra pure supply. The two of us would stand there jabbering mindless wisdom at each other, then take our show on the road, chatting up any women who made the mistake of looking back.

"Sorry, Roy," I said. "You know my rule."

"Whatever," he spat. "Another drink and you'll change your tune. Always do."

I didn't try denying it.

"So, where we headed tonight?" he asked. "You talk to that punk boyfriend yet?"

"Not yet."

"You said the girl's loaded, right? College age, hot party chick? I've got a good idea where she'd go. Boom Boom Room, Provocateur, maybe Southside if she's lame. Shouldn't be too hard to pick up her scent. You got a pic?"

I took out both pictures I'd been given. He leaned in, made a close appraisal.

"Not bad," he said. "She'd have no trouble getting in anywhere."

Roy was a Page Six reporter for the *Post*. Coke should be a tax-deductible work expense for a gig like that. He was expected to go out six nights a week and find bold-faced names in their natural habitats, preferably behaving poorly. He was on a first-name basis with every promoter and club owner in town, but it was his in with the bouncers that really paved the way. Roy was about their size, shared their love of violence, and had the constitution of a mammoth. They respected that.

"So what's the story with this kid, the boyfriend?" he asked. "You said he's some kind of loaded wannabe director?"

"Something like that. Named his production company Scion."

"Fucking tool."

Roy gulped at his beer, his free hand shoved inside his jeans pocket, caressing his little white bag of fuel. "You don't want to turn this shit down, red eye," he said. "Not speedy at all. Super clear." Again he tried to press his palm into mine, and again I resisted. A few painkillers were one thing, no hangover there, but even a bump or two of the blow can leave an ugly impression the next day. And it's never a bump or two. But still, I felt the pull. I wouldn't be able to resist for much longer. I drank the rest of my beer and set it down on the bar with something like conviction.

"I'm gonna go by his place," I said. "I'll keep you posted."

"You go do that," he said. Then he turned and stalked off in the direction of the men's room.

Fealy's apartment was a half block east in one of the finest buildings in the neighborhood. There were lush flower boxes across the base of each floor and high loft windows that looked out onto the prettiest stretch among the alphabet streets. A cracked-out wino lounged by the building's entrance. He raised a can of Four Loco in my direction and guzzled it down. I buzzed Fealy's apartment and waited without response. The temptation to return to Zum's and Roy's goodies was growing.

It wasn't long before an Uber pulled up, and out climbed a kid with a black piece of Tumi luggage. He was college age, dressed carelessly in hoodie and cords, but he couldn't shake the moneyed scent. His blond hair was full of product, and his facial hair was maintained like a Japanese garden. I stepped aside, asked if I could give him a hand. He grunted in response, dug for his keys. I held the door as he tried to shoulder past.

"Hey buddy, hang on," I called. "I'm looking for somebody, guy named James Fealy, you know him?"

He stopped at the threshold. His look said he did, but he mumbled he didn't.

"He's not in any trouble," I said. "I'm looking for his ex-girlfriend. We were supposed to meet up. Appears he forgot. Now I gotta wait down here all night until he shows."

"Sorry, man, can't help you."

He turned his back to me and moved through the small lobby. There was an unattended front desk watched by a camera in the high corner. The kid hit the elevator button three times, slouched and checked his phone with impatience. Just before the front door clicked shut, I slipped a toe against it. I waited until the elevator opened and shut before I stepped inside. There was a stairwell in the back of the lobby. I started to climb the flights to Fealy's. I heard the screaming before I hit the first landing.

By the time I reached him, the kid was out in the hallway in a state of bellowing shock. "Oh fuck, oh fuck, oh fuck!" he cried over and over. He was fumbling with his phone, trying to dial 9-1-1, but not connecting with any buttons. Seeing me coming, he ran at me, blind to the memory of moments earlier. "Help me, man! You gotta help me," he cried. "My roommate! My roommate, he's fucking dead. Somebody, somebody . . . Oh fuck, oh fuck."

I went past him into the open apartment, 3W—the address Cass found listed for Scion Productions. The living room was dominated by a massive flat-screen and a sectional leather sofa. Empty beer bottles littered the glass coffee table. A laptop was open on a long dining room table. Movie posters decorated the walls, the usual college kid clichés: Woody and Quentin and Scorsese.

The bathroom light was on, the door half closed. I approached the room like a man being sentenced for a forgotten crime. Took a breath, pushed it open. I looked down.

James Fealy was lying naked on the shower floor. His throat had been cut almost to his spine. The gash had opened his head from his body like a wide red yawn. There were also stab wounds on his shoulders and arms and a deep slash across his chest. His long body was blocking the drain, and blood was pooled around him in the tub. His dead blue eyes were open and confused. His penis had also been cut. It was thin and flaccid and fell against his thigh, hanging by a few bloody strands.

I stood above him, and I couldn't look away. I had viewed the dead before, as cold slabs in the morgue or in caskets at wakes, when they are pretending to be asleep in heavy makeup, but never like this. Coming across violent death, in a literal bloodbath, is a world away. It is stepping into a dark dimension. You don't come back from it. I was conscious of these things even as I stood there paralyzed. Then I staggered back against the bathroom sink and I felt myself about to throw up. I tried to swallow down the puke, but it was too late. I lunged for the toilet, yanked up the lid, and retched until my eyes burned.

When I returned to his roommate out in the hall, the cops were charging up the stairs.

Chapter 6

The kid's name was Mike. Michael Schwartz, he'd stammered to the cops. He told them he was James Fealy's best friend, that the two of them had lived together since freshman year. He just returned from Montauk where he'd decided to stay another week. The waves were up; the city could wait. He told them he found me outside the front door, wanting to talk to his friend, when he pulled up. Telling them this, he looked over like I was complicit in the horror he was experiencing. The detective turned and gave me a look like she agreed with him.

Schwartz told her that James had no enemies, he was a just a chill, cool guy, man. Then he muttered a few more *oh fuck, oh fucks*, and lost his train of thought. The officer asked him about the girlfriend, and Schwartz snorted, shook his head. "She was psycho," he said. "A total psycho. You don't think? Oh fuck, fuck, man."

His hands shook as he tapped a Marlboro Light from a pack and stared at it unlit between his fingers. The blood had drained from his face, and his eyes wouldn't stay still. They were darting from the detective in front of him, over to me, and back over to the open door of his apartment. A uniformed officer emerged with a wet kitchen knife sealed in a plastic bag. Schwartz let out a sick cry of recognition and sunk to the floor and put his head between his knees. The cigarette fell from his hand and rolled away.

The detective came over. She was short with hard features, built like a former gymnast, and dressed in black jeans, gray blazer. Her red hair was cut shorter than mine in a pixie style. A pair of soft blue eyes belied the rest of her cultivated efforts at toughness. She showed me her badge, told me she was Detective Miller, Homicide. I told her mine and offered a hand that she ignored.

"Could you explain why you were on the scene, Mr. Darley?" she asked.

"I was hired to find a missing girl," I said. "Madeline McKay. She's the ex-girlfriend of the poor bastard in the tub there."

"You were here to question him in her disappearance?"

"That's right."

"And how did you gain access to the building?"

I motioned over to the Schwartz kid. Someone had draped a blanket around his shoulders. "The roommate came home when I was standing out front," I said.

"And he let you up?"

"Yes."

"He said you could come inside and up to the apartment with him?"

"No. I followed him in. Then I responded to his screams and came up the stairs."

"And then what did you do?"

"He asked me to help him, said his roommate had been killed. I went past him and went into the apartment. The door was open. I found the kid, Fealy, in the bathtub, in a pool of blood. His throat had been cut. He'd been stabbed all over his body too. Then you guys showed up."

"You touch anything in the apartment, Mr. Darley?"

"Maybe the dining table as I went by. And I got sick

when I saw the body. You'll find my prints on the bath-room sink and the toilet too."

She didn't react to this, just made a note in a small pad and turned away. An older detective, with standard-issue cop gut and mustache, appeared at the top of the steps. Miller joined him, caught him up as they looked from me to Schwartz to the apartment. He came my way, and Miller went to speak with the uniform holding the knife in the plastic bag.

"You a PI?" he asked without introducing himself.

"No. Friend of the family," I said.

"Family of the dead kid's?"

"His ex. She's missing. Her mother asked me to look for her. The boyfriend seemed like a good place to start."

"We're gonna need all the info you have on this girl."

"Uh huh, sure," I said.

"How long you been looking for her?"

"Since this morning."

He grunted a laugh. "Hell of a first day," he said. "My partner tells me you puked on our crime scene? That's al-ways helpful."

"My apologies."

"Don't be sorry. It's a natural reaction for weak-stomached civilians."

He gave me an aggressive smile of crooked yellow teeth. His mustache had crumbs in it; his skin had the ashen complexion of a life lived under fluorescents and night. I had a few inches on him, but that gut put him in a higher weight class. He was still sweating after the workout up the stairs. He was the sort of sloppy power-thrilled bastard that Cass liked to turn inside out. I flashed an image of her giving it to him with a strap-on and couldn't suppress a smirk.

"Something funny?" he asked.

"Not a thing," I said. "Just let me know how I can help."

"Gonna need a statement, for starters," he said. "And need you to hand over any information you've gathered on this girl. After a day on the job, not much, I'm guessing. Anything the girl's mother may have given you to get started, anyone you may have talked to earlier today."

"Madeline didn't do this," I said. I wasn't sure why I said it, or even if I believed it myself, but I knew it couldn't be easy for an eighteen-year-old girl to damn near behead a man in the shower. Even if she was a nationally ranked athlete whacked out of her mind on drugs.

"Maybe she did, maybe she didn't," he said. "But that's not for you to determine." He examined his fingernails at the end of a puffy, hairless hand. "In any case, we'll find her a lot faster than you will."

I was escorted out of the building by an earnest young uniform that kept putting his hand on my back as we walked down the stairs. A small crowd had gathered around the entrance. A news truck was already on the scene, recording the worried looks and whispered speculation and that giddy lurid energy of breaking tragedy. I spotted Roy Perry talking to a neighbor on the sidewalk. He was nodding excitedly and scribbling notes. Seeing me, Roy walked away from her in mid-sentence and moved toward me. His eyes were wild and wide, his brow bursting with drug sweat. He started to say something but I shook my head and let the uniform guide me over to his cruiser.

It was three a.m. by the time they were finished with me at the police station. I gave them my statement; told them enough, left out some. Said I'd been to Madeline's apartment, didn't mention her stash of drugs hidden in the *Twilight* box set. Mentioned seeing Coach Marks, didn't mention Fred the bouncer guarding the pool deck. They could find out these details with their oh-so-fast police work.

I texted Cass on my way out of the precinct: **Fealy murdered. Saw body. They think Madeline did it . . .**

I decided to walk home. The day's drinks and pills had settled into the soil, and my mind was muddy. My thoughts were not thoughts, only a single grisly image. Forced to describe every frame of what I'd witnessed, the memory of Fealy's slashed naked body in the tub had lodged itself in my brain. I tried to think it through, going back to the start of the day with Mrs. McKay, following the steps that brought me to that moment, but it was no good. You wake up one morning, you go for a swim; someone asks you to look for someone else. You drink, snoop around, and catch up with your past. And all the while, that scene is waiting for you in the night. A dead young man with his throat cut open so deep I could see the bloody spinal stem that connected his head, barely, to his mutilated body.

The bars were still open another hour; drunk kids spilled out of them, smoking on sidewalks and talking too loud. I considered popping into one and pouring whiskey down my throat until they turned on the lights and forced me to crawl home. I kept walking. Detective Miller's partner had told me my job was done. If I had any sense, I'd stay away. Stay out of the water; it's not safe to swim. High, rough surf out there, dangerous rip currents, big hungry fish underneath. But I knew it wasn't a choice. My dark half couldn't wait to paddle out.

As usual there were zero stars visible in the city night sky. A glowing eyeball of moon looked down between nude white clouds, judging the late-night sinners below. An unending row of reds and greens lit First Avenue through the East Village and neighborhoods north. Like most city kids, I'm fundamentally afraid of the dark, the true black dark of the country, the stillness; the unsettling quiet that swallows you out there. In the city, the darkness is all within, within windowless rooms and inside the bodies of desperate souls without lightness, the color of nothing.

When I reached my apartment on East 17th, I sensed Cass's presence before I turned my keys in the lock. Inside, she was standing in the kitchen with her back to me, turning a sizzling skillet. Lucinda Williams played at low volume. *Car Wheels on a Gravel Road.* The small space smelled of stir-fry, soy sauce, and burning white rice. I doubted there was anything else to add to it. The lack of ventilation filled the living room with a ghostly smoke. She was barefoot and had on a loose black sweatshirt and jeans. Cass turned, took a drag from her Parliament and, exhaling, said, "I got your text." Then she went back to cooking.

I nodded, slid past her, and reached for the bottle of Bulleit, gave it a long pour into a dirty glass and drank it down. Didn't even taste it. I set down the glass and leaned against the counter opposite Cass.

"Thanks for coming by," I said.

"You okay?" she asked without turning.

"Not really, but this will help." I refilled the bourbon.

"No, it won't, but this should. I assume you haven't eaten anything?" She turned off the stove and spooned the stir-fry into a soup bowl and handed it to me. "You look terrible," she said.

Cass lit another cigarette while she watched me eat in silence. I asked her without meaning it if she wanted any, and she said she wasn't hungry. She never is. Cass subsists on nicotine and energy bars, as far as I can tell. I don't think I've ever seen her use a fork or order anything off a menu. Doesn't eat, but knows her way around a kitchen; go figure. I finished the bowl with tasteless relish and set it on the counter, then shuffled to the living room and collapsed on the couch. I looked up at the ceiling and felt

Cass watching me like a wounded animal in the dim light. My thoughts started to move and wander again. I started to tell her about it.

When I finished talking, she stood and emptied the overflowing ashtray. Dawn wasn't far off. It was more to-morrow than tonight. A milky gray light filtered through the window. Elvis trudged out of the bedroom, took a few licks from his water bowl, and came over and curled at my feet. Cass opened her laptop and came over to sit beside me.

"There's something you need to see," she said.

Chapter 7

It was a few minutes after eleven when I found myself standing in the airless lobby of Margaret McKay's Gramercy Park co-op. I admired the prewar grace—the ornate crown molding, the black-and-white marble floors, the stained glass entry, the flower stand arranged just so by the ancient elevator. The doors opened, and a well-dressed elderly couple stepped out with a yapping Yorkie between them. They nodded their hellos to Raymond the doorman and limped into the afternoon light as he held the big oak door and averted his eyes.

Raymond was dressed in a bad woolen suit. He was tall and black and courteous and probably hated every resident in the building with a kill-list passion. "You said the name was Duck?" he asked. "Here to see Mrs. McKay?"

"That's right, Duck Darley. Apartment 4B, she said."

He went into a little lobby office and made the call. Ray whispered my arrival into the receiver and came out and pressed the elevator button.

"Go on up. Mrs. McKay and her son are expecting you." And her son . . . Lovely.

I had no intention of telling them what I'd seen Madeline doing online. The videos Cass had discovered played on an endless loop in my mind alongside the image of her

murdered ex-boyfriend. They were something no parent
or sibling should know exists.

I had a copy of the day's *New York Post* with me. I unfolded it as the elevator ascended and looked again at the
front page. PSYCHO SHOWER SLAY, it read. Beneath the headline was a picture of the scene in front of James Fealy's
building. There I was, being escorted into the police cruiser
in the near left corner of the page. Across from that, the
story's lead was published in a small box of copy in the
lower right corner. It read:

> *The murderous psycho slashed him in the
> shower. That's where 22-year-old NYU film stu-
> dent and director-to-be, James Fealy, was found
> with his throat cut open last night. The victim
> was the son of hard-nosed hedge funder Max
> Fealy of Soto Capital. Soon after the body was
> discovered in the bathroom of Fealy's East Vil-
> lage condo, a private investigator happened
> upon the scene.* MORE ON PAGES 3–4.

The elevator doors opened before I could turn to the rest.
Charlie McKay was waiting in the open doorway of his
mother's apartment. He stood with one hand against the
doorframe; the other held a bottle of sparkling water. His
blond hair was combed straight back, his Captain America
face clean-shaven; his skin was tan from summer. He pro-
jected the still confidence of a man who didn't need to explain who he was or what he did. It was assumed you already
knew. He wore khakis and a pressed white button-down,
tucked in. Charlie had always been a tall, ox-shouldered kid.
He remained a chiseled, lucky-gene specimen, the years
doing little to steal away his Olympian's physique. He
gave me a tight smile.

"Hey, Duck," he said, like we'd seen each other yesterday. "C'mon in. Mom's a mess."

The apartment was a sprawling, high-ceilinged affair, room after perfect room posing for the pages of *Architectural Digest*. The décor was English Victorian—all crimson-painted walls with gilded details and Dutch still-lifes. I followed Charlie down a long hall lined with family photos, highlighted by his swimming triumphs. Olympic podiums, in-water action shots, throwing pumpers at the finish . . . I didn't stop to examine them, but not many of Madeline caught my eye, her triumphs to date not quite as frame-worthy. In a dark, ballroom-sized living room, Margaret McKay was standing by a window looking out at Gramercy Park with a glass of white wine in her hands. She did not smile when she turned and saw me enter with her son.

"Sit down, Lawrence," she said.

I followed her order, on a hunter green high-backed sofa. Charlie hovered nearby like an Aryan guard dog. Together, we waited for the next command. Margaret took a drink of wine and walked over, giving off a hot energy as she moved. She was wearing an emerald silk blouse, buttoned low, and black slacks. She stood before me and glared at the paper in my lap.

"You've read the news today," she said.

"Oh, boy," I said. It fell flat.

She stood with her shoulders back and looked at me down her narrow, surgically refined nose. She lifted her wineglass and held it there, sipping with deliberation. Her long, thin neck contracted as the wine slid slowly down her throat.

"Do you know why I hired you?" she asked.

I shrugged, too tired to play along with this servant's badgering.

"For your discretion," she said. "I appreciated our long-ago connection, your childhood friendship with my son, but that is unimportant." She glanced over at Charlie; he nodded along. "I was told that you are very good at what you do—and also skilled at staying in the shadows. And keeping your mouth shut."

"All true," I said.

She reached down and grabbed the paper from my lap and held it close before my face. "You call this staying in the shadows?" she spat. She threw the *Post* to the floor and stalked away. Her body shivered in its aftershock of unaccustomed emotion. "Yesterday morning my daughter was missing and all I asked was for you to find her," she said, hardly above a whisper. "And now, now she is a suspect in a murder investigation that is being splashed all over the cover of the *New York Post*."

"I don't think your daughter killed anyone, Mrs. McKay," I told her.

"Of course she didn't!" She shook her head with fury and finished off what was left of her wine. Then she handed the empty glass to her son. He took it dutifully and marched off to the kitchen for a refill. "Did you know the police have already been here this morning?" she asked.

"I figured they would be," I said.

"The NYPD do not come here, not to this building. We all have our private affairs, our less than perfect children . . ." As if on cue, Charlie returned with a fresh glass of white wine for his mother. "We all have these things inside our homes," she went on. "But they are kept where they belong—in private. What could be more crass than a visit from a cop?"

"I understand, Margaret." She glowered at my use of her first name. "I spent four hours at the police station last night talking to those dumb bastards. I saw James Fealy's body up close with my own eyes. And I—"

"Yes, the entire city knows all about the 'private investigator' that happened upon the scene," she said.

"*Mrs.* McKay," I said. "It was a terrible act, and I sincerely hope your daughter had nothing to do with it."

She looked at me for a long time. There was something dark in the atmosphere, something thick and tense and dangerous. Finally she exhaled and walked back to the window. "What else did you find yesterday?" she asked. "Before you happened upon Mr. Fealy."

I thought of the videos Cass and I had watched online, of her daughter in positions of extreme compromise. She must have seen it in my face. "Just say it," she said. "Do not spare me. If you have found something scandalous about my daughter, just tell me. I'm not sure how it could get worse than that." She pointed to the *Post* and took another drink.

"There was a stash of drugs," I said. "Hidden at her apartment."

She didn't react.

"It was quite an assortment. The usual party drugs: coke, molly, that sort of thing. Lot of pills too. But there was also heroin. That worries me."

Charlie let out a low moan. "Jesus," he muttered.

"We know that Madeline has not made any recent withdrawals from her bank account. We know she has not made any calls or sent any texts from her cell. Mrs. McKay, I say this with all sensitivity, but I have a friend in the medical examiner's office, a pathologist for the city. I'd like to find out if there have been any recent Jane Does."

Another silence stretched between us. Margaret returned to her perch by the window and stared out at the private park beneath her. Glowing green tree light came in through the high window. Charlie started to walk to her, then seemed to think better of it and stopped and sunk into a club chair next to the fireplace.

"Just so we can rule that out," I said with a lame note of false assurance. "Also, this afternoon, my partner has made plans to speak with Madeline's friend, Lucy Townes."

Mother and son nodded from their positions, acknowledging the name but lost somewhere off in their own private worlds.

"I'll report back as soon as I hear something," I told them.

I stood and moved to leave, and neither looked in my direction. Charlie caught up with me in the hall in front of a framed picture of his younger, shirtless self with gold medals around his neck. "Duck, hold up," he whispered. "Hey, let's go get a coffee."

It was a too warm September day, more summer than fall, and everyone on the sidewalks seemed to be regretting their morning choices in clothing. My underarms were wet and bleeding yesterday's toxins. Charlie led me to Taralucci's, just north of Union Square. We didn't speak on our walk, and he maintained a two pace lead as we moved. His shoulders sloped over a wide back that still looked plenty powerful beneath his damp oxford. His blond hair was thinning now, baldness on the horizon in the next few years. He turned his head a few times to make sure I was keeping up as he pressed on at a pitched-forward angle of impatience.

We found a table with some privacy in the back of the café starting to fill with lunching ladies. Charlie asked for a latte; I ordered black coffee for myself. "What the fuck is going on?" he asked as soon as the waitress retreated.

"Nice to see you too, old friend," I said.

"Shit, man, I'm sorry. I know it's been forever. But this isn't exactly the time to catch up. Fill me in on what happened yesterday." He looked at his phone and by some force of will resisted firing off a reply. "Goddamn, I really gotta get back to work," he said to himself.

I opened my mouth, but Charlie wasn't done. "I'm really freaked out about Maddie, man," he said. "I mean, what if she did this? Where the hell is she? I know she's been messed up, but Maddie would never hurt anyone. Anyone but herself, I guess. I don't know, what do you think? You don't think she's in the morgue, do you? I know you only had a day, but did you find out anything at all?"

This time he let me talk. His blithe assumption that she'd turn up had been replaced by a stammering frustration. Charlie still maintained the sharp-edged mind-set of a swimmer. When faced with uncertainty, you could put your head down and train it away, until at some point you needed to look up and see the results on the scoreboard to validate your faith.

The coffees arrived, and I watched as Charlie carefully scraped away the sticking foam from the sides of the mug and licked off his spoon. Then he placed it just right at a forty-five degree angle in the saucer.

"What can you tell me about the last time you saw her?" I asked.

"It was Sunday of Labor Day weekend, up at our place in Rhinebeck. I thought I'd have the house to myself. I went up to get some work done; get a head start while everyone was pissing off on the holiday weekend. Mom was out visiting friends in Montauk. Maddie never uses the place. She hates leaving the city. I was surprised to find her there. When she saw me, she acted really flustered. She hurried upstairs, and came down a few minutes later with a packed swim bag. Then she said she was going back to the city. She called a car and waited out by the road until it arrived. It was weird, man. After she left, I went up and looked through her room, but everything seemed the same."

"How did she look? I mean, physically?"

"Like I said, I barely got a glance. She looked normal, I guess. She was obviously agitated about something, taking off like she did. But physically, I mean, she looked the same to me."

"Did you try to reach her after she left?"

"Of course. What do you think? I called her cell right away. Sent her texts. It went straight to voice mail and she never replied to the texts."

"What do you know about this ex-boyfriend, James Fealy?" I asked.

Charlie frowned, looked down into his half-empty cup. "I introduced them, man," he said. "You know who that kid's father is? I'm praying Maddie had nothing to do with this. Not just for her sake, but for mine too. I could be fucked."

"How long have you and his father worked together?"

"Few years. Max Fealy is one of the partners at Soto. Guy's an animal, worth like one-point-five."

"Billion?"

"Probably even more than that. That's just what *Forbes* reported last year. But guys like that always have more stashed away all over the place."

"And you introduced your little sister to your boss's son?"

"He's not really my boss, we work on separate desks, but yeah, I guess we both introduced them together. It was at a company retreat last year, at Danny Soto's place in Greenwich, the owner of the company. He's real big on crap like that, on trying to pretend his firm is like a big happy family, not just another fuck-your-mother hedge fund. Which, of course, we are."

"And James's father, Max, he was okay with his son going out with Madeline? Did he know about her . . . issues?"

"He knew she was a badass swimmer. And he knew he could trust her family. I'm the one who should have been worried. This kid James was a total fuck-up. Director-to-be, my ass. He was a cokehead party boy. All he did was piss away his trust fund and pretend to make short films. I watched one once; it was total shit."

"How much were you in touch with your sister?"

"Less and less, unfortunately," he said. "I mean, we're sixteen years apart. We both basically grew up as only children, in different households. Sometimes it was like we weren't even related, not really. Mom changed a lot after Dad died, as you might have noticed. I was so into my swimming, it's not like I was noticing much of anything back then. But Maddie, she was so sweet when she was younger . . ."

"How often do you think your mom saw her over the last few months?"

"I don't know how often they got together in person, but I know they talked all the time. If you can call it that. They fought."

"Any idea what about?"

"Everything. Nothing. Obviously I was only hearing it from one side, when Mom would call late at night and ask me what to do."

"And what did you tell her?"

Charlie sighed, took a sip of his latte. He wiped the lingering foam from his upper lip and picked up the spoon and scraped the inside of his mug clean. "I didn't know what to say. I can't even remember." He looked at his phone again and frowned. "I've been so fucking busy. Jesus, I really gotta get going."

"You still in touch with Coach?"

"Of course, man, the guy's like a second father."

"You know he has a bouncer out front of the pool these days?" I asked. "Any idea why?"

He sniffed. "You mean Fred? That guy couldn't guard a saint in a church," he said. "Fred's some old SEAL buddy

of Coach's. Dishonorable discharge or something. I think
Coach is just doing him a favor, helping him get back on
his feet. Besides, you know how Coach can be. He's always had that ego. He probably likes how it looks."

"Like he's someone who needs a bodyguard to protect
his special swimmers."

"Something like that."

"What about Kosta, his loyal lieutenant?"

Charlie shrugged. "They had a falling out last year. The
little Greek decided he should be the boss, demanded to be
called co–head coach or something. You can imagine how
Coach reacted to a challenge to his authority."

"Guess you can't stay an assistant forever," I said.

"Yeah, true, but Kosta got possessive. His distance
group was like a team within a team." A shadow of memory passed across Charlie's face, and it darkened with irritation. "Goddamn it, we're not here to talk about fucking
John Kosta. We can swim through the memories some
other time."

He took out a gold money clip and peeled off a twenty
and set it between us. "Sorry, Duck, but I really need to
run. Listen, it's real good to see you. We'll catch up properly after all this stuff is over. After you find Maddie. I
know you'll find her, right?"

I didn't answer, and Charlie took that as a yes.

"Thanks, man. Really appreciate it. Keep me posted,
okay?"

He was almost at a jog by the time he reached the door.

Chapter 8

Dr. David Burke was an ex-lover of my mother's, after the fall, when I was around fifteen. He used to share his Jameson's with me on Sunday afternoons after he'd stayed over, while Mom slumbered all day in the bedroom and we watched football on the couch. He was a big, lumbering man who dressed in secondhand black suits, even in summer. His huge head was topped with a mess of brown curls always in need of a trim. Even back then his nose swelled with the bulbous red pride of a committed whiskey drinker. He was a decent man who treated me with all the respect I didn't deserve. Of course, I hated him for the sounds that came from my mother in the night.

The relationship had fizzled like all the others, but Dr. Burke had tried to stay in touch. I blew off his kind attempts at contact for years, until I needed something. He didn't hold it against me. His business is the cold and the dead; he doesn't expect much from the living.

I called ahead and arrived at his office a little before two. It's on a doctor-drenched stretch of First Avenue, wedged between NYU Medical and Bellevue, a concentration of the city with too much clinical knowledge of life and death. The Office of the Chief Medical Examiner is at the corner of 30th. Dr. Burke has been there for decades. He can tell you more about the causes of quick death than anyone this side of the grave.

A solemn young attendant led me down to his basement office. He was a skinny, pale kid who looked like he went Goth when he removed his scrubs. Pathology attracts the grim by nature, but those who last, the ones who thrive in the field of the dead, are those with a cheery, unflappable disposition. Dr. Burke grew up in Alphabet City when the far reaches of the East Village still went by that name. His early years were filled with memories of OD'd junkies on sidewalks and random violence so regular you stopped waking in the night to gunshots. Death stopped fazing him early.

In the cold quiet of the basement corridor, I heard him clearing his throat in his office at the end of the hall. Just before we reached the door, his giant frame emerged with a wink and a grin.

"Master Darley," he said with a bow.

"Doctor Death," I said.

He stepped forward and pulled me in for a quick manly hug and a slap of the back. Then he led me into his office as the dour attendant sulked away. Burke settled into a wide, worn chair behind his desk, waved for me to sit on one across from him. Above his head there was his framed medical degree from NYU. Between us, framed in the center of his desk, was a ticket stub from Super Bowl XLVI. I knew which one he was more proud of.

"Good to see you, my man," he said. "What brings you down to the netherland?"

"Missing girl, I'm afraid."

"And here I thought this was a social call." He frowned and put his big hands behind his head and leaned back as the chair moaned under his weight. Despite the chill, there were stains beneath each armpit.

"Pour us a drink, and we can mix business and pleasure," I said.

He glanced down at his desk drawer. "Sadly, the office of Dr. Burke is now a dry zone. Quite a reprimand a while back after the proverbial bottle was found empty in a wastebasket. Tried to tell 'em it steadied the hands, but alas."

"Later then."

"Sure thing. Now, what's with the missing girl? Think she's a Jane Doe?"

"That's what I'm thinking."

"Then you've come to the right place. Let's hear it."

I pulled the envelope from my back pocket and removed Madeline's pictures and placed them on the desk before him. "Eighteen years old. Name's Madeline McKay. Rich girl, mixed up in drugs, found a lot of them in her apartment."

Dr. Burke picked up the photos and studied them with an indifferent intensity. "Pretty girl," he said. "How long she been missing?"

"Little over a week."

He studied them a bit more, then set them down and pushed them back toward me. "Don't recognize her, but let me go have a closer look at the bodies."

He pushed himself up and moved past me with the weary bulk of an old buffalo. I listened to his presence fill the silent morgue as he checked on the lifeless in the rooms down the hall. I checked my phone. No service in this underworld. I examined his Super Bowl ticket stub, remembered Tyree's catch; remembered the Patriots' humiliation with a smile. I returned it to his desk with care and settled back and examined Madeline's pictures again. I thought of those videos she'd made. A reckless one, a self-destructive party girl who was determined to shatter any expectations anyone else might have for her, she'd gone hard around the bend and it was unlikely she could come back, even if she wanted to. If she was alive, and I found her, there would be the requisite rehab, the shaming process. Maybe it would take for a bit, but probably not for long. There would be more hints at the potential and the talent that lay beneath, followed by more relapses, more descents, more disappointments. I was just a courier in a long, sad process. She was beautiful and angry and rich, and she didn't want what she was able to achieve. Yeah, I'd seen that movie. Seen it more than once. No happy endings to that drama.

Dr. Burke returned with a shake of his big, shaggy head. "Girl's not here," he said. He settled back behind his desk and leaned forward on his elbows. "Glad I couldn't help."

"Me too."

"By the way, I saw the *Post* this morning."

"The girl's mother isn't too happy about that."

"I would imagine not," he said. "Sounds like a nasty business."

"Looking that way."

"You think she did it?"

"No." Again, I said it with an unplaced assurance. "I don't know. Maybe. Sounds like she had motive, if you can call heartbreak motive."

"The finest motive of all," he said like a man who knew.

"She was a swimmer, this girl Madeline. Or is a swimmer. A very good one."

"Would that explain the haunted look you're wearing around?"

"That, or maybe it's just coming across a brutal murder." I saw James Fealy again, lying there mutilated in a red pool of his own blood. "She swims for the same team I used to," I said. "Her brother is an old teammate. An Olympic champ, in fact."

Dr. Burke's dark eyes narrowed and he gave a slight frown. "You remember what I told you when you first started in this business?" he asked.

"I know. Never make it personal."

"You can't, Duck. It will torture you. You need to view your clients as I view those lifeless sacks of flesh and organs in there," he said with a wave of the hand. "They are your work, and you have a duty to do right by them, but you mustn't identify with them or personalize your task in any way."

"What happens when it hits too close to home?"

"Then you pass the duty on to someone who doesn't have the same attachment. Move on to the next one." He leaned back and rubbed a puffy, clean-shaven cheek. Burke eyed me like an aging priest who'd lost the faith, made all the wiser. "But you're not going to do that, are you?"

"I don't know," I said. "Maybe I will. But not yet."

I moved to leave, extended a hand, and thanked him once again. I knew Burke felt some kind of responsibility toward me; he was betraying his own advice just by sitting here with me, interrupting his day to assist in my search. I knew why he felt that way, and it set off the usual mix of resentment and gratitude.

"Let's grab a drink sometime," I said. "A few drinks."

"You know where to find me."

He pretended to turn his attention to some papers on his desk as I backed from the office and silently shut his door and moved back up toward the land of the living. Outside, the sky was white and low with a thick humidity to the air. The heat was a miserable remnant of summer, a refusal to roll away for the coolness of fall, the only season worth a damn in this city. I turned down First Avenue and walked against the traffic south, past young docs in scrubs, past sad bus stops full of old folks with walkers and stooped backs. I turned into a bodega at the corner of 18th Street and picked up two six-packs of Beck's, then turned west and headed toward Second with a growing thirst. It was a quiet, tree-lined street, a stretch of restored brownstones with the sidewalks empty before me.

You're supposed to sense when you're being followed. Especially in my line of work, especially with the heightened awareness that aikido training is supposed to provide . . . and sometimes you do. But not always. Maybe I was lost in memories, maybe troubled by Fealy's murder or Madeline's videos. Whatever it was, I wasn't ready. I didn't sense the threat until I heard the voice, and then it was too late.

"Hey Duck," it said in a low grumble.

I turned under a darkened cover of scaffolding. I saw the fist, in fast-moving 3-D, thick, hairy knuckles, but not the face. The punch connected flush with my right eye. My head rocked back and sent me staggering. The bottles dropped from my hands. Another hard lunging hook completed the knockdown as I twisted around and fell to my knees. Then a rough hand pulled a fistful of my hair and forced me to the sidewalk. A series of well-placed kicks to the ribs and kidneys, followed by a few misses to my instinctively covered groin, then a final parting stomp on my head. He straightened up and caught his breath and spat on me. "You're a fucking asshole," he said. Then I heard a car door open and slam and the car speed off. I lifted my head enough to see it was a black SUV, but not enough to catch any details.

The entire assault could not have taken more than twenty seconds. I lay there longer than that, gasping in the heat, before a dog-walking pedestrian approached. He helped me up as his mutt panted on the leash and asked if I needed an ambulance, if I was okay, if I knew what happened. I coughed up some blood and felt my face swelling and disfiguring. I told him I was fine, waved off the concern, and limped away. I forgot my beers.

Truth is, it could have been any number of angry ex-husbands. Or more accurately, any number of angry ex-husbands could have hired someone to give me a beating. Plenty of bankers out there in the big city are a little less rich after I gave their wives proof they were screwing, well, you name it: secretary, boss, nanny, wife's friend, wife's sister, a Chelsea drag queen . . . I caught one guy, a director at Goldman, with two boys from Stuyvesant High. He'd walk over on his lunch break to a rented fuck pad in Battery Park and give the boys a thousand bucks each to hook up with each other while he jerked off. After getting caught, fired, divorced, and shamed, the guy had shot himself in that same apartment.

At least I knew it wasn't him.

I shuffled home getting Quasimodo stares. My right eye was swelling shut, and I could feel the side of my face morphing into a long, nasty bruise. I was pretty sure I'd broken a few ribs; my kidneys felt like they were leaking. Elvis greeted me with concern at the door. He whimpered at my feet and stayed close by as I went straight for the pills pilfered from Madeline. I found three Vicodins, swallowed them down, and poured myself plenty of Bulleit. I wanted to pass out and sleep away the pain. I gulped at the bourbon and while I waited for the pills to kick in, I called Cass. She was not okay.

"Duck, where have you been?" she gasped. "I've been calling. Something's happened."

I hadn't noticed the calls. "I was visiting, um, meeting with

Dr. Burke. No service. No Madeline there. And then . . . What happened?"

"It's Lucy Townes," she said. "We were supposed to meet at Chelsea Piers at two."

"What did she say?"

"She hurt herself, Duck. She was found unconscious at the bottom of her apartment building's pool. A maintenance worker found her. There was a note, addressed to her father. Sounds like attempted suicide. They're at the hospital now." I heard her take a drag from her cigarette. She exhaled.

"When?" I asked. "When did she do it?"

"Sometime between my contact with her and our scheduled meeting. I introduced myself on Facebook, then we emailed. Explained that we were hired to find her friend. She sounded eager to meet. I think she had something to say about Madeline."

Cass's voice was cold and clear; I could hear the rage rippling around its edges. I remembered the images we'd seen of Lucy. She was the bright yin to Madeline's dark yang. Lucy was fair and blond, brimming with the confidence of attractive youth. She didn't look like she'd be a friend of the destructive, drug-abusing Miss McKay, but there was some bond there.

"Is she gonna be okay?" I asked.

"I think so. Sounds like she was found just in time."

"Jesus," I said. "What the fuck is going on?"

A silence stretched between us. Then she said, "Duck, are you drunk? Your voice sounds funny."

"Haven't had a drink today, ma," I said. "Thing is, Cass, something's happened to me too."

The room was closing in with a heavy fog, my field of vision filled with spots. I heard Elvis whimpering, as if from far off, but I saw him right there at my feet. There was a tight pressure in my head, and the screws were turning fast. I took a gulp of whiskey and fought off a wave of nausea. I heard Cass's voice but it kept getting farther and farther away. I heard myself say, "I think something's wrong, wrong with . . . I gotta go."

The phone slipped from my hand. The beating, the pills, the booze, all did their part as I fell into blackness.

Chapter 9

Until I was twelve, my family lived in an Italianate brownstone on the Upper East Side. Not that we needed all that space; I was the only child of my father's second marriage and this was just one of his half dozen residences. But until that year, Mom and I lived a fine loaded life of private chefs and drivers and all the help you could ever need. Then it all went away in a dizzying six months of FBI raids and financial scandal. We fell far, from the Upper to Lower East, into a one-bedroom tenement apartment on Pitt Street, a block from the Hamilton Fish pool. Mom did not adjust well. She fell into a bottomless glass of vodka. One night during my last year of high school, she passed out in the bathtub and slipped under. I'd been staying with friends. I wasn't there to check on her, as I often did when I got home. The next morning our downstairs neighbor complained about a leak coming from the ceiling. They found her blue and lifeless beneath the surface.

Eighteen and orphaned, the weed dealing started up. College wasn't an option. I still had a few friends left from my old rich world, guys like Roy Perry. They became eager customers, started to spread the word. I grew my business, never touching my product, until I was pulling in a few grand a week and feeling pretty good about myself. Then, coming off that subway, I was reminded of the harsh reality that my enterprise was still illegal, and I followed my father's footsteps to the big house.

When I dream, I dream of falling, and I don't need an armchair shrink to tell me why. Sometimes I'll dream of our old house. I'll wander the darkened rooms down to the basement, where my mother sleeps soundly in a single twin bed under a flickering bulb. My concussed and addled brain was dreaming these dreams when Cass shook me awake on the couch. There was a puddle of vomit on the carpet next to me, and one cheek was caked with dried puke. The other cheek felt like I had a pumpkin stuffed in it. Elvis, ever loyal, was curled at my feet giving me his greatest droopy-eyed look of concern.

"My God, what the hell happened to you?" asked Cass.

"Cut myself shaving," I mumbled.

"You look like Cher's son in *Mask*."

"Ready for my closeup," I said. I tried to smile but one side of my face wasn't working.

She sat next to me on the couch and touched my cheek and frowned. She gave me a sad-eyed smile as she ran the backs of her fingernails down my face. "Poor Duck," she said. "What are we gonna do with you?" Then she straightened up and went to the kitchen and returned with cleaning supplies. As she scrubbed at the puke-crusted carpet, she told me I was lucky I hadn't choked on my own vomit.

"A rock 'n' roll way to go."

"You're no Jimi," she said. "You gonna tell me what happened?"

"Jumped," I said. "On Eighteenth and First, walking back from Dr. Burke's. Couldn't give you a description. Memories aren't working. What happened with Lucy?"

Cass recoiled and waved an offended hand in front of

her face. "Could you please go shower? We can trade notes after we get rid of this stench."

I managed my way to the bathroom and took a scalding shower that scorched the pain in my side and face. I avoided any examinations in the mirror.

When I returned to the living room, Cass was sitting with her laptop on her knees. *Coney Island Baby* played at low volume, Lou Reed droning about the glory of love. Cass was watching Madeline's videos with the clinical air of a surgeon studying an X-ray.

"She was high as can be when she made these," she said without looking up. "Look at her eyes, they're dead. She might sound like she wants it, but the eyes say it all. She's punishing herself."

"How'd you find those things again?"

Cass paused the video and minimized the browser. "You know that group I work with? Veronica Life?"

I gave her a blank look; she rolled her eyes.

"Thanks for listening," she said. "Veronica Life is a sex worker's outreach. A sort of watchdog group, named for an escort who was beaten to death by a Russian business-man in a room at the New York Palace. He got out of the country before anyone found the body. Anyway, we try to keep an eye on dangerous practices and people in the city's sex trade. An impossible task, I know, but we do what we can. At a recent meeting there was talk about a madam and porn producer named Angela Jones. Supposed to be a real evil bitch. Owns a company called Fallen Angels. She's developed a reputation for recruiting hot teenage girls in the city. Lurks around the club scene. Feeds them the finest drugs, gets them hooked. Anyway, I texted Madeline's pics to a few of the women from our group. One of them said she thought she recognized her as one of Angela's new girls."

Cass opened the browser again and pressed play. She

pointed to a small graphic in the lower right corner of the screen. "Fallen Angels" was scrawled in a fiery font, branding the production. We watched Madeline's dead high eyes roll back in her head as she arched her back and let out exaggerated moans as a skinny, tattooed hipster pounded above her in amateur frenzy. It wasn't much of a porn set. Angela didn't seem to spend a lot on her productions. It could have been the messy bedroom of any twenty-something dude. Reality porn—it's all the rage these days. I studied the images on the screen, looked past the slapping bodies, out the bedroom's window.

"You want some privacy?" asked Cass. "Stop looking so slack-jawed."

"I'm not, no. Take a look at this." I pointed to the window in the far right corner of the screen. "Right there, you can make out part of a street sign—R-o-e. . . . And there, the corner of that black sign. I think I recognize that. . . . That's right, it's Clem's, corner of Roebling and Grand. Williamsburg. Great bar."

Cass opened a new tab and searched "Clem's" in Google Maps. She clicked on street view and zoomed in until we were looking at the same location. "I'll be damned, well done." She rotated the view until it captured the building across the way, a bland three-story spot with a ground-floor boutique.

"Think we've found the set of our young pornographers."

"Want to pay them a visit?" she asked.

"Damn right."

Cass clicked back to Madeline's performance. Our missing girl was on top now, riding angry and hard. The camera zoomed in on penetration.

She shook her head and closed the laptop and pushed it to the far side of the table like it was infected. Then she got up and walked to the narrow front window, cracked it, and lit a cigarette. She blew smoke in the direction of the opening until she'd sucked it down to the filter. She examined my battered face from across the small room.

"So, you've really got no idea who did that to you?"

"No clue. I remember picking up some beer on my way home, then someone said my name, I turned, and bam. Never had a chance to react."

"Don't remember anything at all about him?"

"I remember seeing a black SUV speed off. Couldn't even tell you what kind. That's it. Tell me about Lucy."

Cass sighed, lit another cigarette. She pulled at it and shook her head like a jaded guidance counselor suffering from the guilt of bad advice to impressionable youth.

"I must have set the girl off on some kind of panic," she said. "We spoke briefly, after our emails. At first it sounded like she was relieved, like she'd been waiting for the call all along, and finally it had come. But then she started to get nervous, asking me to prove my identity, mistrust creeping into her voice. I tried to assure her, and she agreed to meet me. But then she must have had a change of heart." She sucked down the rest of her cigarette, held the final inhale in her lungs. "Thank God someone found her in time," she said through an exhaust of smoke.

"How did you hear about it?" I asked. "You're sitting there, waiting to meet the girl at Chelsea Piers, she doesn't show. Then you find out she tried to drown herself. How'd you get word so quickly?"

"That's the really fucked up part," she said. "Turns out I know the father. He's sessioned with me for years at the Chamber. Sweet man. Michael Townes. He's a widower. Lucy's mother passed away when she was young. Michael has raised his daughter by himself."

"And he called you first about it?"

"No, Duck. While he was waiting for the ambulance, he noticed his daughter's phone. Saw a bunch of missed calls from my number. I'd been calling Lucy after she didn't show. He freaked, thought his relationship with me had something to do with it, and called me from the hospital."

"That must have been a fun conversation."

Cass gave me a look. Her eyes fell shut, her mouth turned down. She shook her head in bewildered sorrow. "He's such a good, sweet man," she whispered. "Always been one of my favorites. For him to think . . ."

Rain began to fall outside; I could hear its faint fizz in the streets. The humidity was finally cracking. Footsteps outside the window began to pick up their pace. A moving van blocked the street in front of our building. A line of cabs behind it began to honk in impatient discord.

"So, I met with Charlie McKay," I told her. "After I was thoroughly scolded by his mother for my appearance in the *Post*."

"What did he have to say?"

"Told me that he's the one who introduced his sister to James Fealy."

She had been looking past me, into the kitchen, glowering in guilt. This got her attention. She came back over and joined me on the couch. Elvis grumbled and jumped down as she nudged him out of the way. The rain picked up into a steady hiss outside. Low growls of thunder rumbled over the city sky. My darkened living room grew darker.

"Appears Charlie and Fealy's father work together at the same hedge fund, Soto Capital," I said. "Sounds like Fealy Senior is some kind of master of the universe. His son met Madeline at a country retreat out at the boss's house in Connecticut. Charlie sounds more worried about his job than his sister."

Cass said nothing, waiting for more. She slipped a pen from her pocket and absently began to click it open and shut. My headache was returning after too much talk. I reminded myself that I should keep ice on the right side of my face. I leaned back and winced as my splintered ribs stabbed my insides. I needed a doctor, but I don't see doctors. Not unless I wake up in the hospital and have no choice.

"He told me about their run-in at the family house in Rhinebeck."

"Last time anyone saw her, right?" she asked.

"Yeah, he says he went up there to get some work done, thinking the house would be empty, said she never uses it. When she saw him, Madeline ran upstairs to her bedroom, packed a bag of stuff, and then took off. She called a cab and waited by the road, he said."

"He didn't go out after her?"

"He said he tried calling and texting her, but got no reply."

"But he was too busy with work to get up and go outside and talk to his sister in person? Isn't that a little odd?"

"Not if you talk to him. It's pretty clear that work comes well before family for this guy."

"What a prince." Cass shook her head, imagining the scene as Charlie described it. "And then she sent that text to her mother the next day?" she asked.

"Saying 'I'm so sorry'—for something she didn't specify."

We both looked over at the closed laptop. "There would appear to be a few potential sources of shame for this girl," she said.

Cass lit another smoke and smiled her sorrowful smile. She reached out and touched my face. Her fingertips soothed the swelling more than any ice could. She looked into my one good eye with a sisterly affection that I hated to acknowledge. "Poor boy, you look terrible. You shouldn't be talking so much. You need to rest."

I shook my head, tried to stand. My head swam in swirling protest. I sat back down. "Don't worry about me, ma," I said. "Not the first time I've had my head kicked in."

"You still need to recover. No drinking tonight, okay?"

"Promise."

"Liar."

She pushed herself up, went to the kitchen and poured the rest of my Bulleit bottle down the drain. She knew I could buy plenty more a block from my apartment, but she couldn't resist inflicting that extra bit of pain to prove her point. She returned with a cruel smirk, stubbed out her cigarette in the cluttered ashtray and stretched, arching her back with her hands on her hips, sighing at the soreness. I felt the usual pangs of lust as I stared up at her long body bent backward toward me. She looked like bottled sex.

At the door, she turned with a final thought: "This James Fealy kid, he had a powerful father and a trust fund worth who knows how many millions?"

"Charlie says one-point-five."

"What do you mean?"

"Billion. He said Fealy's father is worth like one and a half billion dollars."

She considered the ten-digit number.

"Murdered boyfriend, best friend attempted suicide, a little warning assault for you," she said. "Nice start to a case."

On that note, she left me lying there on the couch. Beating or not, I couldn't be alone licking my wounds in the apartment. There was someone I needed to see.

Chapter 10

The Brookshire was one of those pedigreed apartment houses with a co-op board like a secret society. Last names were passwords, and if you have a famous one, don't bother applying, no matter how much you want to pay. Too much attention. Every square foot was priced in the thousands; the maintenance fees were absurd, but if you were bothered by such things, then what were you doing there? The building was old and stylish, with all the original details, and upkeep cost a certain amount. Even to moan about such New York irritations showed you hadn't made it. A curious place for a swim coach to live.

When Marks gave me the Upper East Side address, there was silence for a moment, which he filled by saying that he'd explain when I got there. Back when I was swimming for him, Marks lived in a rent-controlled apartment near the pool in Stuyvesant Town. He told me once that his military service gave him a steep veteran's discount on housing there, which was the only way he was able to remain in Manhattan on a coach's salary. Over the last few decades his job hadn't changed, but somehow his circumstances had.

I got off the 6 train at the corner of 68th and Lex and walked a block west to Park Avenue. BROOKSHIRE was written in a white font across a dark green awning. The rain continued in a steady, dark drizzle, and the evening sidewalks steamed with stubborn humidity. A mosquito landed on my forearm holding the umbrella. I slapped it dead with my free hand, and my ribs burned at the quick movement. The doorman stiffened at my approach. He did not reach for the door.

"Help you, sir?" He said the last word with naked irony.

My one good eye looked down at him; he was a little guy, a good head shorter, with a bad attitude under that doorman's top hat and waistcoat. I felt like slapping him dead too. "Here to see Teddy Marks," I said. "He's expecting me."

"Theodore Marks, in apartment 2C?" he doubted. "Let me see."

I folded the umbrella and waited under the green awning while the little man scurried inside to call Marks. I always seemed to be waiting just outside the gates for approval to enter, wherever I went. Doormen and bodyguards and bouncers all stood by, blocking the way to the rooms that mattered in this city. It was something no tourist would ever grasp about this place, with their "love to visit, could never live there" half-bright comments as they gazed skyward. The city is a giant closed society. Visitors saw nothing.

As usual, this particular guard dog looked defeated as he emerged with head bowed and waved me inside. "He's expecting you," he mumbled.

Marks lived on a lower floor, less exclusive; back when the Brookshire went up in the 1880s, these were the quarters for the help. Fitting, I thought, that it still is. On the upper floors, most contained just two apartments, the floor divided into two 6,000-square-foot mansions in the sky. At the very top, there were three big billionaire's residences, one per floor. American-made billionaires, never foreign in this waspy fortress, who'd inherited some millions, gone to the right schools and banks, and then expanded their already considerable fortunes before taking convenient *noblesse oblige* positions in government to skirt taxes, while slapping their names on museums and hospital wings. These were Marks's new neighbors, but down here on the second floor there were a dozen or so smaller apartments. The cheapest one was probably around $2 million.

I was greeted at the door not by Marks, but by his hard blond assistant. "Anna," she reminded me with an extended hand. "Anna Lisko. It is nice to properly meet you this time, Mr. Duck." She squeezed my knuckles for a bit too long, and I let her guide me in. "What has happened?" she asked, motioning to the wreckage down the right side of my face.

Before I could answer, Marks was by her side, holding a whiskey and a wide-eyed look of horror. "Jesus, man, look at you!"

"You should see the other guy," I muttered lamely.

"Yeah, you give it back?"

"His fists are probably sore as hell," I said. "Feet too."

"Well, something tells me you might have had it coming." He put his arm around my shoulders and pulled me past Anna and through the foyer into his high-beamed living room. "You never were afraid of a beating," he said.

I took a seat on a low-backed leather couch. Anna settled into a club chair next to me while Marks went over to a wet bar in the corner and poured us drinks. He crossed the room proudly, holding a whiskey for me, vodka for Anna. They were offered with a slight bow and wink at his assistant coach. She took her vodka with unsmiling thanks, then leaned back and regarded the two men before her with candid regard. There was a detached curiosity about her, as if she were preparing to watch a play with dubious reviews. I drank my whiskey; she drank her vodka. Marks smiled down at both of us. He took a sip of his drink and wiped some whiskey from his mustache. Some sort of jazz played soft from invisible speakers. Mingus, maybe.

"Nice place," I said.

He looked around, as if admiring it for the first time. "It is indeed, is indeed," he said. A real estate agent would have called it "triple mint" with "old world charm and every modern convenience." Translation: the large living room was bachelor pad perfect, with built-in bookcases around the flat-screen and original crown molding around the perimeter. The space was oddly impersonal, the work of a decorator. A large, dark Oriental rug, a few tasteful Hudson River School landscapes, the palate and the lighting just so.

"How long you been here?" I asked.

"Let's see," he said. "It's been, what, almost eleven years now."

A silence stretched. I looked over at Anna; there was a slight smirk on her full lips, like only she knew how this scene would end.

"It was a . . . gift," he said finally. "A very generous, very overwhelming gift. Some athletes give their coaches their gold medals, others, well . . ." He looked around the room and smiled, unembarrassed.

"Charlie bought this for you?" I asked.

"No, well, yes. It was a gift from the McKay family, from their trust. They purchased it shortly after Charlie won all those gold. I refused it at first, of course. Said absolutely not, I was content in my little place in Stuy Town. But they insisted. Margaret bought it anyway, said it would just sit empty then, until I accepted their gift. And it did, this place sat empty for nine months before I realized she was serious. Margaret McKay . . ." He shook his head in awed admiration. "A formidable woman, that one."

Anna leaned forward and set down her drained vodka glass with theatrical firmness. "Gentlemen," she said, "I must be going. Mr. Duck, it was a pleasure. Feel better. Mr. Coach, I will see you early in the morning, yes?"

She stood and looked down her strong Slavic nose at me. About the same height as Cass, over six feet, but thicker. A rock-solid swimmer girl who'd lost the shoulders but kept the thighs. Everything about her was hard and clean, from her too-toned arms to her crystalline blue eyes that challenged you to look back. I began to stand, and she reached out and touched my chest. She held her hand there until I obeyed. "No, please, do not get up," she said.

I watched her leave; she took her time about it. She kissed Marks on both cheeks and whispered a stern thanks. Then she slipped on a light blue nylon warm-up jacket over her tank top. On the back there was a flag of blue and yellow, two simple bars like an unfinished Rothko painting. Beneath it were the words NATIONAL TEAM. Anna crossed the room unhurried, aware of the eyes following her. She moved in that athlete's slow motion; forever accustomed to conserving energy away from competition. She did not turn back as she opened the door and left us.

"She was a hell of a swimmer, that one," Marks said as the door closed.

I stared through the front door and imagined her waiting beyond us at the elevator, grim-faced and proud, with that private smirk.

"Just missed a medal at the last Games in the two hundred breast," he continued. "Still holds the Ukrainian National records. I hired her a year ago to work with our age groupers. She's gonna be a hell of a coach too, really knows her stuff."

"You always have your assistants over for drinks?" I asked.

He gave a dry, clipped laugh. "Sometimes," he said. "My door is always open. In this case, Anna is having a bit of a problem with her colleague, my other assistant coach, Nick Price. I believe you met both of them on your way out the other day?"

"I did, briefly. They looked like a cute couple," I said.

"Nick only wishes. Seems to be quite a case of puppy love. Anna tells me there was something brief, a forgettable night after a meet and a few drinks; she didn't think much of it. But poor Nick's fallen hard, and now Anna wants to disentangle herself from this 'American boy,' as she calls him, and bless her, she came to me worried that it would upset the professionalism on the pool deck."

"So now you get to tell Coach Nick to leave her alone?"

"I'll mention something tomorrow at practice; he'll get the message." Marks sat down in a beaten black recliner across from me. It looked like the one piece of furniture saved from his last place, a cheap totem of roots that made the rest of the place that much less personal. His face darkened. He set down his whiskey on the floor and looked across at me with that old truth serum glare. "Duck, what the hell have you gotten yourself into? You show up drunk on deck after all that time, then the next morning you're on the cover of the *Post*—at a murder scene. Then you come over here looking like someone stuffed you through a meat grinder."

"You tell me," I said. "I'm looking for one of your swimmers. And, as it happens, one of the owners of the apartment we're sitting in. A rightful heir to the McKay family fortune, I believe."

He stiffened at that. "The apartment is in my name," he said. "I am the sole owner." His pride was too thick to be wounded, but it was clear the subject would always be sensitive. He picked up his whiskey and had a long swallow and winced. "Madeline McKay," he said. "Christ.

That girl has always been a hot mess." He stared into his glass, stewing, trying and failing to suppress his exasperation. Then he turned his hard eyes back to me. "This could really be a disaster, you know? For me, for all of Marks Aquatics, and especially for the McKays. Charlie and Margaret, they're like family to me. Good people, the best. They don't deserve this . . ."

"Don't deserve what? A wild child in the family? What else is going on here, Coach? Madeline McKay is now the prime suspect in a brutal murder—I witnessed the body myself. Someone slashed up her ex-boyfriend. The boyfriend's roommate claims Madeline had gone bunny boiler on him. The police are probably gonna find her before I do."

"I know," he said quietly. "They were here earlier today."

"So what else can you tell me? What did you tell them?"

My head was starting to hurt again; the edges of the room were beginning to blur. I put the whiskey glass to my lips, but it seemed to have emptied itself.

"Here," said Marks. "Let's get us a refill." He stood and took my glass and went to the wet bar and gave us both a splash. Returning, he looked weary, his age and stress starting to crack through the dogged fitness, the veteran's sense of unbreakable self. "I'm sure it wasn't Madeline who killed that boy," he said, handing over the glass.

I swallowed half the whiskey down before he settled back into his seat. "How are you so sure?" I asked. "The girl's a mess, you said it yourself. She's an addict too, from the looks of it. And based on her phone records, she was legitimately obsessed with this kid, James Fealy."

"I don't doubt it," he said. "Maddie has been in a bad way for years, plunging deeper every time we think she's found bottom. But ultimately she's a sweet, sad kid. I just can't see her being violent." He sighed, shook his head at the thought. "I understand this kid Fealy was a poor influence, a partner in crime, so to speak. Charlie hated him from the beginning."

"He told me he introduced them."

Marks nodded, grimaced. "At his company's retreat, was it? He felt horrible about it. Now, well, I can only imagine . . ."

"Where would she go?" I asked. "I thought I'd check out the McKay's country house in Rhinebeck. The last place she was seen, by Charlie over Labor Day weekend. You ever been there?"

He was staring past me, out the dark windows onto Park Avenue a story below. He lifted his glass but reconsidered halfway to his mouth and set it back down and, instead, rose and crossed the room to the window. I shifted on the couch to face him. My sides stabbed at the movement; I needed a Vicodin, more than one, and I was all out of Madeline's stash. I wondered if Marks had anything that could help in his medicine cabinet.

"I went there, once, many years ago," he said. "When Charlie was a teenager, Madeline just a baby. Their father was still alive. Do you remember him, Steve McKay?" I told him I did, but Marks didn't seem to hear. "He was intense, that man. Smart, very smart, clearly, how else does one make all that money? But crazy. Full of animal spirits. Everything was done to excess with Steve. His work, his play. There were drugs and other women—Margaret was aware of both. And he also showed his love in the extreme. When he was around, he showered his kids with affection, his wife too. But then he'd be off again. He would disappear for days at a time. Margaret had him followed once. You're not the first one she's hired, you know? The investigator turned up more than enough. Margaret was prepared to file for divorce, but then Steve got sick. She didn't have the heart to leave him at his bedside."

I got up and went to the bar to help myself to another splash. My legs were unsteady beneath me, and the heavy crystal decanter shook in my hands as I tipped it over. Some bourbon soaked the countertop before it found its mark.

"Sounds like Madeline takes after her daddy," I said.

"That she does. As an outside observer, without children of my own, it is my theory that kids are one parent or the other. They are never a combination of mother and father, even if their genes are a mix. They are one or the other. Charlie, of course, is Margaret's son through and through. They are mirrors of each other. Same character, same temperament. So it was with Madeline and her father. She shares those wild animal spirits. And she absolutely adored him. She was very young when he died, so perhaps the relationship would have fractured with darker truths in later years, but something snapped in Maddie when her father passed away. They were kindred spirits, and ever since, I fear she's been destructively searching for someone to take his place."

A cell phone rang and danced on the dining table. Marks crossed the room and looked at the caller ID and frowned. Then he placed the phone to his ear and spoke before listening. "Let me call you back," he said. "Give me twenty minutes." He walked into the kitchen with the phone. "Wait, what?" he asked. "Oh, my God." His voice dropped. He listened to the caller, whispered distressed replies I couldn't hear. He returned looking ashen. "Duck, I'm sorry, something has happened. I'm going to have to see you out."

"Anything to do with the McKays?" I asked.

"No, no. Nothing about Madeline," he said. "A girl on our team. Lucy. My God, how could she . . ." His voice trailed away. "A swimmer on our team attempted to take her own life today. Now, if you'll excuse me, I need to . . ."

No sense telling him I heard the news before he did. "Is she gonna be okay?" I asked.

"I don't . . . I think, yes. I'm told she's stable, at the hospital now."

As I stood, the room spun, and I had to set a hand on the arm of the couch to steady myself. My vision filled with spots, my temples throbbed.

"You all right there, Duck?" I heard him say from somewhere far off.

I waited for the symptoms to pass and concentrated on my heartbeat. It worked, for the moment. Something like clarity returned, and I straightened up. "Might have a slight concussion," I said. "I keep having these little episodes."

"You should get yourself checked out," he said. "I can put you in touch with an excellent doctor at NYU. Same guy who treats the Giants. I'll send you his contact."

Marks gathered my umbrella and opened the front door. The man was reeling from the news, eager to be rid of me. I asked if I could use his bathroom. He inhaled sharply through the nose and pointed down the hall. "First door on the right," he said, closing the door.

There was nothing stronger than Advil in his medicine cabinet. Not a single orange prescription bottle of any sort, for anything. Was that even possible? Apparently, the man had no maladies. Or hid his meds elsewhere. Closing the cabinet, I had a look at my battered face in the mirror. It looked like I'd gone the distance with a mean middleweight. Marks was waiting where I'd left him by the door, his mind already at the hospital with his troubled swimmer.

"I'll be back in touch," I told him. "So sorry to hear about that girl."

"Take care of yourself, Duck," he said.

Outside the Brookshire, I crossed Park Avenue and waited in the shadows behind a parked black Suburban. I lingered there in the rain, fighting through waves of concussive symptoms. A cab pulled up, and the little top-hatted doorman scurried over and opened the back door. A moment later, Marks came rushing out and ducked in. His silhouette collapsed against the backseat as the cab pulled off in the rain toward the hospital.

Chapter 11

In the morning the pain got to work. The bruising in my face was a mosaic of purples and blues; my right eye was swollen shut, the eyelid puffed out like an allergic reaction. My ribs stabbed, my kidneys ached. I forced myself up and gathered some shreds of life with the help of four Advil, three cups of black coffee, and two Xanax. They wouldn't do much for the pain, but at least they'd mellow out the dread.

I resolved to take Elvis for a walk without my phone. Get the blood flowing, breathe in some fresh air, try to enjoy the mindless clarity of a dog walk. I didn't glance at the missed calls on my way out, didn't want to know; just needed the manic, sniffing company of the hound as we weaved our way down through the East Village. We didn't get far.

At a newsstand on the corner of 14th and Third I caught my first sight of that morning's *Post*. There was Madeline McKay on the cover—her morose yearbook shot from Hewitt. The headline read SICK LOVE; the subhead announced: *Murdered filmmaker's psycho ex-girlfriend sought in slay. Fingerprints "all over" crime scene. Full Story, Pages 3–5.*

I paid for a copy and opened to the story. It got worse inside. There was a sidebar about yours truly, with "reporting by Roy Perry." Thanks, buddy. The piece was less than flattering. It mentioned my "notorious crook" father, my "drug bust" and time in Rikers, and my "reputation in society circles as a go-to divorce detective." There was even an anonymous quote from a woman who claimed I had "bedded more than a few of the ladies he's worked for." A fine bit of reporting by the intrepid Mr. Perry, the prick.

The stories about Madeline didn't reveal much I didn't already know. Her big brother Charlie made an appearance, of course—"a genuine Olympic hero"—and Margaret received sympathetic billing as the "winsome worried widow." The picture of her exiting her Gramercy co-op was a study in scandalous glamour: long black skirt, gray cardigan over high-buttoned white blouse; oversize sunglasses; frosted blond hair glued in place; one hand artfully up and shielding herself from the clicking cameras. The picture of Charlie was older; the *Post* couldn't resist: He was shirtless, hands on his hips, clad only in a Speedo, with that tangle of gold medals on display across his shaved chest.

They claimed that Madeline's fingerprints had been found all over Fealy's apartment. They reported that she had been "stalking" him of late, after an ugly breakup, and that phone records showed a "disturbing pattern of obsession" with hundreds of text messages sent to her former lover in a "desperate bid" to get him back. They quoted Mike Schwartz, the roommate, who expressed his certainty that Madeline was involved. They uncovered a few more mourning friends who added glowing remembrances of the dead.

The last page of coverage was devoted to Fealy's father, the hard-charging hedge fund manager, Max Fealy, whose tax returns showed that in the previous year he had earned $125 million in salary and bonuses. The devastated father had taken a leave of absence from Soto Capital, where he was a senior partner, and he was ensconced with his family—his wife, Sara, and their surviving son, fifteen-year-old Tim—at the family's home in Southampton.

I folded the paper under my arm and set back toward home. Elvis pulled in the other direction, knowing the walk was up. I told him I'd make it up to him with a long one later, but he just lunged at an open trash bag and howled at a passing squirrel. The rain had cleared in the night. It was going to be another humid one. The streets had the sticky, bug-infested feel of an urban rain forest under a moist ash sky. I was miserable with sweat by the time I reached my stoop.

There were nine voice mails, sixteen missed calls, and eighteen texts waiting on my phone. Not a promising sign. Perhaps I should have checked them upon waking, but at least I'd had three blocks of clueless bliss with Elvis before coming upon the *Post*. Most of the missed calls were from blocked numbers—the cops and the media. Both parties were eager to hear from me. Two of the voice mails and a bunch of the texts were from Roy Perry, first requesting comment on deadline, and then apologizing for what went to print. I texted back: **WTF?** and got on to the rest.

In reverse order of urgency, there were calls from other reporters at the *Daily News*, *AM New York*, and NY1. Delete, delete, delete. There were calls and texts from a few concerned divorcées who'd seen the sidebar. There were calls from Charlie, asking to meet as soon as possible. And there were calls from Detective Lea Miller, requesting my presence at the Ninth Precinct at eleven a.m. I looked at the clock on my cable box and saw that it was already forty-five minutes past that hour. I called her back first, said I was on my way.

*   *   *

I found the Ninth on a quiet leafy block in the East Village. A few years back, the Fighting Ninth underwent a total rehab. They gutted it inside and out, bringing it up to modern standards in the early days of Bloomberg's first term. The original white stone exterior was scrubbed and reinstalled brick by brick and a seventh floor of glass and steel was added to the top. The only sign that it's not another new condo building is the annoying cop parking out front. Always perpendicular to the street on precinct blocks; cops don't have time to parallel park like the rest of us. The American flag hung limp over the entrance.

The interior was high and white and antiseptic, a place without humor or germs. A heavy young clerk was behind the desk. She was cranky and bored and smacked at her gum like a disinterested cow. I gave her my name and Detective Miller's and was summarily escorted to the elevators and up to the fourth floor, where the Ninth's Detective Squad was hard at work on the Fealy homicide.

Detective Miller did not smile when she saw me. She was cop cute—a hard little body and utilitarian curves. Her fashion choices were sexless: brown corduroys and worn blazer, sensible shoes, no jewelry, each choice a conscious attempt to erase any spark of attraction around her peers. She crossed the room with a stiff bow-legged strut.

"Jesus, you look like shit," she said. "Rough day at the office?"

"Street toughs," I said. "The gangs of Gramercy Park."

"Dangerous part of town."

"The worst."

"Nice story in the *Post*," she said. "I hear you know that reporter, Roy Perry. Some friend."

"He's no friend of mine," I told her.

She led me across the fluorescent-lit room to her desk. I ignored the usual cop stares—recognized a few of them and knew better than to look back. She motioned to a chair desk-side and settled into her seat with short legs outstretched. She crossed those sensible shoes, a pair of black orthopedic loafers, and reached for a pad and pen.

"So, how do you know him?" she asked.

"Around."

"Around where?"

"He's an old friend, from when I used to be rich," I said. "Oh, and I used to sell him weed before I went to jail."

The blunt honesty tripped her tongue for a moment. She looked past me, across the room at her colleagues, then returned her gaze. "When's the last time you were in a police station, Duck? Bring back memories?"

"All suppressed."

"I didn't think convicted felons were allowed to work as PI's?"

"They're not."

"And yet . . ."

"I was helping an old family friend. Sometimes I like to help people with their problems. Sort of like you."

She ignored this. "You have a previous relationship with Charles McKay, is that correct?"

"We swam on the same team when we were kids," I said. "Before Margaret tracked me down, I hadn't talked to him in twenty years."

Miller looked at me with a wry smile. She made a few notes on her pad, took her time about it. A former gymnast, I thought again, or maybe a dancer, something that left her fit and flexible, and instilled that unmistakable discipline. She was free of any borough accent, had the air of a city girl born and bred. My guess: the blue was in her blood. A cop father who never had a son; daughter made detective early to make up for it. She thought she knew me too.

"I wouldn't have taken you for an athlete, Duck," she said.

"Long retired," I told her. "In another lifetime people thought I was headed for the Olympics too."

"So, what happened?"

"Life."

"That has been known to happen." I couldn't tell if it was empathy in her voice, or mockery.

Before I could ask about her own jock past, we were joined by the less than athletic presence of her partner. His belly almost pushed me out of the chair as he approached from behind. "If it isn't the PI who puked all over our crime scene. How's it going, tough guy?" He offered a meaty hand over my shoulder. "Detective Sullivan," he said. "Mind if I join you two?" He pulled up a chair from another desk and sunk into it across from Detective Miller. The chair creaked and protested under his weight but somehow held its ground.

"Who whipped his ass?" he asked his partner.

"Mr. Darley was just telling me about his illustrious past as a champion swimmer," said Miller.

Sullivan picked some hard candies from a bowl on her desk and regarded me with open disdain. "Was that before daddy was busted?" he asked. He crunched into the candy. I didn't reply, just looked back with my one open eye. "Seems you grew up with quite the silver spoon," he said. "Little Lawrence Darley, a young prince of the Upper East Side. But then one day . . ." He held up his hand over his head and nosedived it in a downward arc, making crashing sounds as it went.

"So, what can I do for you guys?" I asked, fighting off the old rage. Again I pictured Cass giving it to the bastard with her strap-on, making sloppy Sullivan squeal like the pig he was. Made me smile.

The detectives exchanged a serious look. "Roy Perry told us you were drinking with him at a nearby bar, Zum's, before you found Mr. Fealy."

"Nice of him to give me an alibi," I said.

"Duck, he'd been dead for a few days," said Miller.

I shrugged. Sullivan leaned forward into my personal space. "How did you gain entry into the building?" he asked. "And the apartment?"

I looked at both of them. "You know, I already answered these questions the other night."

"Humor us," said Sullivan.

"I slipped through the front door after the Schwartz kid came home," I said. "Then I responded to his screams. The apartment was open."

"So, you were trespassing," he said.

"Yes."

Detective Miller scribbled something else in her pad. Sullivan kept trying to stare me down; I couldn't get the image of Cass railing him out of my head.

"Aren't there security cameras in the lobby of Fealy's building?" I asked. "You guys must have footage of anyone entering or leaving the place."

The partners glanced at each other, looked back at me.

"Madeline McKay was seen leaving the building last Monday afternoon on camera by the building's virtual doorman," said Miller.

A chill coursed through me. So much for my instinct of her innocence. "Does that mean she did it?" I asked.

"Mr. Fealy's parents informed us that their son did not return from Southampton until Tuesday morning," she said. "The body had been there for a few days before you found him, but we haven't determined the exact time of death yet."

"So, his killer must have entered at some point after she left? What else did you find on the security footage?"

"We're looking into it," said Sullivan.

"There appears to have been an electrical problem in

the building," said Miller. "There's a stretch where the cameras were not working."

"Lovely. What's a virtual doorman anyway?" I asked.

"It means some lazy fuck is supposed to be watching the screens from some warehouse in Jersey," said Sullivan. "Helpful, huh?"

Miller made a few more notes. Sullivan crunched into a few more hard candies. They made a fine pair, fit for a TV pilot, the grizzled, overweight old-school cop and the undersized tough broad with the soft eyes.

"When you searched Madeline McKay's apartment, what did you find?" asked Miller, voice now as hard as her body.

"We found her stash of dope," said Sullivan. "Any guess whose prints were all over it?"

"Why didn't you tell us about the drugs in your statement?" asked Miller.

"Must have slipped my mind," I said. "I was pretty shaken up after seeing Fealy's body. As you noted, Detective Sullivan, I have a sensitive stomach. Oh, and I'd been drinking all day."

"What did you take?"

"Just a few painkillers," I said. I motioned to my bruised face. "After this little episode, they've been very helpful."

"Duck, we could get a search warrant for your apartment," said Miller. "I'm certain we'd find more than just pain pills in there. Now's the time to tell us if you took anything else."

"I didn't," I said. "Go ahead and search it. You'll find my hound, Elvis, on the couch. And an empty bottle of bourbon. That's about it."

The detectives exchanged a look of irritation, deliberating silently how to proceed. This little drama was getting old. I helped them along. "Look," I said. "We both want the same thing—to find the girl. I'm sorry I grabbed a few of her pills. She won't miss them. Just tell me how I can help, and I'll stay out of your way."

Sullivan let out a low simmer of steam. He straightened up in the chair and nodded once to his partner, giving her the floor. "You can *help*," said Miller, stretching the word out into two syllables, "by being truthful with us. By turning over everything you lifted from Madeline McKay's apartment. And after that, you can go away and leave this to the professionals."

"Hey Duck, your partner, what's her name again?" asked Sullivan. "Cassandra Kimball, is it?" There was a sudden glimmer to his eye, a rising giddiness to his voice. "She's one of them dominatrix ladies, right? I mean, in her day job, when she's not helping you snoop around. Goes by the name of Mistress Justine?" Sullivan showed me a mouthful of yellowed teeth with deposits of hard candies stuck in the crevices. "She, like, beats men for money? You into that stuff, Duck? You like to get whipped by your lady friend?"

"Don't be ashamed, Sully," I said. "If you want a good railing from my partner, just ask for it. You look like the type."

Chapter 12

I stopped into the first bar I saw, sucked back the rest of the Pabst, and left twelve bucks on the bar. Staggering out into a hard sun, I found a cab heading up First Avenue, collapsed in the back and gave the cross streets. The city swept by off balance as we traveled north. The cheap booze burned in my belly. I should have eaten something. This publicity in the *Post* was bad for business. No one hired a finder that couldn't keep his cases out of the papers. My clientele worshipped privacy like a religion. If they wanted a reality show circus, they'd bring their problems to the cops.

The McKays knew all about the invasion of cameras. Their saddest moments, grieving a father and a husband, had been captured for the world to see, spun into grand Olympic drama. That was the contract you made with greatness. Charlie had touched the wall first in a few very important swimming races; the national anthem had been played in his honor several times; billions watched and were inspired. As such, the champion's family was forced to open its doors to the curious masses. When they discovered cancerous tragedy behind it all, well, all the better. And now the cameras were back, with Charlie and Margaret at the center of another family drama. Except this time it was scandal for sale, not inspiration. The daughter, the forgotten sister of the champion, was damaged and missing and suspected of murder. Her best friend lay in the hospital, an unsuccessful suicide.

I closed my eyes and listened to the chatter of Taxi TV as we stopped and started through the honking gridlock of midtown. A chaos of claustrophobic impatience, I felt sorry for the poor saps forced to work each day in this stressed and soaring part of town. We made it, finally, past 57th and picked up speed as we entered the Upper East Side, the scarred landscape of my youth. I asked the cabbie to let me off two blocks early on 66th so I could walk off the booze. Not that Cass would be fooled.

I found her in a bright, sad waiting room on the fifth floor of the hospital. NY1 aired at low volume on the TV in the corner. Two young parents sat in a pale daze at the far end of the room; the mother was staring at the cover of a magazine without opening it, the father stared off into space. An elderly man sat nearby, looking at his feet in total stillness. He had the air of a prisoner waiting to be called for final rites. Cass sat among them like an angel of death. She was dressed in black from boots on up. Her black hair was combed straight down past her shoulders, parted down the middle. Crimson lipstick was painted on a mouth pressed tight in concentration. She was looking at her phone and tapping on the screen with sharp red nails.

I touched her shoulder and gave her a start, but before we could speak, two doors opened and out stepped a big bearded man in jeans and flannel. His face was wrenched in exhaustion and worry; the weight of the world pressed down on broad sagging shoulders. He approached Cass in three long strides. She stood, and he pulled her into a tight embrace. He whispered something in her ear and she nodded, and he started to cry; then they separated and he looked away. She turned to me and blinked away wet eyes.

"She's going to be okay," she said. Cass turned to the man by her side. "This is Michael Townes, Lucy's father. Michael, this is my partner, Duck Darley."

I shook the big man's hand. His grip swallowed mine, and he avoided eye contact. "I'm so sorry," I said.

He nodded once, looked at me for the first time. "Looks like you had a bit of an accident yourself," he said.

"Slipped on the sidewalk."

"Right. Slipped and fell on a fist." He managed a laugh. "I hate it when that happens."

Aware of his tears, Michael Townes gathered himself, stood a little straighter. He ran a hand through his beard and rubbed at his eyes. He searched the waiting room like a man lost in a foreign land.

"Thank God she's going to be all right," said Cass.

His expression fell from sorrow to anger. "She's not all right," he said. "My daughter tried to kill herself."

"It was a cry for help," she said quietly. "And now you're going to get her the help she needs."

Cass rubbed at his back. Townes swatted her arm down, moved a step away. "How do you know what she needs?" he asked. "You've never even met her."

"I was waiting to meet her, Michael. She might—"

"He's right, Cass," I said. "We have no idea what she needs, or what's going on." I turned to Townes. "I hate to say it, but I have some experience with what you're going through right now, with what your daughter tried to do. The last thing you want is for someone to tell you it's going to be okay," I told him. "At least in my experience."

"That's the last thing you want to hear," he said, making eye contact with his mistress.

Cass seemed to shrink a step behind me, unaccustomed to a scolding from her longtime slave. She managed a submissive nod. "I'm sorry," she whispered.

"We'll get out of your way in a minute," I said. "As Cass probably mentioned, we've been hired to find Lucy's friend, Madeline McKay, who's now a suspect in a murder."

"The boyfriend," he said. "I saw the papers."

"Lucy's attempt and this killing could be connected. If possible, whenever she's ready, we'd really appreciate it if we could talk to your daughter."

He thought about it for a moment. "You know, Madeline McKay can go to hell as far as I'm concerned. She was a horrible influence on Lucy."

"I'm sure she was," I said. "The girl sounds like nothing but trouble. But now we need to find her before she pulls anyone else down with her. That's why it's really important that we speak to her, whenever she's able."

He sighed. "I'll ask her. If she's up to it, maybe. Just one of you, though; my daughter doesn't need a grilling, not now."

"Of course," I said. "If it's okay with you, it's probably best if Cass speaks to her then. Woman to woman."

Townes looked back at his mistress. The energy crackled between them as the power dynamic began to shift back toward their preferred roles. "That's fine," he said.

Then he stared off at NY1 in the corner: a report on the heroin epidemic said to be sweeping Staten Island. When it went to commercial, he turned back to us and said: "We used to be so close, Luce and I. I really thought I did right by her, after her mom died. She always got good grades, never gave me any trouble. She was a great kid. Until . . ." His voiced trailed off, remembering when the wheels began to come off his daughter's life. "Until, I don't know, a year ago? She started hanging out with that McKay girl. She stopped communicating with me. Her swimming went south. Even Coach Marks couldn't get through to her."

A young, white-coated doctor emerged from the double doors and approached our threesome. He addressed Townes.

"We're running a few tests," he said. "She's still getting her bearings." He gave us a tight-lipped smile. "She's a lucky girl."

Outside, we crossed the hospital entrance and walked down 68th toward the water. Cass was already to the filter of her first cigarette and was fumbling with her pack for a second. She flicked the stub away, and we paused as she lit the next one. There were sounds of slow-moving traffic on the FDR below and smells of the East River, dirty and placid, with the wasteland of Roosevelt Island just beyond. I considered, not for the first time, that Cass and I shared little but the crimes and the confusion of others. We spoke and worked together when there was strife, when there was something to solve, dirt to dig up, someone to make pay. I had never been to her apartment, knew only that she lived in Chinatown. I knew nothing of her life outside of our partnership, apart from what she did at the dungeon, and even that was mostly conjecture. I thought I remembered her saying once that she was from Baltimore, but I couldn't even be sure of that. Yet Cass had keys to my apartment and knew more than anyone else about my past and my problems. I always found the imbalance unsettling, but not enough to ask her any personal questions.

"Thank you," she said. "For what you said back there. I was just making it worse."

"No, you weren't. You were just saying what everybody says. Sucks that I can speak from experience."

"You handled it perfectly, Duck. I know Michael appreciated it." She took a quick drag, exhaled from the side of her mouth. "He's always been one of my favorites. Such a kind, honest man, and when he really needed me . . ."

"Stop beating yourself up," I said. "He won't hold it against you."

"I doubt that. I'm sure I won't be seeing him again—in our professional capacity. Not that it matters. I'll just miss him, I guess." She drained the second smoke, flicked it into the street. We walked half a block in silence. "So, how were they?" she asked. "The demeaning detectives?"

With a few exceptions, my partner shares my general belief about cops. They're dim, rule-crazy men and women obsessed with their authority. To be fair, most also have a certain inherent sense of bravery and honor, some more than others, but they're best treated like bears in the woods: powerful and capable of violence when threatened, always keep some distance.

"They have Madeline on camera, leaving Fealy's building that Monday, before she dropped out of contact."

"Jesus," said Cass. "Then it had to have been . . ."

"No, Fealy's parents confirmed that their boy didn't return from the Hamptons until the next day. They're still determining the time of death. Had to have been sometime last week: they said he was dead for a few days before I found him."

"So, what was she doing there? She was distraught about something, and she goes and lets herself into her ex-boyfriend's place?"

"Too bad we can't ask him."

"What else did they have to say?" she asked.

"Apparently there's a gap in the security footage in the lobby," I said. "Something about an electrical problem in the building."

"For how long?"

"They didn't say. I was surprised they even offered that."

"Interesting." She took a drag, held it in her lungs. "Anything else?"

"They're pissed I didn't tell them about Madeline's drug

stash," I said. "I took a few of her pills. They found my prints."

She stopped walking, gave me a disapproving look. "Why did you do that, Duck? What the hell were you thinking?"

"When I took them," I said, "I didn't know Madeline was about to become the lead suspect in a murder investigation."

She shook her head. "Maybe not, but you still weren't thinking. No, that's not true. You were thinking—only about yourself," she said, stalking off.

I caught up to her at the dead end overlooking the FDR and the river. She was staring off across the water, a new unlit cigarette in her hand. A police boat moved against the current, headed south toward lower Manhattan. Planes drifted north over Queens, in their long queue toward La Guardia. Traffic slowed to a standstill on the FDR below us.

"I'm sorry," I told her. "It was stupid, I know that."

"You need help," she said. "You used to have things under control, but now . . ."

"Jesus, I just grabbed a few Vicodin," I said. "It's not like I'm jabbing needles in my arm. What's with the judgment?"

She ignored my question. "So, where you headed next? The nearest bar, or are you capable of doing some sober work?"

"Work," I told her. "From here I'm headed over to see Charlie McKay at his office. He's been storm calling since this morning. How 'bout you?"

"I think I should hang here until Michael lets me talk to his daughter," she said. "Then I thought I'd see what I can get out of the Schwartz kid."

Cass fished out her phone and tapped a quick text.

"Had to cancel a session this afternoon," she said. "A regular too. He is not happy." She stared at the screen, read a reply, fired off another message.

Her crimson lips parted, and she started to say something but swallowed it. We turned and headed back toward the hospital. She gave off a low heat next to me. There's a hot energy that radiates off of certain women. They're the ones that other ladies hate, the ones looked at with loathing and a jealous fear that sparks at first sight. Too tall, too striking, too in command of her own sexuality, a woman capable of taming the most unbroken man. In these women, there is a deep well of loneliness. They're aware of the looks, the claws-out cattiness of fellow, lesser women. Men fear them, women want to be them and despise them instead. Cassandra Kimball's cross to bear . . . We reached the entrance and stopped alongside a line of yellow cabs.

"Check in in a few hours?" I asked.

She nodded, lost in thought, an emotionless look on her lovely face. I went in for a hug, and she went through the motions.

"Jesus, Duck," she said, pulling away. "You reek of booze."

Chapter 13

The offices of Soto Capital were on West 57th, on the forty-fourth floor of a glass tower with 360-degree views. I was ushered upstairs with a security photo just as the markets were closing. The Soto receptionist—brunette, big-chested, Southern—greeted me with a flirty drawl and led me to a leather couch next to floor-to-ceiling windows. She asked if I'd like anything, then swayed back behind her desk, showing off an ass in slacks long accustomed to the eyes that followed.

A large Andreas Gursky photograph of a frenetic trading floor was framed above the couch on the far wall. It was a vast, disorienting bird's-eye view of money changing hands in a paper-bound past. Now the old exchanges were stripped down to skeleton crews as money was made or lost at the speed of Bloomberg based on intricate algorithms down halls like these. Out the windows, Central Park stretched out like a great green masterpiece, framed by the most valuable real estate on earth. The Hudson was visible to the west, with the George Washington Bridge out in the distance, the main northern artery in and out of this inscrutable island.

"Hey, Duck, there you are," said Charlie, hurrying toward me with manic energy. "Thanks for coming up.

What a day, right? Fucking hell. It's been intense. Come on back."

I followed him down the hall to the Soto trading floor where Charlie's workstation was arranged with OCD precision. Other desks were littered with empty coffee cups and candy wrappers; Charlie's had bottled water, Fiji, resting on a coaster and an untouched green apple. A pen and notepad were arranged parallel to the keyboard, in front of his Bloomberg terminal.

"Markets just closed," he said. "Woo! Hot damn, hell of a day." He let out a sudden laugh and shook his head in disbelief.

He had the buzzing aura of a poker player who'd just raked an all-in full house, knocking out a few players in the process. Charlie was dressed trader casual—pressed khakis, monogrammed white button-down, sleeves rolled up to the elbows. A navy blue blazer hung over the back of his ergonomic swivel chair. His tasseled shoes looked handmade, with the soft pressed leather molded to his big, wide feet like royal clown shoes. He picked up the apple from his desk and bit into it with a crisp, juicy crunch that made other traders look in our direction.

"What a fucking day," he said again. "Sorry, Duck, I'm still coming down. Give me a sec while I pack up my stuff. We're supposed to have a postmortem meeting down in the conference room in a minute, but Danny said it was cool if I missed it. I gave him the download on you."

As if he'd been waiting offstage for his cue, a slim, black-haired man appeared at the end of the hall and approached us in quick purposeful strides. As he moved he seemed to vibrate on the silent frequency of serious wealth. He had an irrepressible smile across an intense, bony face. His eyes did not share the joy; they were ink black and untrusting. He wore a bespoke black suit over a black shirt, no tie. He had a dark complexion, an exotic ethnicity of something unplaced.

"Master McKay," he said, squeezing Charlie's shoulder. "A fine day indeed, a very fine day. Well done, my man."

"Thanks, Danny," said Charlie. "I was dialed in today."

His boss gave a low whistle. "That you were, that you were," he said. Then he turned to me and extended a long, bony hand. "Daniel Soto," he said. "Pleased to meet you. You must be the investigator, Dirk Darley, was it?"

"Duck," I said, returning the too-long shake. "What did Charlie do today?"

We both turned to him. Charlie took another bite of his apple and smirked. "What did he do?" asked Soto. "He made this firm a great deal of money, a great deal indeed. And my definition of a 'great deal' is higher than most, I can assure you. I am told it is our third biggest P and L in the firm's history."

I nodded dutifully. "Not bad," I said. "Particularly in light of all that's going on."

Soto was waiting for me to make that point. "But don't you see!" he exclaimed. "That is exactly *why* this man had such a successful day. The great ones perform at the highest level at times of highest stress. This is when they separate themselves, when their ability to focus and to execute becomes so clear." He put a hand over his dark eyebrows and turned and scanned the rest of the trading floor like a sea captain looking for land. "And where is Max Fealy today?" he asked. "Oh, that's right, at his big home in the Hamptons. Not here."

"His son was just murdered," I reminded him.

Soto scowled at me while Charlie looked at his big shoes, trying not to smile. "I know this," said Soto. "Yes, we all know this, and tragic it is. But you do not hear my point. Perhaps you can't, you are not cut from that cloth. The cloth that Charlie and I are cut from."

"Perhaps not," I said.

"But you will help this man, won't you," said Soto. It was not a question. "You will help him find his sister, and clear her of any wrongdoing in this unfortunate matter."

"I'll do my best," I said.

"Your best?" said Soto. He looked at Charlie like this was some private joke. He was beaming from his boss's praise; I had the sense that it was more valuable to him than all the money he'd made that day. "You will do neither your best nor your worst," said Soto. "You will only do—and you will do it until it is done, yes, Mr. Dirk?"

"Yes, Denny, I will."

"Excuse me?"

I turned to Charlie. "What do you say, buddy? Should we go get a drink and toast your good fortune?"

"I don't drink," he said. "But we can find a bar to talk things over, if you want."

"Take him to Whiskey Park," instructed Soto. "We will call down and have them reserve a table where you will have a private place to talk, yes?"

"Okay, thanks, Danny," said Charlie. "Sorry about missing this meeting."

"No, Master McKay, thank *you*. And do not worry about a meeting. You performed like a champion today. Now go and let this man help you take care of your family."

Whiskey Park was at the corner of Sixth Avenue and Central Park South, a low-lit lounge filled with crimson leather and cocktail waitresses auditioning for thousand-dollar tips and after-work invitations to banker lofts. It was still early, and the crowd was still light. There had been no need to call ahead, but the moment we'd walked in we'd been greeted like visiting royalty by the hostess and ushered to a back corner next to a high, tinted window. A short stretch of velvet rope was placed in front of our area. A leggy Japanese cocktail waitress approached dressed in fishnets, stilettos, and a barely-there black dress. She held eye contact until it hurt.

It wasn't on my dime, so I asked on a lark for Pappy. Remarkably, they had it. Charlie ordered a ginger ale and failed to appreciate the presence of that rare, luscious bourbon on their shelf. I was moving up in the world—Pabst and Jack for lunch in some downtown junkie bar, and now here I was behind a velvet rope with a glass of the mighty Mr. Van Winkle on its way. Twenty-three-year, bet your ass. It was enough to make a man feel charitable.

"So, how much did you make today?" I asked.

"Plenty," said Charlie. The gambler's buzz had faded and, removed from the frenetic cocoon of the markets, he was beginning to sulk. The messiness of the rest of his life was starting to elbow back in.

"Like a million?" I asked. "Five million?"

He snorted, insulted by the low-balling cluelessness. "Like I said, plenty. Look, Duck, we're not here to talk about my work, and besides, everyone starts at zero again tomorrow. I guarantee you Danny's already forgotten about it. If I lose tomorrow, he'll be up my ass with no memory of the profits I made him today."

"But you don't start at zero," I pointed out. "You guys get to keep the money you made today."

"You just don't get it," he said.

The waitress returned with our drinks. She made equal ceremony of setting down the ginger ale and the Pappy, but when she delivered mine, she gave a low bow of respect. I watched her drift away, wondered what time she got off. Dylan's "Visions of Johanna" played soft over invisible speakers. She seemed to move with the song's wistful cadence. I turned back to Charlie and found him staring into his bubbles and ice.

"I got called into the cops today," I said. "Talked to two detectives investigating the Fealy murder."

"And?"

"And, let's see, I made the *New York Post*? Nice little sidebar on yours truly. You see it?"

"Yeah, Duck. I saw it. So did my mother. Two days in a row. She says she never should have hired you. The cops and the media—I don't know which one she hates more. That's what I wanted to talk about. You gotta keep both away from us."

"Unfortunately, both of those fine estates can be rather stubborn when they get hooked on a crime," I said. "Like, say, the brutal murder of a rich white kid."

He thought about that for a moment, took a drink of his ginger ale and set it down carefully on the cocktail napkin and wiped his upper lip. He crossed his legs and gazed out the window at passersby. I waited, had a slow sip of the Pappy. Let it linger on my tongue. Savored the amber bliss.

"I know it was a long time ago," he said, lost in a memory. "But what do you remember about him? You remember what he was like?"

"What who was like?"

He turned from the window. "Coach," he said.

"Coach Marks? I'm not sure I know what you mean."

He didn't like the sound of that, turned back toward the window and sulked. "I think you do," he said.

"Listen, Charlie, I quit the team when I was thirteen. It was another lifetime. As far as I recall, Marks always did right by me. And I certainly thought that was true for you. Shit, the man lives in an apartment you bought him."

"My mother bought him that place, not me." He drained

the rest of his ginger ale and put his hands on his knees. "I should go," he said, pushing himself to his feet. "I thought we were on the same page, but I guess I was wrong."

"Sit down, Charlie," I said. "Sit your ass down."

He bristled at the command, but when he looked down at me he relented. I was perfectly willing to make a scene in this swank place, Pappy be damned. Charlie sat.

"Thank you," I said.

He crossed his arms and sunk low in his seat. "So, how are you going to find my sister?" he asked.

"Tell me about Coach Marks," I said.

"You really don't remember anything?" he asked. "Think about it, Duck."

"Didn't your mother tell you? My mind is so addled with booze that I can't remember what I had for lunch yesterday. Stop dicking around and tell me what it is I'm supposed to be remembering."

Charlie motioned to our waitress; she was perched over us in seconds. "Another round, gentlemen?" she asked. Charlie nodded and handed her his empty glass and looked at mine. It had emptied itself. "Sure," I said. "Another of the same would be lovely." Her eyes gave me a knowing smile, and she took my glass and turned on her heels. Watching beautiful women walk away: one of life's loveliest diversions.

"I think she likes you," said Charlie. "That or she's getting wet thinking of the fat tip you're gonna leave on eighty-dollar shots of whiskey."

"I didn't think you drank?"

"I don't, but I can read," he said. He picked up the cocktail menu on the low table between us. "I think you can cover this tab from the advance my mother gave you."

"Fair enough." I shrugged. "I know how you're hurting for cash these days."

He wasn't listening; he'd taken out his phone and was

frowning as he scrolled through new emails. He removed a second phone from a separate pocket and did the same. Then he placed both devices on the table before him, taking measured care to position them parallel to each other, a centimeter apart.

"Tell me about Coach Marks," I said again.

The waitress returned with our refills. She recognized the tension between us and set them down without looking at either of us. The Pappy didn't taste quite as good this time.

"Let's just say he likes them young," said Charlie.

"Who? You mean girls on the team?"

He nodded. "Don't pretend like this is news to you."

"How young?" I had that feeling of history shifting beneath my feet like quicksand. It was a sensation I was familiar with, and I didn't like it.

"Not, like, children," he said. "He's not that sick. Teenagers. His eye starts roaming right around the time they start looking back."

"He wouldn't be the first," I said.

"It was pretty common knowledge that stuff was going on back in high school, with a few of the girls my age."

"And later, after you were gone, do you think it continued?"

"No reason to think he'd stop," he said.

"And you think . . . Madeline. You think your sister may have been involved with him."

He bit his bottom lip and looked away. He nodded almost imperceptibly. "My mother has no idea," he said. "Obviously, she doesn't. She's been in love with him since my father died. Maybe even before that."

"Wait, your mother and Coach?" I asked.

"Convenient that she left that part out."

"Hence, the apartment," I said.

"She would never set foot in that shit hole he used to

live in," he said. "And Coach told her he wasn't comfortable going to her place. I wonder why, with my sister down the hall. So my mother went out and bought them a love nest."

"Why didn't you mention this stuff when we met the other day?"

Charlie agitated in his seat. He pulled at his collar, wiped sweat from his brow. His eyes darted out the window, then around the bar, searching for something to distract his thoughts. "Do you have any idea how hard it is to admit this shit?" he asked. "This is the man who coached me to four gold medals. After my dad died, Coach Marks basically became my stepfather. My mother was head over heels for him. I owed him my success. What was I supposed to do?" He seemed to deflate before me. His chin fell to his chest.

"You were supposed to protect your sister," I said.

He didn't look up.

"Charlie, do you have any idea where Madeline might have gone?" I asked. "I assume someone has been monitoring your family's home in Rhinebeck."

"Of course. We have a caretaker up there that looks after the property when we're away. He and his wife have been living in the big house ever since my mother got worried. If Maddie had been back, they would know."

"Any friends, relatives you think she might turn to?"

He shook his head. "Both of our parents were only children. We have no aunts or uncles. Grandparents all died a while back. As for friends, I wouldn't know. Being so much older, I never knew Madeline that well, never knew that part of her life anyway."

"How do you know about her relationship with Marks?" I asked.

"Because I know *him*," he said. "I know him really well. I went to watch her at Junior Nationals two years back.

That's when I first noticed. It was the way he talked to her, the way he hugged her after a good swim, the way he whispered to her after a bad one. I'd seen it before. So many times before, growing up. Every sign was there, trust me, I'm sure."

The memory seemed to spark an electrical current that coursed through Charlie's body. His knees began to bounce up and down, his fists clenched; a shiver seized his upper body. He inhaled deeply through his nose, tried to calm himself with a slow exhale.

"But you never said anything?" I asked.

"I said something to her, yeah. I confronted her about it right after the meet. She told me I was crazy, denied it completely. Then she stopped speaking to me."

"And Marks, did you ever approach him about it?"

Charlie took a drink of his ginger ale from a shaking hand. He checked his phones and eyed the growing crowd in their power ties and perfect makeup, released from their cages and ready to play. He studied them like a foreign species, curious of their habits but repelled by their basic nature. Four men in identical blue suits shouted with laughter at the bar. They toasted their whiskeys with puffed chests and puffier cheeks.

"No," he said. "I didn't. You don't understand."

Before I could reply, one of his phones lit up on the table before us. The name of the caller read *Mother*. He picked it up. I watched his face as she spoke. It darkened like an approaching storm. He told his mother he was on his way. Then he ended the call and looked at me with wild eyes.

"My mom," he said. "She's having a hard time. I gotta run."

Chapter 14

I was waiting by the entrance before dawn as the swimmers approached. Lanky teenage boys with bed heads and a sullen, shuffling air; huddled teenage girls pulled parkas tight around their long, uncertain bodies. They came off the steps of the subway in safe packs of threes or fours or ducked out of Ubers by themselves. They were just past the age of independence, free to move around the city without parental accompaniment, and they moved with that New York air of jaded over-maturity. They looked like children despite themselves.

A few of the girls eyed me warily. The guys paid no heed. One nodded in my direction with vague recognition, his head an unnatural shock of blond-green straw. We stood together in the predawn darkness as we waited for their coach's arrival. Rain was in the forecast again. A light drizzle started to fall, and they began to herd under cover by the door.

Charlie had rushed away and left me sitting there with more questions than answers, along with a stupidly priced whiskey behind a velvet rope on the edge of Central Park. The cocktail waitress was unimpressed by my tip. In the cab on my way home I texted Roy Perry, thinking he could earn my forgiveness with many rounds of drinks and maybe a bump or two. But when he failed to write back I was thankful. This wasn't the time to unravel into coke-fueled weakness and mindless mania. Instead I went home, walked Elvis, and did some homework.

I knew there had been scandal in my sport, and plenty of others, swirling around inappropriate coach–athlete behavior, but until I started Googling I had no idea how pervasive. It was damn near an epidemic, with mounting lawsuits coming out of teams all over the country. Youth coaches were being lumped into an unholy trinity with Catholic priests and Boy Scout troop leaders. Based on the search results, it sounded like a long-dormant sickness now bubbling to the surface. There was a task force set up by swimming's governing body, devoted to investigating every last rumor.

And there were rumors about everyone. Old-school coaches like Marks would say those were different times, and they were—a time when statutory rape and abuse of power was par for many pool decks. After a few hours of online research I was convinced I'd never look at a coach the same way again. I was also inclined to believe Charlie's allegations. I set the alarm for five a.m., looking forward to a predawn confrontation.

I was proud to have acknowledged the wake-up call in the darkness. These kids were too young to be impressed by their commitment, but someday they would be. It takes a certain obsessive insanity to wake this early to go follow a black line up and down a swimming pool before school while your classmates slumber. But it was the right madness, and they'd all be better for it—no matter who loomed over them on deck.

At 5:34 a.m., a low agitation began to spread through the group. There were hushed whispers and the checking of phones and a hint of merriment at the prospect of no practice. Marks was nowhere to be seen, and his swimmers were eager to get back to their beds. A tall, freckled girl approached.

"Are you here for practice too?" she asked.

"Here to talk to your coach," I said. "He late?"

"Yeah." She looked across the street to the subway entrance, then back to her pack of friends. "He's never late."

"Weird," I said. She agreed and went back to the herd.

Five minutes later, just as the guys were starting to speak up and call the morning off, a cab came to a stop before us. A dashed groan went through the group as a tall blond woman emerged in blue nylon warm-ups. She regarded them with a supercilious smirk.

"Teddy is not able to make it this morning," she said. "I will coach you. Let us go, we are late."

She strode between them with painted pink toes in her flip-flops and unlocked the door and waited by it as the procession marched downstairs to the pool. I waited until the last one entered before I approached.

"Mister Duck, that is you?" she asked. "I see your face is improving, yes?"

"Nice to see you again, Anna. Where's Marks?"

"Sick, I am told. I receive text early this morning, asking me to run workout."

"Does he miss practice a lot?"

"Never," said Anna. "It is very unusual."

"Strange, indeed," I said. "Do you mind if I watch?"

"Of course, Mr. Duck. Come."

She turned and walked down the steps as the rain opened up behind us. The smell of the waiting pool was like a warm chemical balm. The sense memory set off the usual associations of pride and peace of mind. Associations I was starting to question after Charlie's accusation and my previous night's research.

The air on deck was hot and heavy. Anna stripped down to cycling shorts and a black halter sports bra, enviable

abs between them. She tied her blond hair back in a ponytail and spread her legs and began to stretch. I watched,
sweating, in my jeans and polo, feeling like a poorly dressed
intruder. Anna tossed her muscled arms in lazy circles,
twisted out the morning kinks, then walked to a white
board behind the lanes and began to write out the warm-
up in red marker.

The swimmers began to trudge out of the locker rooms
dragging mesh bags full of boards and buoys and paddles
and straps. They pulled at caps and goggles and moved
their mostly naked bodies like colts in the morning mist.
The guys looked like young anatomy charts. The girls
wore a bit more flesh on their bones. They were no less fit,
but they carried their fitness with an artificial broadness,
like it was a temporary condition. Most walked with arms
covering their chests, careful of angles and the bleary-eyed
stares of their male teammates. Anna eyed each body with
naked judgment. When they were all assembled behind
their lanes, she pointed to the warm-up on the board and
told them to leave at the sixty.

I settled onto a bench along the side of the pool and
watched them swim. They moved with such splashless
ease, stroking and flipping and streamlining up and back,
lap after lap, with languid carelessness. I wondered what
Marks saw when he watched these kids: flaws and critical
assessments in every movement, picking out certain ones
for special attention. And perhaps others for private attention that had nothing to do with their performance in the
water?

Anna led the workout with Eastern European efficiency.
She did not smile, did not praise, and did not raise her
voice. She delivered her commands and then stalked the
deck, watching their strokes like an impatient piano teacher
hearing all the wrong notes. If she was aware of her sexuality, she did not show it. Her body was an aggressive fact,

and she carried it as such. There was no reason for me to stay. I didn't expect Marks to show. But I liked watching Anna, and she knew it.

At the end of practice, she released them, and the swimmers filtered away, wet and exhausted, to the showers. Anna approached. We hadn't spoken since we walked together onto the pool deck two hours earlier.

"How did they look, Mr. Duck?"

"Very impressive," I said. "Tired just watching them."

"It was not so good, the effort, I think. When head coach is gone, kids, they do not work as hard."

"Guess that's inevitable."

"Inevitable for American children, yes. They need their hands held to be good at anything, it seems." She erased the workout in quick swipes from the white board. Then she gathered her warm-ups and pulled them back on and looked back at me. "I am very hungry, Mr. Duck. Would you like to join me for breakfast?"

I was too quick to accept.

She insisted on cooking. Her apartment was in Soho, and we made the two-mile walk in the rain, huddled under cheap deli umbrellas that covered little but our heads. The city was coming alive for the workday, the sidewalks a brigade of black umbrellas. Harried men crouched beneath them, eyes on iPhones. Well-dressed women waved down cabs or teetered down steps to the subway in their heels. This was the part of morning workout that I always liked best: the afterglow. The smug satisfaction in knowing that you had already done something worthy with your day, while the rest of the world yawned and sucked at their coffee and fought their way to their little beehive offices. Of course, I had done nothing but sit on a bench and watch a few dozen teenagers slog through their sets.

"Do you have a very busy day ahead?" she asked.

"We'll see."

"Well, you will give me just a little bit of your time, won't you? I am excellent chef. I will make a special Ukrainian hash. You are not a vegetarian, no?"

"Not a chance," I said.

"Yes, good. I do not understand those who do not eat meat."

We walked in rainy silence past the perpetual construction on Houston. Then she steered me onto the cobblestones of Mercer Street and stopped half a block down in front of a classic cast-iron loft building. "This is me," she said.

The keyed elevator opened onto a cavernous expanse. Gray rain light filtered through tall, arched windows, giving the space a sorrowful sense. Her aesthetic was minimalist to the point of irony. It was furnished like she lived in a jewel box studio that had mysteriously come with an extra two thousand square feet that she wasn't quite sure what to do with. A loveseat where there should have been a sprawling sectional; a four-top dining table where there was space to seat a dozen; a small thirty-inch flat-screen on a wall sized for a movie projector. The rest of the walls were artless and empty.

"My father works in petrol," she said by way of explanation. "I know what you are thinking—this is not the apartment of an assistant swim coach, is it?"

"No one knows where the money comes from in this city," I told her. "We just assume."

"Not like where I come from," she said. "There, everyone knows." We reached the back of the loft, and she pushed open a door. "And this is the bedroom," she said with pride. It was the one area that had been appointed with care, in dimensions that suited the space. There was a king-size bed set into an ornate wrought-iron bed frame. A large antique chest sat at the foot of the bed. There was a burgundy high-backed chair in one corner, an imposing mid-century armoire in the other.

"I see where you spend most of your time," I said.

She gave a wicked grin and led me back out. "Come, Mr. Duck, I am hungry. First, we must eat."

Anna was good to her word: she knew how to cook. The Ukrainian hash was outstanding. She served it with a dense, dark, braided bread and good strong coffee. Her appetite surpassed mine, and we said little as we ate across from each other at her little table. She sat with well-bred posture; after each bite she wiped the corners of her mouth and took a sip of water with quiet formality. When our plates were clean, she stood and gathered our dishes and went to rinse them in the sink. "Tell me," she said, turning on the faucet. "When will you find this girl, Madeline McKay?"

"Wish I knew," I said. "I was hoping you could help me with that."

Anna refilled our coffees from the French press, splashed more milk, added heaps of sugar, and returned to the table. She looked across at me with frank, unblinking eyes.

"And how would I help with this? I have only seen her maybe two, three times at practice since I began coaching. I know nothing of this person."

"But I think you know plenty about Coach Marks," I said.

"And why do you think such a thing? Because you found me at his apartment that night?" She smiled to herself, sipped her coffee. "You were quite a sight. So beat up and crazy-eyed."

"Why were you there?"

"To discuss a private matter with my boss." She shrugged, bored by suspicions.

"I hear your young colleague has fallen hard for you."

"Nicholas?" She gave a guilty smile. "I am surprised

Teddy told you this, but yes, it is true. American boys are so eager, like untrained puppies. And sweet, you are all so sweet. But this is not something many women find attractive, yes?" She picked up the cloth napkin in front of her and absently folded and unfolded it. She looked deep in delighted thought.

"What about Marks?" I asked. "Is he that way? Over-eager for your affections?"

"I am not sleeping with him, if that is what you are asking. Besides," she said, "I think I am not Teddy's type."

"What type would that be?"

She considered this for a moment. She tipped her Slavic face to the side and pressed her full lips together. "He can be very flirtatious with the girls, you know."

"I'm told it might go beyond flirtations."

She shrugged. "Maybe it has. It is not my business. I had a coach, once, home in Ukraine. He was this way. He had sex with my friend when she was fourteen. Some coaches, they are like this, yes? But, no, I think with Teddy it is only flirtation. Besides, he is with Mrs. McKay, yes?"

"I didn't know that was common knowledge," I said.

She gave a sudden laugh at this. "People like to talk, you know?"

"That they do."

Again, that laugh, darker this time. "What does this have to do with finding this girl, Mrs. McKay's daughter?"

"Maybe Teddy's taste runs in their family?"

Anna leaned back in her chair, examined her pink nails. "Mother and daughter? This would be very scandalous, Mr. Duck." She reached for her water glass, dipped her fingers in, and brought out an ice cube. She placed it against her lips and sucked at it. Then she slipped it into her mouth and crunched it between her teeth. I held her eyes.

She rose and crossed the table and leaned across me

with lazy intent. She picked up my empty cup, gazing down at me. "Would you like anything else?" she asked. "Something stronger, maybe?" She did not wait for my reply. She went and removed a frosted bottle of Stolichnaya from the freezer. She took down two shot glasses and filled them both with the cold, clear liquid and brought them over.

"*Nasdrovie*," she said, standing over me. She knocked hers back without waiting for our glasses to touch. I swallowed mine down. I felt the delicious warmth sliding past my breastbone, down into my stomach. Then I felt Anna's fingers on the back of my neck. She stood behind me and began to dig into my flesh. "You are very stiff, Mr. Duck. Very sore," she said. She let her hands slide down my back to my waist. They slipped beneath my shirt. My entire body quivered at the sensation.

I turned and kissed her hard on the mouth. Her breath was fresh and tasted of icy vodka. She returned the kiss with hunger and drew back and laughed lightly into my mouth. "You taste very good," she whispered. "Come with me." She took my hand and led me off toward the bedroom like an unhurried huntress.

I was stripped without words and pushed onto my back on her bed. Anna shed her clothes with a solemn air. She was one of those women who looked much nicer in nothing, without effort, and who looked foolish when they spent too much time in front of a mirror. Her body was thick and powerfully built; the pink nipples on her full chest were hard and pronounced. She stood before me without self-consciousness. She was the sort who feels most comfortable naked, who wants the lights left on. Then she allowed herself a private smile, and she climbed across me.

Anna straddled my waist and guided me inside. She pressed herself down hard, forcing me up into her as deep as I could go. Her hands pushed down on my chest, and she arched her back as her eyes closed. I watched her find her rhythm, a self-contained motivated grinding against my pelvis, knowing precisely how to bring herself close. My hands reached around and tried to clutch her but she swatted them away. Instead, she grabbed my wrists and leaned forward and pinned them over my head. Her breath quickened; her nails dug into my skin.

It was after eleven when I woke in her bed. Anna was seated in the high-backed burgundy chair in the corner, watching me slumber, empty shot glass on the low table beside her. Outside the bedroom window, the rain had stopped. Sunlight streamed across the room like I'd awakened in a new Technicolor reality. The air was still, suspended. Anna sat with an eerie calm. She wore a light blue silk robe that fell open as she crossed her legs and revealed acres of smooth, hard skin beneath.

"Nice rest?" she asked.

"Mmm, nice morning," I said.

She nodded at this with unemotional agreement. "Yes, I am glad you decided to come by the pool this morning." Anna stood and tied her robe tight around her waist. She took a step toward the bed and regarded me with a look that said it was time to go.

"We should do this again," I said. It elicited no reply. She watched as I gathered my pile of clothes at the foot of the bed and then scurried off to the bathroom like a scolded dog. I made the usual silent sweep of the medicine cabinet, was unsurprised to find no prescriptions of interest. When I emerged, she had left the room. I heard the clinking of glasses in the kitchen.

Anna did not turn as I walked down the hall. She was wiping down countertops with vigor, indulging an apparent passion for cleanliness and order. I watched her bend in concentration, scrubbing at a stubborn stain, as her robe inched up the backs of her thighs. I had the urge to go to her, to press myself against her and coax her back toward the bedroom. She must have sensed my motives. She turned to face me.

"Thank you for your visit, Mr. Duck," she said. "I enjoyed myself very much." She managed a smile; it lacked warmth.

"Any word from Coach Marks?" I asked.

She resumed her cleaning. "No, I have not heard from him. Not since early this morning."

"If you do, would you mind letting me know?"

"I do not think I have your number," she said.

"Would you like it?"

She shrugged. "You may leave it if you like. My phone is dead, it is charging, so I cannot enter it now."

I slipped a business card from my wallet and set it in a dry spot on the kitchen counter. As it left my fingers, I remembered her pocketing an identical card when we first met, on my way out of the pool. Now she had two. I doubted she'd keep either.

"You mind giving me yours?" I asked.

Her body tensed: another overeager American boy. She turned and, without looking up, scribbled it on a Post-it note and handed it over. We kissed awkwardly on both cheeks as she called for the elevator. Then I was thrust out into the too bright Soho sunshine.

Chapter 15

The bar at the Old Town was mostly full with the early drinking lunch crowd, but I found two open stools in front of the taps, with just enough space for a pint glass on the stained wooden bar. It had once been named one of the "coolest bars in America" by a men's magazine, a dubious honor that was now taped to the front window. It brought an unfortunate crowd of tourists during the holiday season and was usually too crowded for peaceable drinking in the after-work hours, but during weekdays it remained a fine, comfortable place of wide-bellied regulars and boozy publishing types who worked nearby. The tin ceilings were high and the porcelain urinals were huge; it often functioned as my office.

I was a few minutes early and found a discarded *Post* for company. The Fealy murder had been pushed from the front page, thanks to a school shooting in the Bronx. On page ten, there was a story about the grieving Fealy family, how they were still holed up in the Hamptons, with father Max on indefinite leave from Soto Capital. The piece made no mention of Charlie's monster day in the markets. It noted that the police continued to search for Madeline McKay as a person of interest, but reported that sources indicated the NYPD was pursuing other suspects as well. Thankfully, I received no further ink.

When Cass came in through the swinging saloon doors, I was finishing the box scores and taking the first sip of a second pint of Paulaner. I saw her before she saw me. She was at the front of the room, dressed in a long-sleeved black lace dress and combat boots, pretending not to notice the usual stares. Her face was made up in scarlet lipstick, rouge, and heavy black eyeliner and mascara. It was clear she had just come from a session; she had that lingering look of high heat, like water coming down from a boil. I raised an arm, and Cass came toward me. We did not greet each other.

"What's with the shit-eating grin?" she asked.

"Huh?" I didn't realize I was smiling. "Guess I'm just happy to see you."

"Bullshit. You look like you just got laid."

My face told her good guess.

"Well then, good for you," she said. She slid onto the stool and motioned to the bartender. "You certainly needed it. Who was she?"

"I went to see Marks this morning, early, at the pool. I've got some stuff to tell you about. Anyway, he wasn't there, but his assistant coach was, the Ukrainian girl I mentioned? The one who was at his place the other night?"

"So, after practice, she dragged you back to her place for a little morning lay? Nice."

"Something like that. What about you? You look like you just tamed a tiger."

"Not so far off," she said. "Had an intense session this morning. Guy was a masochist to the extreme. I can wield a whip, but nothing I could give him was hard enough. He was a big bastard too, a former NFL lineman." The bartender set down her Pinot and pretended not to eavesdrop.

"Anyway, guess he missed the pain." She took a sip and set down the wine and wiped her top lip. As usual, the red lipstick stain on the glass stirred something in me. "So, what do you have to tell me? I've got a bunch for you too."

We decided on our lunches: tuna melt for me, a Clif Bar from her purse for her. She waited until my meal came, and then she peeled open the wrapper and chewed each bite slowly as I told her about my meeting with Charlie. When I mentioned his allegations about Marks, she did not seem surprised.

"So the guy has an affair with our client, the mother, scores a two-million-dollar apartment out of it, then starts messing with the teenage daughter?" Cass nodded to herself, as if she'd heard this story before. "And the perfect son is wise to both relationships, but he doesn't say a thing?"

"Marks was like a father to him," I reminded her. "Not to mention the man who coached him to all those gold medals."

"I'd say someone has some conflicted feelings about the *paterfamilias*," she said.

I chose not to relate.

"You mentioned a bodyguard or a bouncer at the pool before?" she asked. "Some kind of rent-a-cop stopped you when you first went by there the other day?"

"Yeah, guy's name was Fred Wright. That was bizarre. Marks brushed it off, told me it was because stuff was being stolen from the locker rooms. Apparently, Fred's an old Navy SEAL buddy. Charlie seemed to think it was just Marks putting on airs."

"Was the guy there this morning?"

"He was not." It hadn't occurred to me. I'd been too busy taking in Anna.

"Is it possible that Teddy Marks is being threatened?"

We looked at each other's reflections in the high mirror

above the amber bottles. I stared at the rows of whiskey before me, standing shoulder to shoulder like soldiers, proud to serve. I resolved to order just one when my beer was gone.

"Threatened by someone who knows and resents his secrets?" I asked.

"Uh huh."

"Perhaps, but it's not like Charlie was the only one who knew. According to him, everyone knew what Marks was up to. Sounds like it was an open secret on the team. It wasn't like Madeline was the first swimmer he set his sights on."

"Sure, it's easy to overlook when it's someone else's sister, or mother."

"Or when you're immersed in training for the Olympics."

"Right, but when you come up for air, see your sister become totally fucked up on drugs . . ."

I thought of Margaret McKay. The woman had hired me to track down her errant daughter. Until that moment, the sins swirling just beyond her sight had been kept hidden under water. But the moment I inserted myself into the equation and started asking questions of those closest to her daughter, violence had bubbled to the surface. Her ex-boyfriend murdered, her best friend attempted suicide. A ring of death circling around the drain of her damaged young life. Perhaps Madeline had confided in the two people she trusted most. Perhaps Marks was feeling increasingly cornered by threats from her brother. There was motive, and the man in question was a trained killer from the SEALs. But none of this got us any closer to finding Madeline McKay.

"So, this morning," said Cass. "He calls Fred the rent-a-cop and tells him he won't be there, no need to come in? Then calls his assistant and asks her to cover for him. No need to protect her, I guess."

"Stolen stuff from the lockers, my ass."

"After practice, did you and this assistant talk about any of this? Before you had your way with her?" She smiled sideways and knocked her knee against mine.

I neglected to tell her that she had it backward. "We did. Anna has seen how flirtatious he can be with the girls. She knows how common it is with coaches, seems she witnessed some dark stuff herself back home. But she thinks with Marks, it stops before he crosses any lines."

"You believe her?"

"I think so. She's very matter-of-fact, very direct. You know how Eastern Euros are. If she thought there was something there, I think she would have said so."

We finished our meals in contemplative silence, turning over the emerging details. I had once been convinced that Madeline was dead, that we were searching for a corpse; now I wasn't so sure. I remained convinced that our girl wasn't a murderer. A heartbroken addict, unstable and damaged, and yes, her prints were all over her ex's apartment, but I couldn't acknowledge her capacity to inflict that kind of violence. I pictured her far away, on a beach in Mexico, getting clean, getting away from the mess her life had become in the big city. If that was the case. then I wondered if I really wanted to find her.

"Your turn," I said. "You said you had shit to tell me too."

Cass rolled her eyes. "You've set the bar high, my friend. I hardly know where to begin." She was folding the wrapper of her Clif Bar in smaller pieces. When she was satisfied that it couldn't be folded again, she tucked it delicately back into her purse.

"You talk to Lucy?" I asked.

"I did. Her father didn't give me much time, and she was pretty out of it, but she was able to talk a little."

"How was she?"

"Hiding something, that much is clear. She kept apologizing, over and over. Said she would rather die than share her secrets."

I thought of the last text Madeline sent to her mother before she disappeared. *I'm so sorry . . .*

"Was her father in the room when you spoke to her?"

"He was," she said. "A nurse too. They wouldn't allow me to speak to her alone."

"No way she's spilling any secrets with her father listening," I said. "Did he happen to mention what was in that note she left him?"

"He told me that she said she just couldn't take it any more, that he'd never understand. And that she loved him."

"Jesus. Poor guy."

"He's shattered, Duck. I've never seen a man so completely broken and confused. And I've seen men in plenty of dark places."

"Did she mention anything else? Anything about Madeline?"

"Just that Madeline was the mess we thought she was. Seems their friendship blossomed around rebellion. Madeline's a year older and apparently quite the bad influence. Sounds like Lucy injured her shoulder last year, and it kept her out of training. Seems she filled some of that free time partying with Madeline and Fealy."

"Maybe she was in love with her friend's man? Tried to kill herself after hearing about the murder?"

Cass shrugged, finished the rest of her second glass. "It's possible. Would be typical, I guess. But I don't know. When I asked her about James Fealy, she barely reacted. She just said it was all so sad. Unfortunately, her father made me leave before I could ask her much more."

I discovered my pint glass was empty before me. My eyes fell to that waiting row of amber. The bartender was already approaching, an old pro accustomed to reading thirsty habits. "Double Maker's," I told him. "Just a bit of ice." I felt Cass watching without approval. "Another glass?" I asked her. She shook her head.

The bourbon was set before me like a sacrament. I lifted it and took a sip and closed my eyes and felt it burn down my throat. When I opened my eyes, Cass was sliding from the stool and gathering her things.

"Meet me at your place at five, okay?" she said. "Try to stay soberish, I might need your help with something."

"What something?"

"After I left the hospital yesterday, I tracked down Fealy's roommate, the one who let you in the building."

"The Schwartz kid?"

"Yeah, Mike Schwartz. Total punk. He's on some kind of tragic bender since his friend died. I found him coked up at La Esquina late last night. He wasn't too hard to find. He posted his whereabouts on Instagram. Social media's making our job too easy."

"So what did the punk have to say?"

"Plenty," she said. "I cornered him right after he came out of the bathroom, rubbing his nose and sniffing without shame. I let him hit on me for a bit, then acted like I recognized him from his picture in the *Post*."

"What did he say about Madeline?" I asked, knowing the answer.

"Nothing nice. I believe 'stalker slut' was his favorite term for her."

"He convinced she did it?"

"I asked him straight out," she said. "He hesitated. There's something he's keeping to himself. Even high on coke, there was something he managed to hold back."

Cass removed a twenty from her bag and set it on the bar. She eyed my double serving of whiskey dessert, thought about saying something. I noticed bruises on her forearm. Her left wrist was red and swollen and bore the traces of fingers that had squeezed it tightly and refused to let go.

Sometimes I worried about her, alone in those dungeon rooms with conflicted, pain-crazy men. She could take care of herself, and reduce any man to a weeping wreck, but in the presence of a hulking NFL lineman, she wasn't as dominant as she thought she was.

"So, what's the story at five? The Schwartz kid coming by my place?"

"No," said Cass. "But his dealer is."

Chapter 16

Iarrived home at quarter after five to find Cass and the dealer seated on my couch, chatting like old friends. The dealer was an oddly shaped man with sallow skin and a big, bald head that balanced over a small body like a bowling ball on top of a pin. He tensed when I entered, and Cass set a reassuring hand on his thigh. "This is my friend, Duck," she told him. "This is his place."

"Oh, okay. Right, cool. What's going on, man? I'm Pete." He pushed himself up and extended a small, clammy hand. I shook it and moved past him to the kitchen, opened the fridge and fished out a Beck's. Elvis came over and knocked at his empty food bowl. I filled it and rubbed his neck and apologized for the lack of steady walks. He didn't seem to mind.

Cass was telling Dealer Pete about her work at the dungeon. Pete was enthralled and becoming more turned on by the second. Cass crossed her wrists and held them up, demonstrating some bit of bondage, as Pete nodded along with eager understanding.

I suspect there's no finer complement to our job than to work in a dungeon. Nothing can shock her, and everyone opens up to her. She hears the darkest, strangest pleadings

of lust and buried desire on a daily basis. Her clients confess to her. That is what they do first. Then she does as
they wish, and she does it with the exact levels of pain and
cruelty that they request and require. She winked when I
joined them and ended her description by setting her hands
primly in her lap and sitting up straight with a naughty
glint to her eye.

"So, how do you two know each other?" asked Pete.
"Are you, like, in that scene too?" The bastard could hardly
contain himself.

"I'm a finder," I told him. "Like a private investigator.
When Cassandra here isn't busy with her whips and chains,
she's my partner."

This took some of the wind out of Dealer Pete's sails.
"Private? You mean, like you're not a cop."

"No, Pete," said Cass. "Relax. He's not a cop." She
rubbed his thigh and gave him a mischievous smirk. It didn't
take much to get him back to fantasyland.

"I feel the same way about cops," I said. "They're the
enemy. Now, what do you have for us today?"

He looked over at Cass for approval. She nodded once,
giving him permission to speak. Good boy. "What's your
pleasure?" he asked. "I've got all sorts of goodies. Coke,
molly, Oxy, you name it." He gave us a conspiratorial
smile and leaned forward and opened a small black backpack at his feet. "H?" he asked in a lower, excited voice.

Cass set her hand on his. "First, we were wondering if
you'd—"

"You have any Vicodin?" I asked.

"I do indeed," he said. "How many would you like?"

"Let's say twenty."

Cass sat back on the couch and crossed her arms and
watched as Dealer Pete dug through his bag for the pills.
She shook her head, unimpressed. I tried to make eye con-

tact, but she ignored me. She called Elvis over. The disloyal hound jumped onto her lap and rolled onto his side for a good rubbing. He looked at me with disapproval too.

Dealer Pete counted out twenty white vikes, mouthing each number, and sealed them for me in a plastic bag.

"Two hundred," he said. "Ten bucks a pill. Sure you don't need anything else?"

I told him I was good with the painkillers and reached for my wallet. Had eighty on me. I looked to Cass for help. Still no eye contact. "Honey? Could I . . ."

"No," she said, not looking up.

Dealer Pete looked at me, then back at his drugs. They still weren't mine. Decisions, decisions . . .

"Okay, just give me eight for now," I said.

Pete shrugged and unsealed the bag of pills and counted out a dozen, dropped them back in his stash. An eyeball estimate told me there must be three hundred in there. I wondered, of all the goodies in his bag, which was his drug of choice. Probably the smack, by the sound of his voice when he'd whispered that letter *H* like it was porn. Probably considered Vicodin the stuff of amateurs, Opiate Lites.

"Okay, so that'll be eighty bucks," he said.

I handed over all my cash.

He pocketed it and asked, "You guys mind if I use your bathroom?"

I pointed down the hall. He took his backpack with him.

"Have I mentioned that you need help?" asked Cass the moment we heard the door close.

"You remember the beating I took? These things are medicinal. Besides, you were just gonna grill him without buying anything? How rude is that?"

"You have problems," she said.

"So, now it's plural. What the fuck, you can't lend me a few bucks?"

While she went on shaking her head and rubbing Elvis, I remembered the envelope of expense cash from Margaret McKay. Screw my righteous drug-judgy partner. I had enough on hand to get myself good and glazed for days.

We continued to sit there in stony silence while Pete took his time. He was taking more than a piss. Finally we heard the requisite flush, and he emerged looking like he'd just found enlightenment. He gave us a blissed-out smile and floated down the hall on a new plane of higher, or lower, consciousness.

"All right so, like, you have my number," he said. "Give me a ring whenever, but not after midnight; that's when I make my last delivery."

He was almost to the door when Cass stood up. She crossed the room and held the door closed just as his hand touched the knob. "Hold up, Peter," she said. "Just one more thing."

The look on his blissed-out face said he knew something was about to mess with his high.

Cass led him back to the couch with a hand on the back of his neck. The flirtation had left her; she was entering mistress mode, and she was one disappointed dominatrix. "Sit," she snapped. Pete obeyed.

I leaned back in my chair, sipped my beer, and felt bad for the poor bobble-headed punk.

"Peter, I want you to know that I have no problem with your profession, per se. In some cases, you seem to perform a valuable service to certain broken souls." Cass glanced my way; now it was my turn to avoid the eye contact. "However, we must have standards, am I right?" Pete nodded nervously. Cass took a sip of her wine, settling into her performance. "You can deal to drug-abusing idiots like my partner here all you like. It's his life, and it's yours too. You can go shoot up in a stranger's bathroom every night, for all I care. There's no judgment, do you understand me?" She began to pace the room, idly rubbing her hands together. Her long crimson nails looked like the bloody tip of a well-used weapon. Even Elvis started to cower at the dangerous energy she was giving off. "However, you must understand that there are things I do judge. There are things that are just not acceptable. Do you know what sort of things I'm talking about, Peter?"

"Whatever it is," he stammered. "Whatever it is I did, I'm sorry. But I don't know what you're talking about."

Cass stopped pacing and stood above him with her hands on her hips. In those combat boots she was six and a half feet of black-laced menace. She shook her head. "I think you do, Peter. I think you know that not all clients are created equal. Like, say, drug-addicted teenage girls? Sometimes dealers need to just say no too."

"Look, man, if someone OD'd, I mean, someone you know, I'm sorry. I know it's not cool to say, but it comes with the territory, you know? Buy the ticket, take the ride, and all that shit."

"No one OD'd, Pete," I said. "At least not that we know of."

Cass glared at me, not welcoming my appearance in her scene. She walked over to the kitchen counter and returned with a manila folder. She opened it, placed a picture of Madeline on the coffee table in front of him. "Do you know this girl?" she asked.

Pete nodded, averted his eyes. "Yeah, I've sold to her. She's a reg. Did something happen to her?"

"She's missing," said Cass. Again, she reached into the folder and took out a photo. "Do you recognize this man?" she asked.

Pete jumped at the image. I leaned forward and took a look. Wished I hadn't. Somehow she had secured a crime scene photo of the mutilated James Fealy in the shower. "What the fuck!" he cried.

"That is, or was, a young man named James Fealy," said Cass. "He was this girl's boyfriend." She pointed back and forth to each photo. "Clearly you don't read the papers. You see, she is missing, he was murdered, and you have dealt to both of them."

Pete's high was evaporating as he began to grasp his role in this particular darkness. "Look, I haven't seen that dude in a while. Last time I sold to her, chick told me he quit." He said it like an alibi, with the first glimmer of hope in his voice since he'd sat back down.

"When was that, the last time you sold to her?"

"Weekend before last. Saturday, I think."

"You go to her apartment?" I asked.

"Her pad in the West Village? Nah, man, not this time. She asked me to come out to Williamsburg. I usually don't do bar hand-offs, too risky, but she promised a big buy."

"What bar was it?"

"I don't know, man. It was a bar, random place near the Bedford stop."

"What bar was it?" Cass asked again.

"Let me think, what was the name again? I suck at names. Wait, I got it. It was Clam's. Like oysters? Except there wasn't no seafood there. But that was the name. Clam's."

"Clem's?" I asked.

"Sure, whatever. Clam's, Clem's, you know the spot?"

Cass and I glanced at each other. A big drug buy across the street from the porn studio, a day before her last sighting. I knew where I was headed next.

But Cass wasn't done with him yet. "Last night, did you make a delivery to a young man named Mike Schwartz?" she asked.

"I don't do last names," he said. "And every other dude I deal to tells me his name is Mike."

"Curly blond hair, early twenties, skinny, with a hipster

beard. Used to live at 259 East 7th, but you probably sold to him elsewhere last night."

Pete nodded. "Oh yeah, I know that dude. He was at some penthouse on the Upper East last night, never been there before. He said it was his uncle's. Dude was acting strange. Bought five bags of blow from me, around eleven. Kid's usually friendly, but last night he didn't even look at me. I been dealing to him for . . . Wait, oh shit." The smack cloud had finally lifted enough for Pete to complete the connection. "They used to live together, those two guys—Mike and that guy who . . ." He looked again at the picture and almost retched. "Jesus, those two, they were roommates."

"Very good, Peter," said Cass. "It appears we are making progress."

"Do they have any idea who did it?"

"They have suspects," I said. "There are always suspects. Including you, Pete."

"My partner is right, Peter," she said. "You're the go-to drug dealer for a rich, well-connected white kid who was brutally murdered. That does indeed make you a suspect. You also dealt to the dead man's girlfriend, who is now missing. And to top it off, you continue to deal to the dead man's best friend and roommate. These are all things that I'm sure the NYPD would love to know."

"I thought you said cops were the enemy?" asked Pete with a desperate croak.

"No," said Cass. "My partner said cops were the enemy. He has always had problems with authority. I'm sure the two of you can relate. However, I have dear friends who are members of the NYPD. How do you think I was able to get these crime scene photos?"

Pete slumped back into the couch. He held his drug-filled backpack tight to his chest like a bullied fifth-grader.

He closed his eyes and breathed through his nose. "What do you want from me?" he asked quietly.

"Last time you saw her, at Clem's, what did she buy?"

"Whole bunch of stuff. Like six bags of blow and a bunch of molly. I think the chick got some H too. Must have been a big night."

"Big night for you too," said Cass. "What did all that cost her?"

"It was a bunch. Let's see, hundo each for the blow, that's six. I think it was like three bills of molly. And a few bags of the H. A little over a grand, I'd say."

"You must have been thrilled, selling all that to an eighteen-year-old addict," she said. Then she stepped forward and slashed the dealer across the face with her sharp red nails. Blood sprang from his cheek in jagged lines. He cried out, grabbed at his face and fled head down for the door.

"When we find her," she called, "you better hope she's not dead."

Chapter 17

You might think that a professional dominatrix falls into an alternative category of prostitution. Cass would be quick to explain the distinction of her craft. Yes, it is sexual in nature, and money changes hands. And sure, the client is often naked. But a dominatrix is more a well-dressed therapist than prostitute. She is never penetrated and never ever touches the client's cock. Release, as they say, must be manual—if the mistress permits it.

The role gives her a unique perspective on the sex industry. It allows her to see it from an informed remove, yet also up close, viewing the types of men who will forever line up to pay for the fulfillment of their needs. The murdered escort her outreach group was named for, Veronica Life, was a one-time mistress who made the leap. She had spent a short stint at the Chamber with Cass. Veronica was a young, gorgeous Latvian girl who was sending much of her income home to her mother and sister each month. Mistresses earn a fraction of what well-paid escorts can take in; she hadn't wanted to go that far, but the offer came and she needed the money. Then along came that murderous Russian john who left Veronica strangled with his leather belt on a hotel bed. He was seated in first class, flying somewhere over the Atlantic, by the time the maid found her.

Cass was reminding me of these things again as I prepared to leave for Clem's and the makeshift studio across the street. She is disgusted by porn, thinks it's a sickness of society, the voyeurism of prostitution; says it destroys honest interaction between the sexes: this from a woman who will tie you down and clamp your body in clothespins, if that's your honest pleasure.

"Angela Jones, that vile bitch," she said, examining the blood under her nails. "Do you have any idea how many girls like Madeline she's lured in, gotten hooked, and used up? Eighteen-, nineteen-year-old party girls—that's her target. It's criminal."

"There's also a large market for it," I reminded her. " 'Teen' must be the most searched word in porn."

"I realize that," she said. "Penises will always be the true problem, the things that make them hard. But women like Angela, the ones who facilitate it in the worst ways—there's a special circle of hell reserved for those cunts."

She shook her head and checked her phone. "Shit, I have a session in an hour, I gotta run." Cass pushed Elvis from her lap and tossed her leather bag over a shoulder.

I felt sorry for the poor guy. He didn't know what was in store for him behind those padded dungeon walls.

"Keep me posted," she said.

I watched her slam the door and stalk off through the window. I remembered a story about the Old West, about the white man's battles with the Native Americans. I read that the worst punishment a captured cowboy could receive did not come from the Natives he was battling out on the plains. It came from their women. That was the torturous fate reserved for the true white devils. When the most vicious, painful retribution is required, pray that they don't hand you over to strong women.

I swallowed down three vikes with a last gulp of beer, then brewed some coffee for clarity and took Elvis out for a quick evening walk around the block. Despite the violence and the madness of the previous days I found myself almost giddy over what lay ahead. The prospect of that porn studio, the evil madam, the opiates already working their way into my brainpan, all of the illicit thrills on the horizon. There were worse ways to earn a living. Returning home, I unleashed the hound, tossed on a sport coat over my pitted T-shirt, and moved back out into the dusk, headed for the L train.

The stench of self-conscious hipness hits you as soon as you walk up the subway steps at Bedford. The young masses of Williamsburg have it all figured out. Scrawled alongside the subway exit it read *"Now it's bridge and tunnel in reverse."* This borough needed to get over itself. When Sinatra sang about making it here, he wasn't talking about fucking Brooklyn.

I moved among them until I traced my way to Grand and Roebling. It was an ugly block, for decades a fringe neighborhood of lower-income immigrants. But no longer: now those same cheap railroad apartments were rented for five grand a month by graphic designers and tech kids, and your occasional enterprising porn entrepreneur.

Clem's, at least, was trying to rise above the hipsterness. The crowd was older; dads slouched over whiskeys under the high copper ceiling. This wasn't a place that catered to the kiddies. An attractive Asian bartender was staring up at a Premier League soccer game on the TV in the corner. She approached without taking her eyes off the screen and set down a cocktail napkin in front of me. I asked her for a Bulleit, one cube, and she poured it without acknowledgment. The pills were starting to kick in. I turned on my stool and watched the building across the street through the blinds of the bar's long windows. Not a bad spot for a stakeout.

I was finishing my third drink, feeling the rush of the vikes, when the bartender decided to speak to me.

"You been staring out that window for some time," she said. "You waiting on someone?"

"You could say that."

"Looks like you been stood up."

"Not sure she knows I'm waiting."

"You some kind of stalker?"

I turned to her. She had a kind, wide face with full lips and a smirk to her thin, dark eyes. "You know what goes on over there?" I asked.

"Over where?"

"Where I've been watching for the last hour," I said.

She reached for the whiskey bottle, refilled my glass. "This one's on me," she said.

I let her drift away and make her rounds, pouring more drinks for the growing crowd. I had resolved to downshift to beer by the time she returned.

"You looking for work?" she asked. "Over there, I mean."

She made eye contact for the first time. Her smirk was gone.

"More like looking for someone who works there," I said.

She glanced down the bar at a few raised arms looking for refills. I wouldn't have her attention for long.

"Looking for a missing girl," I said. "Tall, athletic eighteen-year-old. She's done some work over there."

"Likely story," she said. "Look like a stalker to me."

I turned in my seat, pulled up the side of my sport coat and shirt. Showed her the bullet scar just below my ribs, where my spleen used to be. "See that?" I asked. "A stalker gave me that a few years back. Shot me point blank. I'd like to think I'm on the non-creep side."

She looked from my scar to my battered face. I let her size me up. "Hang on," she said.

When she returned, she was holding a felt pen and a cocktail napkin. She leaned before me on the bar and scribbled something down, then folded the napkin and pushed it over to me. "Ask for Angela," she said. "Give this to her. Tell her you're interested in work. She'll like you. Apartment 3C."

I opened the napkin. It read "Enjoy!" in red ink that leaked through the thin layers. It was signed with a K and a winking smiley face. Time to go apply for a job.

My legs were unsteady beneath me as I stepped out into the warm night. The vikes filled me with a sense of gauzy fearlessness, an invincible cloud around my consciousness. I approached a rusted entry gate alongside a graffiti-covered garage door. Before I could reach for the buzzer, two girls came tripping and giggling out of the building. They were dressed in little but their tattoos and just enough cloth to count for public decency. The brunette had a high beehive hairdo that needed tending. Both arms were covered in tat sleeves. When she lit her cigarette, her smeared lips sucked down a mighty drag. Then she coughed it out and shared the lighter with her friend, a waif of a redhead with translucent skin and a high air about her.

"How's it going, girls?" I asked.

"Rad," said the redhead. She turned her back to me, and the brunette rolled her eyes.

"Hey, I was just going up to see Angela," I said. "It's 3C, right?"

This got their attention. Both turned and examined me up and down like a pair of art appraisers. "You know Angie?" asked the brunette.

"No, not yet, I mean. My friend put us in touch. I was gonna look for some work."

The redhead laughed, took a drag, placed her hand

against my chest. She moved in close and peered up at me. Her eyes were glazed as a Dunkin' donut. Definitely high. "You're a big boy, aren't you?" she asked.

"Settle down, Juli," said the brunette, slapping her friend's narrow ass. "Excuse her," she said to me. "She's in heat."

Both girls laughed and sucked down the rest of their smokes. Then Juli grabbed my hand and buzzed the apartment. "C'mon," she said. "Come with us."

If not for the collection of video equipment positioned across the living room, the apartment was your average crappy one-bedroom: small open living space with kitchenette against one wall, bedroom and bath behind cheap drywall. Two muscled red-faced guys in boxers lounged on the leather couch, sipping at Coronas. Another pair hovered over a cutting board by the sink. They were schlubby, bearded, and dressed—the ones operating all that equipment. One was slicing limes, the other lines of coke. They looked up as we entered. The room tensed as all eyes fell to me.

"Yo, where's Ang?" asked Juli, now holding my hand.

"The fuck is that?" asked the one cutting the limes.

"Where's Angie?" asked beehive.

"Bedroom," yawned one of the dudes on the couch. He was young, ripped, and blond, with the look of an off-duty construction worker.

Juli dropped my hand and rapped on the bedroom door. A husky voice called, "Hang on," and took her time about it. Beehive looked over at the little man busy with the coke. "Hey, Marco, you better save me one," she said.

"And why should I do that?" he asked.

She leered at him. "I think you know why."

The bedroom door opened, and I was presented with the ample Angela. She was rubbing the inside of a fat forearm. Perhaps a performer a decade and a hundred pounds ago, Angela had now filled out to roughly the size and shape of a newborn elephant. She was wearing a dark gray dress with a black sash wrapped around her wide waist. Her black hair was swept back in a ponytail, presenting a puffy face that had reeled in the years. She gave us a sleepy look before her eyes settled on me and stayed there. She waited for some explanation.

"So, like, this guy was coming up to see you," said Juli. "He says he was referred by a friend." She squeezed my arm and snuggled in close. "Can I work with him, Angie, please?"

"What friend?" asked Angela.

"The bartender across the street," I said and handed her the folded cocktail napkin.

She took it, read it, and smiled. "Please step into my office," she said, stepping back from the doorway. Then, to her performers outside, she called: "You guys ready to go again?"

"Damn right," said one. The other just grunted and swallowed back his beer.

"All right then, Marco, Eddie, you guys know what to do. Girls, look alive."

Juli and Beehive nodded their heads, then moved fast for the lines on the cutting board. They'd be looking more than alive in no time. Angela waved me into her room and shut the door.

It was a small space that the elephantine woman filled at the foot of an unmade queen bed. The wall behind the headboard was spray-painted with an abstract black-and-red mural that I recognized from Madeline's past performances in this room. Angela reclined on the bed. She propped herself up on an elbow and bent a leg like a side of beef. "You're a friend of Kim's, huh? She does like those finder's fees."

The bartender's willingness to share was starting to

make more sense. I felt myself squirming before this large, lascivious mass.

"So, let's see what you've got," said Angela.

"What I've . . ."

She motioned to my belt buckle. "Off," she said. "Need to see the equipment. Don't worry if you're not hard yet. Even if you're a grower, I'll be able to see what we're working with."

"Listen, do you mind if I ask you a few questions first?"

Angela sighed. Her mouth turned down in reproach. "Baby, if you're not willing to drop 'em without a thought, then what are you doing here?"

Thanks be to the vikes for my fearlessness. "Okay, fair enough." I reached for my buckle. "But can I ask you some questions after?"

"Honey, if you meet my approval, you can ask me anything you like," she said.

Before I could feel shame, I closed my eyes and dropped my pants. I stood there swaying with my hands on my bare hips. I felt Angela examining me in silence. The bed creaked and groaned as she climbed across the mattress toward me. She cupped me in one hand, lifted and tugged with the other. When the violation was complete, she exhaled and slapped my ass. I felt her hot breath against me. "Okay," she said. "You pass. On the small side for this biz, but you'll do."

I opened my eyes and leaned down and pulled up my jeans. "Thank you," I muttered.

"You sure you want to do this?" she asked. "You don't seem too eager. But I wouldn't worry. Little Juli will get your blood racing. She can't wait to get with you. A live one, that little redhead."

"Listen, about those questions," I said.

"Shoot."

"I was wondering about a girl who's done some work

here. Tall, young, only been eighteen for a few months. Likes her drugs."

"Honey, you're describing every girl who walks in here."

I removed her picture from my back pocket, the one of Madeline posing with James Fealy at Bowery Ballroom. Showed it to Angela. "Name's Madeline, though she may go by something else here."

Fat fingers snatched it from me. She glanced down at it and handed it back. "Oh right. Maddie. Aka Charlaine Black. The lips on that one—made for this biz. Loaded with talent too, if she can keep her shit together. Likes to party, you know? What do you want with her?"

"I was just hoping to talk with her. You know how to reach her?"

"Why?"

Dropped trou or not, Angela was starting to get suspicious.

"Friend of a friend," I said. "I heard she was up . . . for anything."

"Well, anyone who's seen her work knows that," she said. "Tell you what, you shoot a few scenes with us, we get to know you a little, and next time Maddie comes calling, I'll make sure to introduce you two. Sound good, soldier?"

"I was hoping to . . ."

"Good, settled then. Let's go see how they're doing out there."

"Actually, no good. I need to find her."

Angela held my gaze. A crooked smile played on her mouth like a crocodile at the water's edge. "Let's see how it's going out there," she said again. Then she hefted her bulk from the bed and moved past me to the bedroom door.

Sounds of slapping and soft moans were audible from the living room. I hesitated there alone in the bedroom, considered a retreat back to Clem's for more fortification before I joined Angela on the makeshift set. As I crossed the threshold those sounds of pleasure turned to sharp pain.

"Ow, fuck!" shouted one of the male performers. "Fucking bitch! What the—"

I came into the room to find him grasping at his crotch, blood visible between his fingers. He looked wild-eyed across the couch at Juli, who was wiping a smear of blood from her chin like a rabid vampire. The rest of the room was frozen in suspended disbelief. Angela was the first to snap out of it.

"Juli," she said calmly. "What the fuck?"

Juli was off the couch now, grabbing for her things. She pulled on a tank top, shorts, tossed a pink purse over her shoulder. Tears spilled down her pale cheeks. "I'm out of here," she cried. "Fuck all of you."

No one blocked her path as she fled for the door and slammed it behind her. Instead of tending to the wounded man on the couch, all eyes turned to me. It appeared my arrival had sparked some bad energy on the scene. It was time for me to go too. I met Angela's eyes. "See you soon," I said. Then I raced out, down the stairs and outside in pursuit of Juli.

She was halfway down Roebling, walking fast in bare feet. Her high heels dangled from the straps in her left hand. Her right arm was half raised as she searched down the street for a passing cab. I called out her name, and she picked up her pace. I caught up to her at the corner of South 1st Street. My hand touched her bare shoulder. She spun around, flung her shoes against my side.

"Not now, man, okay? Not now."

"Hold up," I said. "What happened back there?"

"Fucking prick," she said. "I can't believe he said that shit."

"Said what?"

Juli looked up at me for the first time. Her pretty face was ruined with tears and streaked mascara. The cocaine made her eyes look like an empty, wet well. Her forehead glistened with sweat beneath damp red hair. She removed her phone from her purse, looked back down, and tapped at an app.

"Just leave me alone, man," she said. "I'm calling an Uber. Maybe some other time, okay?"

"Can you tell me what happened?" I asked.

She tried to gather herself. Straightened up, wiped at her eyes. "You have a cigarette?" she asked. Before I could shake my head, she reached into her bag and produced one of her own. The lighter quivered in her small hand and refused to spark. I took it from her and lit it and waited until she had a few calming drags.

"I'm sorry, man. There's just some shit that triggers . . ." She shook her head, decided not to complete the thought. "Some words just set me off," she said.

"What did he say?"

"Don't worry about it, okay?" She blew smoke out of the side her mouth. Her shoulders deflated. "What did Angela have to say?" she asked.

"That I was on the small side," I said. "For the biz."

"Wouldn't worry about it," she said. "That fat bitch is a size queen."

"Can I buy you a drink?" I asked.

"I'm really not in the mood to ball tonight. Not after that, okay?"

"Just asked if I could buy you a drink."

"What do you want, man? You obviously weren't looking for work."

"How can you tell?"

"You followed me out here," she said. "After I bit that asshole." She remembered her actions from moments earlier. "Jesus, hope I didn't hurt him too bad. Guess that fucks my chances of working for Angie again." She flicked the spent butt of the cigarette into the street. "So, what were you really after?"

"I'm looking for someone," I said. "A girl about your age. Really tall, athletic, name is Madeline, but I think Angela said she goes by Charlaine or something?"

"Maddie," she said. "Sure, I know her. That chick's wild. We've partied together a few times."

"Seen her recently?"

Juli nodded. "Weekend before last," she said. "We went out after we shot a few scenes at Angie's. Maddie ordered a bunch of stuff for this party we went to."

"Where?" I asked, blood racing at the warm trail.

"It's called the Day of the Lord party," she said. "Goes from midnight Saturday to midnight Sunday. In a different spot every week, in like old warehouses? Last time it was at this place in Gowanus, next to the canal."

"Was Maddie a regular at these things?"

"Seemed like it. She knew a whole bunch of people there. It was my first time going. I got so fucked I barely remember it. I left sometime Sunday afternoon. Don't know when Maddie left. We lost each other at some point."

"Any idea where this party is being held this week?"

She shook her head. "Why you looking for her, man?"

"She's been missing, from her family at least, for a little while," I told her. "Her mother is worried. She hasn't been back to her apartment, no one's been able to reach her."

Juli shrugged. "Like I said, I just hung out with her at that party. Who knows why she hasn't been home. Maybe she's with a client."

"A client?"

"Yeah, man, that's where the real money is." She reached into her bag for another smoke. "Everybody watches those videos for free these days, Angie barely pays us shit, but guys will spend a ton to be with an actual porn star. You have no idea. That's her main business, madam, porn producer, it's all the same thing. She says the videos are just like promotional."

"So Madeline is also working as . . ."

"An escort," she said. "Sure, sometimes. It's not like a regular thing for us. We're not hookers, but the money's so good it's worth it every once in a while. Sometimes guys'll give us like ten grand to spend the weekend with them."

I neglected to point out that Madeline McKay already had a trust fund and a monthly allowance that made escorting money irrelevant.

"How can I reach her, Juli?" I asked. "She's not answering her cell or emails. Hasn't been home. How can I find this party?"

She shrugged again. Her tears had dried, and whatever trigger had sparked her biting blow job was being pushed back beneath the surface. She lit another cigarette, this time with a steady hand. "No clue, man, that was Maddie's scene," she said. "I'm sure she'll turn up."

She lifted her arm as she looked over my shoulder and moved toward the street. "I think this is me," she said.

I turned to find a black SUV slowing to a stop behind me. The ubiquitous Uber "U" was not visible beneath the windshield. The driver's door opened, and out climbed an unfriendly man in a gray tracksuit and dark glasses and a black Yankees cap pulled low over a heavy skull. He was about my height, but spent a lot more time in the gym. In his right hand, he held an aluminum bat. I glanced back at his car and saw no one sitting shotgun. One-on-one, I liked my odds.

"Get out of here," I said to Juli.

She didn't respond, didn't move.

"You don't learn," said the man in a guttural Russian accent. The sense memory placed it. Last time I heard it, I was lying on a sidewalk in a pool of broken beer bottles and blood.

He tapped the head of the bat in his other hand as he approached. Juli let out a light whimper like a kitten in a corner. I worked through my aikido progressions, willing myself to remember something. I used to be a regular at the dojo, but I lost the discipline. Never felt the spiritual side of the art. It was the attacks that did it for me. Literally translated from the Japanese, aikido can be defined as "the way to combine forces." Figuratively, they say it's all about unifying our energies in harmonious movement. But in action, at the moment of attack, it means that you can take on any sized fucker and use his own strength and aggression against him.

He didn't hesitate, and neither did I. The arc of the bat came at my head with a mean home run swing. Moving forward, I swept one hand low, the other high, catching his wrist and executing a fine heaven-and-earth throw. It sent him flying onto the sidewalk. His weapon clanged away in the street.

Now, at this point, my aikido training had done its job. I'd disarmed my attacker by using his aggressive energy against him, and now I was safe from further harm. An aikido master would have the discipline and purity of spirit to walk away. But I'm no master. I'd also been knocked down by this guy once before. If he'd connected with that swing, my head might have burst open like a busted watermelon. I also had enough booze and pills in my system to cloud even a monk's best intentions.

So, instead of getting away with Juli, I walked over to the guy, just getting warmed up. There was a cut above his eye where he'd landed, but beyond that, he was unharmed by my throw. He looked up at me and tried to scramble to his feet.

I kicked him once, hard, in the stomach and sent him

back down. Before he could catch his breath, I kicked him again in the mouth. He choked back broken teeth, tried to lunge at me. I caught him by both ears, and then slammed his head back down on the curb. Did it a few more times. Softened the back of his skull on the pavement.

"Who are you?" I heard myself shouting. "Who hired you?"

He smiled a ghastly smile through a bloody mouth as the fight went out of him. I heard shouting down the block, getting closer, shouting at me to stop. I gave his skull one last crack, and then I grabbed Juli's hand and got us out of there.

We ran in a random maze through the streets until I was sure there was no one behind us. We finally came to a stop along the waterfront, under the Williamsburg Bridge. We stood there panting for a while, bent forward with our hands on our knees. I straightened up and looked across the still black water to Manhattan staring back at us with detached judgment. I heard a cigarette sparking next to me, followed by the grimy scent, and the lingering plume of smoke. She stood there smoking in silence before the questions began.

Chapter 18

My answers changed her mood. By the time I'd finished explaining myself, the little redhead was purring about not wanting to be alone tonight. She was a sweet kid, claimed to be twenty-one, born and raised on Staten Island. Suffered the usual abuse, responded with the usual rebellion. Wanted to be an actress, and now she was one. A bad dream come true.

I managed to pack her off in a cab, resisted the urge to join her. The perpetual worry of transmitted disease was one thing, the thought of trigger-word bitten castration quite another. She promised to call if she heard any word from Madeline. I promised to call if I ever wanted to reconsider my adult film debut.

It was midday when I woke, and a rude September sun shone through my bedroom window. My knuckles were cut and crusted over with dried blood. They must have connected with sidewalk during the repeated softening of the guy's skull. The unlucky bastard was hurting somewhere right now. When he woke, if he woke, I doubted he'd start talking. I cursed myself for failing to get his license plate. Elvis whimpered at the foot of my bed. I staggered to the back door and let the hound out in the garden. The cruel light of day hit me full in the face as I stood in the doorway and watched him piss on a dying tree. Then he trotted back inside, went to the kitchen, and started beating on his bowl. Hangovers wait for no hound. As he ate I checked my messages and tried not to make any fast movements. A few texts from Cass, eager for updates. One from Juli, wishing I were there.

There were three missed calls from a random number— 845 area code, upstate. One voice mail, a long one. Before I could bear the sound of another human voice, I brewed a pot of strong coffee and swallowed down four Advil. While I waited for the water to boil, I considered the previous day. A predawn start in search of Marks at the pool; a cold morning lay at Anna Lisko's sparse Soho loft; drinks at Old Town, as Cass and I caught up on the case; our visit with Dealer Pete; then, an introduction to the hipster porn scene and a humiliating audition; only to end the night with a curbside assault, followed by fleeing the scene with a damaged but eager porn star. I needed about twenty-four hours of silent soul-cleansing recovery to work it all out. When I checked the voice mail, I knew that wasn't going to happen.

The message was from Marks, calling from the McKay house upstate in Rhinebeck. He was staying with Margaret, he told me. There were things they both needed to discuss with me. Could I please drive up this afternoon? It was looking like a beautiful fall weekend up there, he added. Margaret would very much like a progress report. She wouldn't be getting all of it.

I called Cass first. I told her about my examination at the hands of hefty Angela and confirmed her worst suspicions about the scene. Then, about that impromptu assault . . .

"I can't believe you had the presence of mind to execute that move," she gushed. "I have to say, I am impressed, Duck. The heaven-and-earth? That is no easy defense.

And wasted as you surely were? I couldn't do it. Sometimes I really do underestimate you, my friend."

She didn't need to hear the rest of it.

"Amazing what comes back to you in the moment," I said.

"When's the last time you were at the dojo?"

"Got me. Few months?"

"Incredible." She was silent for a long moment. I could hear the pride in her breath. "I don't know, you really amaze me sometimes. Just think what you could be with a clear head."

"Wouldn't be me," I said.

"No argument there."

"So, listen, can you do some research on this Day of the Lord party? Shouldn't be too hard to locate. Looks like I gotta head upstate to see the Mother and the Master."

"I'll track it down, no worries," she said. "You gonna be back in time to join me?"

"Should be. Curious to hear what they have to say up there."

"You gonna tell them about Madeline's escorting?"

"Wasn't planning on it."

"This girl is seriously damaged, Duck. It's not like she's doing this stuff for the money."

"Maybe she's just a nympho?"

"Like your new little redheaded friend? Most of these girls are running from something."

"I realize that." I was thinking about Marks, about the way Charlie had seen him with his sister, the way their coach had behaved with other young girls on the team.

"So who was this guy with the bat?" she asked. "Same one from the other day, you're sure?"

"Positive. Same accent, same black SUV. A Tahoe. Can't believe I didn't get the plates."

"It was probably good you got out of there. We don't

need to waste time with more questioning cops. Besides, after your performance, I doubt that's the last you'll be hearing from him."

That is, if he regained consciousness anytime soon.

We wished each other luck, said we'd keep each other posted. Cass told me to take the Benz on my road trip to the country.

She kept it parked in a lot beneath the Manhattan Bridge. The attendant was an ex-con named Ping Pong who'd worked out a deal with Cass: one free session at the dungeon each month in exchange for free parking. His years in prison had left him with a certain submissive streak, and now Cass filled his conflicted desires with a strap-on and some therapeutic role-play. Ping Pong was seated on his usual stool at the entrance to the garage. He made no effort to conceal the joint smoldering in his right hand.

"Meester Duck," he said in greeting. "The beautiful bride. How is your husband doing?"

"Careful with that," I told him. "Cops'll toss you in the Tombs."

"NYPD can suck Ping Pong's fat dick," he said, grabbing at his crotch. He took a long drag, didn't offer to share. "Let them send me back, you think I care?"

"Guess not."

He sat there inhaling it down to the fiery butt, showing no inclination to retrieve the car. A Caribbean nanny walked by the garage pushing a white baby in a stroller and gave him a reproachful look.

"Fokking bitch judge me?" he muttered. "Go take care of somebody else's baby and keep your eyes to yourself."

When he'd taken the last puff possible, he sighed and stamped it out on the driveway and lazily pushed himself to his feet. "Be right back," he said.

Cass's Benz was an '81 Mercedes 300SD sedan, turbo

diesel. Silver body, burgundy leather interior, just 80,000 miles. Each new mile was carefully considered. And no overpriced oil from the pump for this beauty; Cass filled it with vegetable oil, procured in barrels from Chinatown restaurants. The fact that she offered it for a hundred-mile drive upstate showed just how impressed she was with my aikido. It drives heavy to the ground, with the low rumble of a well-made tank. Made before the age of airbags, you'd rather get into a head-on collision in this steel machine than any of today's fiberglass toys. I guided it onto the FDR and pointed it north.

The drive was bumper to bumper in the late afternoon Friday traffic. We inched along the East River as I sweated out the booze with no AC in the old Benz. On a helipad at 34th Street, a group of black-suited bankers huddled into their waiting ride. The helicopter began to spin its long arms in slow revolutions, gradually speeding faster and faster, before lifting off and out to the Hamptons. Nice commute, if you've got the coin. I rode it once at the end of my last case with my newly single and achingly grateful client. It was $695 for the half-hour trip. You'll never find a higher concentration of fuckwits than at the waiting lounge of that place. On board, the seats were cramped, the takeoffs nauseating, but hey, at least they provided complimentary plastic cups of rosé for the ride.

I sipped my Gatorade, needing more hydration than a marathoner, and remembered Marks's voice when I rang him back after Cass. I pictured him speaking from the stillness of the McKay mansion in the rolling hills of Duchess County. "There are some things, ah, that we feel we need to share, Duck," he'd said. "Madeline really is a good girl, despite what you've heard. Despite what, ah, you might have already turned up. Problem is that she's too smart for her own good. And lacks discipline, yes. We know there

---

are some good reasons for this, some things we probably should have shared previously. But, well, we would like to share them with you now."

"We?"

"Margaret and I."

"You might have started by telling me you were a couple."

"We didn't see the relevance, honestly. In retrospect, we could have been more up front with you from the start."

"There are a few things I'd like to discuss with you too, Teddy. Some probably best discussed in private, away from Mrs. McKay."

"We have no secrets, Duck. She can hear whatever it is you have to tell me."

"I doubt that. But after we speak, I'd also like to speak to her one-on-one if you don't mind."

"Whatever helps your investigation," he said. "How soon can you be here?"

I told him it would be early evening, anticipating the soul-crushing traffic I was now stuck in. If it was true what Charlie had said, about Marks and Madeline, then the man was making a bold bluff with the no-secrets bit. If it wasn't true, well then, Charlie had made one hell of a false accusation. Marks hung up with an awkward formality. He thanked me for my discretion, muttered how it would all make sense soon.

I sat for a sweaty hour on the Harlem River Drive marinating in the filthy fumes. Over the shoulder of the road, a pair of fat black women jabbed their fingers in the chest of a stammering Latino man in front of a grocery store. They couldn't have been more than ten feet away, but to the sealed climate-controlled fleets of BMWs and Range Rovers around me, they existed in a silent parallel universe. With windows down in the old Benz, I took in the shouting, enjoyed the raging righteousness of the women;

considered pulling off for some malt liquor to get me through the drive. Then, finally, we were gliding over the George Washington Bridge, the colossus of Manhattan shimmering down river to my left like the Emerald City on steroids. I veered off onto the Palisades, made it to the Thruway without a ticket from lurking Jersey cops, and settled onto I-87 with hangover-approved jazz playing at low volume.

It was after seven by the time I crossed the Kingston-Rhinecliff Bridge and consulted Google Maps for the final leg of my journey. The McKay mansion was three miles outside the tony town of Rhinebeck, on a winding country road with the old estates set up on green hills well back from the roads. This was where city wealth used to summer, in the Edith Wharton days, before the Hamptons took over as the sun-drenched playground of rich lemmings. I gave the McKays points for taste, in choosing this as their second home, as I slowed at each stone archway and sought their address.

It was known as Owl View Farm. I turned through the open wrought-iron gates and drove up a long driveway lined with white birch trees like pale-suited soldiers. The temperature had dropped leaving the city. I breathed in the cool, clean country air and felt something closer to normal. The sun was low in the sky, with magic hour light, and the dusk colors gave the property a crisp, still sense of posing for its portrait. The main house was a stately Georgian affair with long, white Corinthian columns across the front. It was the kind of place that fulfilled a man's image of himself before ever setting foot inside. Off to the side, there was a low white brick guesthouse, and down a gentle hill, a pool house that looked modernized and enlarged by its present owners.

I pulled the Benz past a shining black Range Rover and

parked directly in front of the main house. As if on cue, the high front door opened and out stepped Teddy Marks and Margaret McKay like the perfect gentry couple.

Marks smiled broadly beneath his well-kept mustache, and Margaret held his arm with mannered grace. She was wearing tan riding pants, black boots, and a white blouse that billowed out in the evening breeze. Her hair flickered across that surgically stretched face like the wind was in on the scene. Marks was dressed in white linen pants and a light blue oxford, with no socks on his loafered feet. I felt embarrassed for him. They could have been posing for the cover of *Town & Country*.

"Welcome," said Marks.

"Nice place," I said.

He shrugged, gave me a wink, and Margaret gave me a tight smile as I walked up the wide white steps.

"We appreciate you making the drive," said Margaret. "Was traffic very bad?"

"Horrible. Two hours up the FDR."

Marks looked me up and down, processed my appearance. "Late night last night, Duck?"

"Not too bad," I lied.

Margaret turned her eyes up at her lover, her sharp profile set off in the twilight. He held her look for a beat, communicating something between them, before turning back to me.

"You'll stay the night, won't you, Lawrence?" asked Margaret. "We've made the guesthouse up for you."

"You're the boss," I said. "Sounds good to me."

"Wonderful." She squeezed his arm and turned him back toward the house. "Do come in," she said. "We have dinner waiting."

Chapter 19

We were seated in a tall, dark dining room full of fresh cut flowers, Hudson River School landscapes, and a big stuffed buffalo head over a stone fireplace. The eyes of the buffalo looked like translucent cue balls. They looked down over the long oak table with clear-eyed disdain. Three places had been set at the far end of the table, with Margaret seated at the head, Marks and me on either side. A chandelier of stained glass offered a low amber light over the table, keeping the rest of the room in shadows.

Marks was making a show of pouring the wine. A Barolo of some sort, full-bodied, earthy tone, long finish, the man presented it with insufferable enthusiasm. Margaret sat still with hands in her lap, eyeing both of us with a look of blank regard. Reminded me to get Botox and a facelift the next time I went to Vegas; she had a flawless cosmetic poker face. When Marks filled her glass she nodded with grace and sat back in her chair. We made a silent toast as a sturdy gray-haired woman set out bowls of butternut squash soup.

"Thank you, Nina," said Margaret. Then, to me: "You're in for a treat, Lawrence. Nina is a fabulous chef."

She was right. The soup was insane. With the first spoonful I almost forgot how bad I was feeling. I was informed that Nina and her husband, Ernest, lived at Owl View in a converted stone barn. The couple took care of the property in the McKays' absence, with Nina keeping the main house and Ernest tending the grounds.

We chatted through the soup with the loaded hum of small talk: the brilliant weather this time of year, the Yankees' latest failures, the sense of relief in crossing the GW and leaving the city. The empty words only added weight to the conversations that loomed. Nina cleared our bowls with a downward gaze and returned with lamb chops and assorted root vegetables as Marks refilled our glasses. When he finished pouring, she lifted the empty bottle from the table and asked Margaret quietly if we would like another of the same. I noticed Nina's body language; her hip turned away from Marks, making clear she took direction only from the lady of the house.

"Nice wine," I said, taking a healthy gulp before cutting into the chop.

"Is indeed," said Marks. "There are some truly fantastic vintages down in the cellar."

Margaret stiffened at the possessive way he said it. He noticed too. "I'm afraid to touch some of them they're so good," he said with a self-conscious laugh. Margaret bowed her head toward him in forgiveness. Then she leveled her gaze at me.

"So, tell us, Lawrence. What have you discovered over the last few days? I understand it's been quite eventful."

I held up a finger as I chewed a succulent bite of lamb, savoring the juices, wanting to hug Nina in appreciation. I washed it down with another gulp of wine and wiped my mouth. "Eventful, yes." I nodded. "I've been attacked, twice. One win, one loss. Witnessed a murder scene, visited an attempted suicide at the hospital, and heard some troubling details about your daughter and those closest to her." I looked straight at Marks as I spoke the last line. He did not react.

"Hell of a week," he said, cutting into his lamb. "Good to see those bruises on your face are healing. You were a wreck last I saw you."

"Poor Lucy," said Margaret. "She was always such a sensitive girl. I do hope she's recovering." She set down her knife and fork and took an imperceptible sip from her glass. "Now, Lawrence, have any of these violent adventures led you any closer to finding my daughter?"

"Perhaps," I said.

"Oh?"

"I've been informed that your daughter was seen at a party the weekend before last. My partner and I plan to attend that same party tomorrow night. Seems she might be a regular."

"Didn't Charlie see her here, at the house, that weekend?" asked Marks.

Margaret added nothing, only waited for me to continue.

"Right, which means she must have come up here the next day. Charlie says he saw her the Sunday before Labor Day?"

"That's correct," said Margaret.

"And she left almost immediately," I said. "As if she was troubled by something. Then she sent you that text the next day, and Coach, you missed a call from her."

They nodded together.

"Does Madeline drive?" I asked.

Margaret shook her head. "She never expressed an interest. She said there was no point, living in the city."

"Can I ask how that's relevant?" asked Marks.

"Well, Charlie told me that after she left the house she went out by the road and waited for a cab to pick her up. Presumably to go back to the train station?"

"I suppose," said Margaret. "It's only two hours from the Rhinecliff station back to Penn."

"Still, it seems like quite a trek, to come up here and leave so quickly, especially after a night of partying. Whatever she had to pick up, it must have been important."

When neither chose to reply, I added, "I'm not sure if the police have informed you of this, but there is security footage of Madeline leaving James Fealy's building the next day."

Margaret's chin fell to her chest, her hands dropped to her lap, shoulders sagged. She reached for her wineglass and swallowed down the remains. "I did not know that," she said quietly.

"This doesn't imply any guilt," I added. "Fealy's parents confirmed that their son was with them in the Hamptons until the following morning. Evidently, Madeline was inside an empty apartment. It's confirmed that neither Fealy nor his roommate were home."

"What else did they see?" asked Marks. "On the security. If they saw Maddie coming and going, they also must have seen the someone else entering the next day?"

"It appears there was an electrical issue in the building," I said. "There's a gap in the lobby's security footage." When that failed to elicit a response, I asked, "How much do you know about her relationship with this kid?"

"We were aware he was a poor influence, almost from the start," said Margaret. "Charlie introduced them, at a company party of his. James was the son of a senior partner at his firm. I approved at first. He was from a good family, after all. But soon after meeting him, I suspected trouble."

"How so?"

"Madeline was already . . . struggling. I knew she was using drugs, and she'd had her problems with depression.

But her self-destructive behavior escalated when she took up with that boy."

"How long were they together?"

She flipped through the pages of the calendar in her mind. "It was just a few months, I suppose. I recall that party of Charlie's being in the spring."

"Was the relationship serious?"

"She thought she was in love," said her mother, sighing. "She told me as much after she introduced me to him in June. I was quite sure they were both high."

Marks cleared his throat, set down his knife. "If I may," he began. "It's relevant to point out that Madeline's commitment to her training, while spotty to begin with, took a significant turn for the worse soon after she started dating this boy. By summer, I suspected she was done with the sport for good."

When he got no response from either of us, he frowned and drank from his glass.

Nina appeared with the new bottle, and conversation stopped as we watched her uncork it and pour a splash into Margaret's glass. She tasted it, and gave a quick nod, and watched her glass fill with the rich red liquid. She drank off half of it before Nina reached our glasses. Then she pushed back her chair and stood before us.

"Please continue eating," she said. "I must excuse myself for a moment."

We watched her walk across the room and disappear down a dark hallway into the shadows of the house. Her footsteps echoed on the hardwood floors until they faded like dying breaths. A heavy silence settled over the dining room.

"This is killing her," said Marks. "You have no idea how hard this has been on her."

"I can imagine," I said.

We ate for a minute or two in quiet. Despite our less than happy circumstances, I was rejoicing in the meal. I let each bite of the lamb sit on my tongue for a few seconds before biting into the perfectly seasoned meat. "Hot damn, that woman can cook," I said through a mouthful.

"Huh?" said Marks, looking up, startled.

"I spoke to Charlie," I told him.

"I know, you mentioned that when you came by my apartment. We were hoping he could come up this weekend, but it appears he has to work."

"No, I mean I spoke to him again," I said. "After I saw you. He had a lot more to say."

"Oh yeah?"

Sometimes you have to throw it out fast, before the window closes. "He told me about you and Madeline."

"How so?"

I studied his face like a good earnest gambler. Got nothing in return.

"About your relationship with the younger Ms. McKay."

"Duck, I'm afraid I have no idea what you are talking about."

There was something rehearsed in his oblivious denial, as if he'd already heard and replied to these lines in a previous take prior to my arrival. He cut into his meat and took a bite. "You're right," he said. "That woman sure can cook."

"Listen," I said. "I realize honesty is out of the question at the moment, since Margaret may be back any second, but maybe we can talk after dinner?"

"As I told you, Margaret and I have no secrets. Whatever it is you heard, you can say in front of her."

Okay then. "So you want me to tell your girlfriend that I heard you're also fucking her daughter?" I asked. "And that I heard this rather troubling accusation from her beloved son?"

He almost choked on his lamb. Then he lowered his knife and fork and looked at me with the calmness of an assassin. In that look, I saw what the man was capable of. He sipped at his wine, sat back, and crossed his arms.

"Why would Charlie say such a thing?" he asked.

"I'm asking you the same question."

I watched him trying to compose the words, some reply that could explain away the allegation. His lips were starting to part when Margaret returned to the dining room.

"My apologies, gentlemen," she said. "This is all quite overwhelming. I needed a moment to gather myself." Then, seeing the look on Marks's face, she gave a curious smile. "What have you two been discussing?"

Marks turned to her, all love and honor. "Margaret, do you think Charlie will be able to make it up this week-end?" he asked.

"He says not," she said, taking her seat. "A black tie with the Sotos, it seems. Did he tell you about his big day this week?" Margaret's face brightened at the subject of her son.

"I haven't spoken to him," said Marks. "But I'd like to." He cut into his lamb with a tightened fist, took another bite and chewed like he was grinding bones between his teeth. "Something happen at his work?"

"Oh, yes," said Margaret. It appeared she'd temporarily forgotten about her black sheep daughter. "It sounds like he had a day for the ages, one of the most profitable in the firm's history, he says." She sipped her wine with a new glow. "He's always been remarkable under pressure, that boy. As you well know. Indeed, I suppose he has you to thank for that—you trained him to be that way, after all."

"That's one quality you can't teach, I'm afraid," said Marks. "One of those innate gifts you're born with. It's in the genes. So, I suppose it's you that Charlie has to thank." He attempted to smile.

"Yes, well, in any case, it appears Danny Soto has taken a heightened interest in our boy. Tonight, Danny is hosting a benefit for his wildcat conservation society. I hear the Schwarzmans and the Kaplans are going to be there." She beamed, thrust out her high, firm chest. Then, as an afterthought to me: "The Sotos are one of the world's biggest benefactors of protecting natural cat habitats—tigers, jaguars, snow leopards. Their numbers are diminishing across the globe."

"Sorry to hear that," I said.

She gave me a quizzical look.

"About the cats, I mean. They're lucky to have Mr. Soto."

"Margaret, do you think Charlie might be persuaded to drive up tomorrow afternoon, after this benefit? It might be helpful for Duck to speak to him at the house, where he last saw her. Something may come back to him, some detail he may have forgot."

"I'll ask him," said Margaret. "It sounded like a very brief encounter. And he is so busy these days. But if you think it might help."

"Duck?" asked Marks with something dangerous in his eye. "Perhaps you could tell Margaret what you told me while she was away?"

As Sun Tzu would say: "He who knows when he can fight and when he cannot will be victorious." (*The Art of War*. If it was good enough for Gordon Gekko and Tony Soprano, I figured I could learn something.) If I were to drop that particular bomb right then at his request, two things would happen: shock and denial. Neither would get me any closer to the truth. Margaret would gasp at the allegation. She would insist I was mistaken or making it up. Privately, she would begin to doubt her lover. She'd believe her son in her heart. But publically, she would shut things down. Dinner would end abruptly, and she'd insist on hearing it from Charlie. Then she would want to hear the denials in private. I'd be shut out of the equation. No closer to finding Madeline, or the truth.

So instead I told her, "I was just saying how strange it feels to be back in all of your lives, after all this time."

"Yes, a lifetime ago," she said.

A happier one at that.

"I wondered if I might have a look through Madeline's bedroom?" I asked.

"Of course," said Margaret. "When we finish, I'll show you up there."

"Thanks, though I have to say, I agree with Coach. Having Charlie walk me through their encounter here could be helpful."

Margaret considered that. She looked from Marks back to me. Again I envied her inscrutable frozen face. She gave a small nod. "I'll speak to him tomorrow, see if he might join us."

"It might help," I said. "Though I'd also like to get back to the city for this party tomorrow night, where Madeline was last seen."

"Of course," she said. "That would seem like an important avenue to explore." She spoke with a matter-of-factness that I appreciated. Beneath her glossy false shell, there was something sharp and genuine. She looked at me with those ink-colored eyes for a long while, making quiet judgments and quick calculations.

Marks was looking at me too. Something told me he'd studied *The Art of War* more than I had.

Chapter 20

It was the room of a young girl frozen in development at, say, twelve: all pinks and hearts and bulletin boards full of BFF pictures of fresh-faced girls posing in various states of happy innocence. The bed, a queen covered in a purple spread, still had a few stuffed animals propped among the pillows. At the foot of the bed, there was a locked chest. Atop the dresser, a few framed photos of the McKay family in sunnier days. The largest and most prominent was a picture taken before she would have remembered, from when her father was still alive. Madeline was maybe three. The family was posed on the porch of Owl View, laughing on a fall day. She was sitting on her father's lap, holding a dripping cup of ice cream, her thrilled face covered in chocolate. Charlie, about nineteen at the time, stood behind them with a shaved head and a smirking smile. His mother stood off to the side, taking in her family with a look of utter contentment. She had not yet begun her plastic journey under the knife, and she looked striking in her natural motherly beauty. The health and wealth and good fortune on display was almost nauseating—if you didn't know what came next.

"Steven was diagnosed about a month after that picture

was taken," said Margaret from the doorway. She walked toward me and took it from my hands and placed it precisely where it had been on the dresser. She looked down at it. "Another lifetime," she said.

"She was close to her dad, wasn't she?"

"Adored him. He walked on water. Now, of course, he's forever sainted in her mind. She believes all the problems she's had since are due to his early death—and my failings as a mother."

"I'm sure that's not true."

She gave me a look that said if I only knew. Then she began to circle the room as if it were a lost artifact, a space only recently uncovered by archeologists. "As you can see, Madeline hasn't spent much time here over the last few years. I was very surprised when Charlie said she'd been here. I can't remember the last time she came up." She examined the bulletin board of pictures and frowned in remembrance at photos she'd likely taken. "Around the time she turned thirteen, she lost interest, but Maddie used to love coming here. For a time, it was every weekend, and entire summers, just the two of us. After Steven passed away, and Charlie was off in school, or swimming all over the world, Maddie and I used to come here and just hunker in and eat junk food and watch movie after movie. When she was ten, we almost moved here full-time, leaving the city behind. I'd enrolled her at Rhinebeck Day, and we were prepared to begin a new life in the country." She looked out of Madeline's window, at her reflection in the darkness. "Now, of course, I wish I'd gone through with it."

"Why didn't you?"

"Her swimming," sighed Margaret. "Maddie was starting to show promise, and of course, she was the sister of the great Charlie McKay, Olympic champion, so big things were expected of her. When I told Teddy we were considering the move, his heart about stopped. He was really the one who convinced us to stay in the city. He was sure Maddie would follow in her brother's footsteps."

I tried the lock on the chest at the foot of her bed. "I'm sure the key is around here somewhere," she said without turning. "If not, you're more than welcome to break it off." She turned and looked down at it like it held the secrets of the lost ark. "I fear I've given my daughter too much privacy over these years. I always tried to respect her space, tried not to pry, and look where it's gotten us."

"Mrs. McKay, if it's all right with you, would you mind if I had a look around Madeline's room in private?"

She stiffened at the suggestion and crossed her arms beneath her high chest.

"It's just that I know her room stirs up so many memories for you. I might be able to make more progress if I could look through things alone."

"Very well," she said. "Please close the door on your way out. When you're finished, Teddy said he'd like to have a word with you in the study."

She left the bedroom on unsteady legs. I suspected she'd taken something to go with the wine when she'd left the table. Her manner since had been slightly out of focus, her speech a little less crisp than usual. I wondered if there was a way to sneak a peak at her medicine cabinet.

Alone in the room, I felt Madeline's unhappy presence lingering, a shadow just out of sight. Her closet contained clothes that would no longer fit, shoes meant for a preteen. Her dresser was full of T-shirts and cotton underwear and long-dry swimsuits. On her bedside table rested a worn copy of *Pride and Prejudice*, beneath it an unopened journal of empty white pages. I inspected the pictures on the bulletin board, recognized Lucy Townes in a few shots. The rest of the kids were strangers, forgotten friends from the forgotten days before puberty. I made a cursory attempt to locate the key to the chest, and not finding it in the obvious places, I lifted my knee and kicked loose the lock. There were a few picture albums, a few tattered notebooks. The albums contained more photos of family and friends. There were beach vacations, trips to Radio City to see the Rockettes, birthdays, swim meet shots of girls and boys in caps and goggles, huddled on pool decks with towels wrapped around bare shoulders. The notebooks contained the drawings of a talented young artist: steady-handed sketches of dolphin and whales and mermaids and underwater worlds. Further inspection revealed the artist's growth, as the pages turned to still-lifes and landscapes and, finally, portraits of her young friends. Based on the age of her posing models, the drawings appeared to stop around age twelve. Around the same age this house and this room were left behind, frozen in happier times.

I closed the chest and made one more pass around the room. I got down on my hands and knees and peered under the bed. More discarded swim bags, some pink leather luggage made for a little girl. I was pushing myself to my feet when I noticed a short white cord beneath the dresser. I crawled over, reached under, and retrieved it. It was a USB cable, the sort used to connect cameras to laptops. I pushed it down my jeans pocket, finished my search, and found nothing else of interest.

I walked downstairs wondering about the cable, when it was lost beneath the dresser. I was feeling rattled and too in touch with her lost innocence. A lot of kids get angry as they enter their teenage years, tossing aside their talents with clueless disrespect. A lot of city kids go a little crazy and choose drugs and partying instead of the prosperous path. And a few unlucky ones also get to deal with the loss of a parent on top of it all. Sad and tragic, but plenty typical. Yet there was something else there with Madeline. Something had dragged her down into the abyss, and she was still somewhere deep beneath the surface. If that something had been her coach, I intended to make him pay.

I found him in a darkened study at the end of a long, dim hall. The floorboards creaked in the stillness. The hall was lined with small Flemish paintings in ornate frames. Portraits of long-dead gentry, domestic scenes rich with symbolism, studies of fruits and flora—Madeline hadn't had to look far for inspiration. There was a faint light beneath the high, heavy door to the study. I knocked twice and heard his baritone from within. "C'mon in."

He was seated with legs crossed on a deep leather couch, holding a whiskey in cut crystal. "Have a seat, Duck," he said. "The bar's over there; pour yourself a drink." The room had an unsettling similarity to his apartment. The same landscape art, the same masculine furniture of dark woods and leather, even the marble bar felt like it must have been salvaged and restored from the same old hotel. Margaret had ensconced him in a replica of her dead husband's most personal space. She had taste, I had to hand her that. Though I was starting to wonder about her taste in men. I poured myself a whiskey from a heavy decanter with an engraved spade on its side.

"It's Hirsch, twenty-year," he said from the couch. "You'll like it."

I tasted it and did. I raised the glass in his direction and found a seat in a Stickley rocker across from the couch.

"So," I said.

Marks didn't reply. He sat there looking past me at the rows of books on the far wall. He sipped his bourbon, wiping his mustache after each tip. Off at the other end of the house, I heard a door open and shut. Must be Nina headed home for the night. I stared over at him, waited for him to speak.

"I never touched that girl," he said finally.

"Then why do you think Charlie would say such a thing?"

"I have no . . . it feels like a betrayal of the deepest sort." He looked down into his glass for answers, shook his head at the rich amber.

"How do you think he could have gotten that idea?" I asked. "He said he saw something at a meet, the way you spoke to her after a race or something."

"On deck at a meet? Hell!" His voice broke through the quiet like shattered glass. "What does that boy think he saw?"

"You tell me. He seemed awfully convinced."

"Duck, as you might remember, coaching is a highly personal profession. I am closer to these kids than most of their parents. I see them every day. I know their dreams and their fears. I know what makes them tick. Whatever he thinks he *saw* . . ."

"Coach, Charlie mentioned that there were others. That everyone knew there were other girls on the team, through the years."

He pushed himself up from the couch on old knees and walked over to the books. He set his whiskey on a shelf, stared at the spines of hardcovers. "Unbelievable," he muttered. "Un-fucking-believable."

"You're saying there's no truth to those rumors?"

He shook his head, took down a book from the shelf, and opened it. Then, he slammed it shut and slid it back in place. "Duck, I was twenty-eight years old when I started Marks Aquatics, back in the eighties. I'd done five years in the SEALs, right out of college. Saw action in Grenada, spent time in Afghanistan, Albania. Experienced some heavy shit at a young age. But when I got out, I was still a kid. I was a big, strong warrior, but I didn't have a clue about life. I went straight from a swimming pool to the

SEALs, where they took discipline to a whole new level. You have no idea. They made us into well-programmed machines, but where does that leave you when you enter the real world—in New York City, of all places? I've never been sure why I chose the city. Ego, I guess. You can make it here, you can make it anywhere and all. I was a clueless kid who thought he knew something. I had the All-American honors to prove it, had the old SEAL stamp of approval. So, I set up shop in that dungeon pool, and I convinced some kids to work hard for me. But I wasn't prepared for the girls, Duck. I wasn't prepared for them at all."

I could hear his breathing close behind me. He was pacing the dark room, stirring up the buried memories, muddying the long still waters. I resisted the urge to turn and watch him.

"Age is a funny thing, don't you think? Those linear numbers are highly subjective. The number of days you've been on this earth says so little about one's true emotional age. Do you understand what I'm saying?"

I didn't answer, didn't suspect he wanted one.

"I think of myself, just starting out, a clueless veteran in his late twenties, all bluster and empty leadership. The boys were impressed by the SEAL stuff; they knew I used to be pretty fast myself. It didn't take much to get them on board. And they were willing to put in the work. Not like nowadays. Back then, I give a sixteen-year-old kid a ten-thousand-yard fly set, he just nods and cranks it out. But the girls? They saw right through me. They saw me as a peer—as a catch. Take a seventeen-year-old girl born and raised in Manhattan; then take a late-twenties kid from upstate New York. Who do *you* think has the power?"

I heard him refilling his glass at the bar. He set down the heavy decanter with a clumsy crash, and I could tell he'd been hitting the whiskey hard.

"Ah, hell, Duck. You know where I'm going with this.

It was a different time. You ask me about the rumors? Well, there you go. Way back then, in those circumstances I just described? Yeah, I crossed the line a few times. With some girls, sixteen, seventeen, pretty high school girls who wrapped me right around their pretty little fingers. I can't say I felt much guilt at the time. I certainly wasn't in control of the situations. But you know, as one gets a little older, those girls, they stayed the same age. Wasn't that in a movie? Anyway, by the time I'm pushing thirty, getting a bit of city wisdom under the belt, starting to have some real relationships with women my own age, all that stuff just went away. Had no interest in them any longer. I guess I saw them for what they'd always been: kids just playing grown-up. It's been twenty-five years since I even looked twice at a swimmer on my team. That's the God's honest truth."

"So you think those old affairs have followed you all these years? That's the source of these rumors?"

"What else could it be? Kids talk, pass things down; embellish it as they go. But I certainly never thought Charlie believed that stuff. And for him to think I had any intentions with his younger sister? It's almost too much to digest."

"Tell me about Fred, Coach."

"What about him?"

"Why is a Navy SEAL sitting out front of the pool whenever you're on deck? Seems a little overqualified for that detail."

"Man's fallen on some hard times. He's grateful for the work. I told you, things were getting stolen from the lockers. The school doesn't give a damn, so I asked Fred to help us out."

"You were doing so well with the truth serum," I said. I got up and went to the bar and helped myself to a refill. The wine and the feast and the whiskey were cutting through the hangover like a fine Ginsu knife. Marks had stopped pacing. He was standing in front of the window, looking at his reflection in the night glass. Standing in a dead man's study, sleeping with his widow, living in décor so close to the dead, so deeply entwined in the lives of the man's children . . . He looked lost in that well-dressed reflection, unable to comprehend how he'd consumed this other man's family.

"I'm being blackmailed," he said.

"For how long?"

"Couple of months."

"What do they have on you?"

"What do you think?" He cast a look over his shoulder. "That ancient nonsense. It appears some of the girls, all grown up and jaded now, want to dredge up the old flings. They've seen the scandals with other swim coaches in the news. They see a chance to cash in on past indiscretions. Playing the virginal teen victim . . ."

"Why not just go to the press, hire lawyers like the others?"

"That would mean coming forward, out of the shadows. They're too cowardly for that. These women are likely married with kids by now. They don't want their names and faces splashed all over the news. They just want the end result: money."

"Then why not call their bluff? Refuse to pay."

"Duck, in case you haven't noticed, my profession is being compared to pervert priests and Boy Scout leaders these days. Coaches are everyone's favorite suspected pederast, thanks to a few true sickos out there. There's no such thing as innocent until proven guilty with this stuff. All it takes is one public accusation and you're finished. My life's work, my team, all of our accomplishments—ruined. I've never held another job in my life, never wanted one. One whiff of an accusation, even an anonymous one, and I'd be banned from the sport for life."

"So you've been paying them off quietly for how long now?"

"Since the spring, but now they're asking for more money than I have left. I haven't been able to meet their demands."

"Any idea who's behind it?"

"I have my suspicions, but I've only dealt with a 'representative.' He calls from blocked numbers, emails from untraceable accounts, with instructions on the next payment. Always a wire transfer to a numbered offshore account."

"I meant the girls, how many were there? Who are they?"

"I can't remember how many. It was decades ago. It was a few. A handful, hell, I don't know the number. But I was told that if I tried to reach out to any of these women, anyone I might have had any relationship with at all, then the information would be made public that same day. I chose to believe him. So, I've been paying ever since. Or at least I was until I ran out of funds."

"Ever wonder if it could be a scam?" I asked. "Someone playing you for the old rumors? Maybe these women aren't even involved."

"Possible, I suppose. But I'm not exactly in a position to call a bluff. Like I said, all it takes is one public accusation. The truth of things is pointless."

"This representative, any clue who it could be? You recognize the voice?"

"He uses one of those voice manipulators when he calls. Believe me, I've taped the calls and tried to study the voice. It's no use. The emails can't be tracked either. It goes back to an anonymous IP address in the Philippines. You'd think a Navy SEAL could track down anyone. Hell, our boys caught Bin Laden. But, Duck, I haven't got a clue about this stuff. I hardly know where to begin."

Marks returned from the window and sat down heavily

on the couch. He placed his whiskey on the coffee table before us and leaned forward with his elbows on his knees. "And now, with Madeline missing. That murder. Not to mention poor Lucy Townes. I can't help thinking this is all connected to the blackmail."

"Don't forget the two little visits they paid me," I reminded him.

"Jesus, that too." He reached for his drink and swallowed down the rest. Then he fell back into the leather and stared up at the dark ceiling. "What the fuck is going on?" he muttered.

"Coach, getting back to Fred, your SEAL buddy. How does he fit into this?"

He continued staring up into the darkness as he spoke. "When I failed to pay the last few times, I was told there would be consequences. There were. At first it was just some theft and vandalism in the lockers. A computer was stolen from a locked locker, some iPhones, a few wallets, that sort of thing. Then, one of our swimmers had an accident on the way to the pool. He was pushed down a flight of subway stairs, broke his arm. Out for the season. The kid's a junior, starting to get recruited by the big schools. The worst possible timing. Then, last week, another swimmer, a fifteen-year-old girl this time, was mugged on her way home from practice one night. She was thrown onto the sidewalk, broke her hand on the way down. They took her purse, but it was found a few blocks away—with everything still in it. That wasn't the point. Duck, no one gets mugged in Manhattan anymore. Christ, the girl lives on the Upper East Side. They were sending me a message. If I don't pay, they take it out on my swimmers." He sat up and looked me straight in the eye for the first time since I'd entered the study. "They know that if they came at me, I'd kill them," he said. "I've been out of the SEALs a long time, but some things you don't forget. Whoever it is, he knows better than to tangle with me. So, instead, the spineless bastard wants to take it out on my swimmers. Innocent teenagers—with dreams and talent." He shook his head at the cowardice.

I refrained from pointing out the irony.

"So you brought in Fred to do some digging, help you keep watch."

"He's a good man. As fearless as any human being you'll ever meet. He knows how to hunt things down . . . and to kill, when necessary."

"Coach, you switched from *they* to *he*—who are you referring to?"

"What are you talking about? When?"

"A second ago, you were saying how *they* were sending a message. Then, you said how *he* knows not to mess with you. Who's the spineless bastard? Who do you suspect is behind this? Who's working for these girls, who knows enough about your past?"

Through the dim light of the study, I could see the soldier that he had once been. It was the look of a man willing and able to kill. A look that said he had killed before and did it without hesitation or remorse. There were some situations when that was what was required. His blackmailers had picked a dangerous target.

"You remember John Kosta," he said. "My former assistant."

"Of course. The Greek. We talked about him—I asked you why he left."

"Yes, I remember. And I told you the truth. Kosta wanted my job; he was tired of being called an assistant, thought he deserved more credit. The usual power struggle. He left on bad terms."

"How long ago?"

"Little over a year."

"And you think he resurfaced, bent on revenge, after talking to those girls from your past?"

"He is certainly the most likely enemy," he said.

"Have you tried to reach out to him?"

"I did. Sent him an email early on, when this first started, tried to feel him out. Told him I'd like to make amends for the way things ended. Asked if he'd meet me for coffee. He declined."

"And then?"

"And then I followed him. He lives out in Brooklyn, Fort Greene, works as a photographer now. Shoots weddings, family portraits, and such. Pathetic. Got married late, to a short, fat girl. Young kid." He got up and returned to the bar and brought back the decanter. He topped mine off and filled his glass, long past the need for ice. "I let myself into his apartment one day last spring, had a look around. Didn't find anything, but that doesn't prove anything." He took a drink, settled back down. "I've had Fred following him, waiting for the prick to slip up."

"You could go to the police, you know. With tapes of the calls, copies of the emails, the wire transfers. Proof of the blackmail. They might help."

He looked at me like we'd just met, and he'd decided this stranger was a fool upon shaking. "And turn myself in? Hell, Duck, I know you're smarter than that."

"On second thought . . ."

He laughed at that. Then he pushed himself up and took two unsteady strides toward me. He stood hovering over me and placed his hand on my shoulder. I looked up and met his watery eyes through the dim light. They were out of focus, and he swayed lightly before me on sea legs.

"Listen. What do you say about coming to work for me? I could really use your help on this. You and Fred could work together and get this fucker. What do you say?"

I considered the offer. Drank my drink. Looked at his hand on my shoulder until he removed it. "One job at a time," I said.

"I can respect that," he said without respect.

"There would also be the matter of my fee."

He looked around the room with a smug air of possession. The look said he wasn't quite out of money after all. "I'm sure something can be arranged," he said.

"Speaking of which, when we spoke on the phone, you mentioned that there were no secrets between you and Margaret. Can I assume that wasn't entirely true?"

Marks looked down at me with those steely SEAL eyes. The watery drunkenness seemed to pass. He was suddenly sober, and determined to regain control. "I appreciated your discretion at dinner, when I gave you a bit of a challenge. And I would appreciate your continued discretion now. It would be wise. For all involved."

Chapter 21

It was late morning when I woke in the guesthouse feeling worse than the day before. I thought of Madeline's arrested bedroom, like the preserved space of a dead child. The girl was somewhere out there in a bad way. A murderer, maybe. Or perhaps she was next, as soon as yours truly flushed her out. Did Marks's blackmailers have her? Was this his final warning—pay up or we kill her? The man had painted quite a picture of ancient sins he couldn't quite bury. Or maybe they weren't so ancient. I remembered the rehearsed sound of his denials about Madeline. His version of the "God's honest truth" was filled with plenty of holy holes, I was sure of that.

I looked around the room. Walls of light amber wainscoting; an oil painting of a seascape above the dresser; high standing mirror framed in rustic wood in one corner; my bed, cradled in a distressed wrought-iron frame. Through lace curtains, a cool fall breeze blew through a cracked window. Outside it was a gray and dreary day, the clouds low in the sky, considerations of rain.

I climbed from bed, pulled the lace aside, and stood looking out for a time, my thoughts a disconnected mess. Across the lawn, a layer of steam hovered over the McKays' heated pool. I pictured Charlie knifing into the still waters and swimming through the mist.

Then I went over to the mirror and looked at myself with rare honesty. It was a grim sight. I was a big puffy-faced disaster with swollen whiskey cheeks and hollow eyes, on top of an overgrown body that had seen better days. I looked like one of those *before* shots in ads for the latest fitness regimen. I sucked in my stomach, stuck out my chest, and tried to flex. It wasn't much, but it was an improvement. A tan and a week or two on the MX 5000 workout videos, and I'd be ready for my *after* shot. I told myself it was time to shape up and start flying right, the way I always did on mornings such as these. I got down on the ground and cranked out twenty pushups on the hard-wood floor. Then I went and felt sorry for myself in the shower, before slipping back into my clothes and going off in search of coffee.

I found Margaret alone in the kitchen setting flowers on the windowsill above the sink. She was wearing a blue knit dress with a cream cardigan around her shoulders. She turned her head and nodded toward a French press half filled with dark coffee. I gave silent thanks, found a mug, and filled it black. It was lukewarm, had been sitting out for some time. I drank it down fast.

"Sleep well?" she asked.

"I did." I refilled my cup with the dregs from the press. "I had a good talk with Teddy last night," I said.

"So I heard."

Doubt you heard the half of it. I thought about coming out with all of it, vomiting up every last dirty detail until Margaret stood before me a shattered, shell-shocked woman. Maybe I would once I found her daughter, but to disclose any of that now would be beyond my capacity for cruelty.

"Is he here?" I asked.

"Teddy left at dawn. He said he needed to get back to the city for practice. He intended to stay the weekend, but any more than twenty-four hours away from the pool deck and the man starts to get restless." Her expression was resigned, the look of a woman used to her man putting work first. "He asked me to thank you . . . for hearing him out last night. I have to say, he came to bed in better spirits than I've seen in a long time."

"Glad to hear it." Just call me Father Darley, ready to hear your deep, dark confessions. Go say a thousand Hail Marys, and your soul will be freed, yes indeed.

She motioned to a breakfast nook that looked out over green hills. The contours of the Catskills rolled across the horizon. It started to rain, a sad, silent drizzle that seemed to leak from the low clouds. "Could we sit?" she asked. She slid into a floral patterned banquette and regarded me with eyes that were aging faster than the rest of her. I took the chair across from her.

"I know about Teddy's past, with those girls, when he was just starting out." She said it like it was a simple matter they'd disposed of long ago. She noticed the look on my face. "You didn't think I knew, did you?"

I shook my head.

"I understand how this has become a very serious issue, in today's current . . . climate. There are coaches out there who have no business around these young athletes. But I am also able to distinguish between the regrettable behavior of a mature young woman and an immature young man, and, well, the evil behavior of men who prey on children.

"Teddy has always beaten himself up about these 'old indiscretions,' as he refers to them. He knows how dangerous relationships can begin, without either party knowing what they're getting into. I think that's why he was always so protective of Madeline, always so forgiving. You know how he can be with his swimmers. He has little patience for those unable to show the commitment he demands. But with Madeline, there have always been endless second chances. He's as worried about her as I am."

"She's also Charlie's sister. That has to count for a lot."

"Of course it does. Teddy has been a surrogate father to both of my children for some time now." She touched her neck and fingered a thin gold chain hanging down over her dress. "I suppose it was inevitable that we would be together. A man that is good to your children can become very attractive."

"Did he mention anything else that we talked about last night?"

"He said he told you about that stuff, that history, and that you discussed your progress last week. Lawrence, I want you to know, I do appreciate your efforts—and the violence you've encountered. Perhaps I was unfair to you, the morning after James Fealy's murder. I know it wasn't your fault we ended up in the tabloids."

"It's an overwhelming time," I told her. "So, is that all? I mean, that's all Teddy told you about our talk?"

"What else would he have mentioned?"

Maybe that your son is convinced that the man is also sleeping with your daughter . . . Or maybe that he's being blackmailed for those "old indiscretions"? The ones you don't seem to care much about.

"Nothing in particular," I said. "We talked about Charlie too."

"Oh? How so?"

"He's worried about him. He thinks he's almost too good at being able to focus under stress. To the point of repression."

She nodded vigorously. Somehow that spontaneous load of shit had hit the mark. "He's right, of course. It can be so effective—in sports, and now, in business. But it's not healthy, is it?"

"Probably not."

"I don't know where it comes from. His father, I suppose. Steven was very skilled with that same compartmentalized focus. The building next door could be on fire, but if Steven was zoned in on work, he wouldn't even smell the smoke. He was very proud of that. He taught his son to be the same way. Or, in any case, he passed down the genes that gave Charlie the same ability. But sometimes I wonder . . ."

"If it's too cold-blooded?"

She bristled at the implication. She could find fault with her son, but that didn't mean outsiders were allowed to do the same. "No," she said. "It's not cold-blooded. That would imply he lacks empathy for those around him. That's not it at all. It's that he's been conditioned to think that extreme focus is a virtue. It makes him more of a man or something, to be able to rise above any external chaos and perform whatever task is at hand. Teddy is right, though—it's a form of repression. A little worry and despair would be good for him once in a while."

"I'm sure he's just as worried about Madeline as you are. He just expresses it differently."

"Expressed by going to work and earning millions of dollars?" She allowed a smile despite herself. "If only we could all cope so well."

"If only."

"When did you last see your father, Lawrence?"

I wasn't prepared for the hard right. A chill went up my spine.

"Been years," I said with a forced casualness.

"Despite everything that happened, you really should go see him. When he's gone, you'll wish you had."

"He's already been gone a long time."

She looked at me with something that must have been sympathy. She cupped her coffee mug in both hands and sat a little closer with her shoulders rolled forward. Despite the surgeries, she suddenly looked like a wistful grandmother. "I remember him at swim meets, when you and Charlie were boys," she said. "He would always insist on being a timer in lane number four—so he could be behind the blocks in his son's lane. He was such a presence back then. You both were."

"And then we weren't."

"That was a terrible time, just terrible. How is your mother these days?"

"Dead," I said. "Died my senior year of high school."

"I'm sorry, I didn't . . ."

"How would you? We weren't rich anymore."

She frowned into her mug and got up from the table. The grandma's air vanished as I watched her walk to the sink. Her hips swayed like a woman half her age.

"I should probably be getting back to the city myself," I said.

"Very well."

"Were you able to speak with Charlie this morning? I assume he won't be making the trip to Rhinebeck."

"I did, yes. And no, he's unable to get out of the city. However, he said that he'd like to speak with you when you get back to town. He asked that you stop by the house later. Have you been there?"

"I haven't."

"It's something else. Wait till you see," she said. "He's very proud of it. He just bought it last spring. Thirteen Leroy Street in the Village."

"I'll look forward to talking to him . . . and seeing the place." The *house*, not the apartment. In the West Village. Do the math. Start at eight figures.

At the door, Margaret gave me a lingering hug and a

kiss just off the lips. The corners of our mouths touched, and I tasted a hint of what she must taste like to Marks: rich moisturizer and subtle fragrance and something else, something full of need beneath the carefully crafted shell. She placed a hand on my chest and looked me in the eye. "I look forward to the good news, when you find Madeline," she said. "Do keep me posted."

I said I would and looked away and walked down the front steps.

She had closed the front door before I started the Benz and guided it back toward the city.

Chapter 22

The steady drizzle turned to a driving rain with sheets splashing sideways against the windshield. The wipers panicked to keep up like a squeegee man at a changing light. Despite the poor visibility the Benz took the turns with low, casual confidence. I guided it down the backcountry roads until it found the Taconic. Google Maps had advised me it would be a faster route back. It was a fine scenic highway in blue skies; a narrow, shoulderless death stretch in night and bad weather. NPR was playing a weekend blues marathon. I turned up Muddy Waters, "Born Under a Bad Sign." The radio gods were mocking me.

Marks had provided his lover with the plea-bargained version of his sins. Admitting to old, previously confessed crimes, leaving out the more troubling present . . . I admired his ability to walk that line. He knew that I'd go right along with it, following his lead for the sake of Madeline's worried mother. There was a reckoning coming between him and Charlie. I knew he hadn't sped back to the city to return for swim practice; he was going back to confront his former champion.

I tried to picture Charlie's place. Would it be your classic West Village brownstone with the perfect redbrick façade, the original crown molding in the high-ceilinged parlor, with marble fireplaces in every room? Or would it be your modern gut job? Say a former carriage house, now converted to a minimalist masterpiece of floating stairs and design piece furniture? Based on the McKay country house, my money was on the former. It would be a restored gem, the former home of some turn-of-the-century tycoon. It would fit Charlie's image of himself.

A few miles onto the Taconic, I realized I was being followed. An old Jeep Wagoneer was tailing me two cars back, one lane over, huffing and puffing to keep up. Mid-seventies model from the look of it, with the wood paneling and the big, boxy frame; the body was cream colored and maintained with care. The same car had been in my rainy rearview on the road from the McKays'. The Benz is a stylish, rugged machine, good for many things, but losing a tail is not one of them. It has little pickup left in its vegetable oil–fed engine, and it's hardly inconspicuous. It sticks out in a crowd. So does a vintage Wagoneer. We were stuck with each other, so I figured I'd have a little fun.

At the next sign for an exit, I put on my blinker a mile early and slowed to thirty miles an hour. It earned me some nasty looks from the on-rushing traffic, but the Wagoneer wasn't quite sure what to do. It slowed too, until there was no use hiding. When he was right up on my bumper, I looked in the rearview and got a good look at my friend. An older man, thinning white hair, white beard, looked nervous, less than professional. I stuck my arm out the window, gave him a wave. He didn't wave back.

Then, right at the exit, I turned off the blinker and floored it. The Benz gave a grumbling roar of objection. It did what it could. I burned a few gallons of vegetable oil trying to get it back up to seventy. He labored to keep up, a couple of old folks playing tag, as we continued together on our merry way toward the city. Signs for the next exit appeared seventeen miles later. I repeated the process. His expression in the mirror wasn't amused. He looked like a scolding grandfather who couldn't wait to give the young folk a piece of his mind. I could tell he was bracing himself for another juvenile maneuver, but I was already bored with the game. I veered off the exit, and he followed. I found a Stewart's station a half mile up the road and parked in the back. He pulled up alongside me and we got out.

"Howdy," I said.

"You drive like shit, young man," he said.

He was a big old guy, country strong, as some might say. He was dressed in jeans, work boots, a red flannel shirt. He had large, gnarled hands that did real work for a living, and which were now balled in fists, like he planned to deliver a deserved beat-down before he came to his point.

"I wasn't trying to hide," he said. "There was no need to be cute."

"I don't like being followed," I told him. "You're lucky I felt like being cute, not cruel."

"A regular big city tough guy." He grinned through that white beard and showed me a set of decayed yellowed teeth. He had a wad of chewing tobacco wedged in his lower lip. He spit a thick stream of dip juice at my feet.

"What do you want, old man?"

"Thought we'd have a talk," he said.

"Who are you?"

"Ernest." He stuck out one of those gnarled paws. I shook it. His grip swallowed mine. What is it about shaking a giant powerful hand that makes you feel like less of a man? Never mind, I can answer that myself.

"The caretaker?" I asked. "For the McKays?"

"My wife and I manage the property, yes."

"Your wife's one hell of a cook," I told him.

"That she is," he said. "Now, about that talk. Could you spare a few minutes? I have some things you'll want to hear—about the girl you're looking for."

"Lead the way," I said.

There is a vaguely sinister air to your average upstate Stewart's; whispers of meth and despair beneath the fluorescent lights and relentless bargains. I watched a fat denim-covered biker gathering a collection of king-sized Kit Kats and peanut butter cups. He added a thirty-two-ounce Mountain Dew to his bounty of sugar and pushed past me. I lowered my shoulder and pushed back with some aggression. He turned and eyed me with quick accustomed rage, ever ready for a fight. I returned the silent challenge. He considered it, glanced down at his armful of snacks, and muttered, "Watch it" and stalked toward the register. I grabbed a bag of salt-and-vinegar chips and a Bud tallboy, and found Ernest waiting in a booth by the ice cream counter.

"You okay?" he asked.

"Lovely. Why?"

"You don't look so good. You were talking to yourself on the way over."

"Was I?"

"You look like you could use some sleep, son."

"I'm fine. Got eight deep hours in the McKays' guesthouse."

I cracked the Bud and sipped off the foam while he considered how to begin.

"I've known Madeline her whole life," he said. "Nina and I have lived on the property ever since Steven McKay bought the place eighteen years ago. Maddie was just a baby, her brother Charlie was in high school. Never got to know Charlie too well, he was always off swimming, then working . . . But Maddie, we got to see her grow up at Owl View. After Steven died, she and Margaret used to spend an awful lot of time there. Almost moved up full-time when Maddie was ten or so."

"So I heard."

"So you heard," he said. He looked down at the table, lost in a memory. He scratched at his beard and, after some time, looked back up and met my eyes. "Mr. Darley, I'd like to tell you about something you probably haven't heard."

I sat back and crossed my legs and waited as he gathered himself.

"Six years ago, there was a tragedy at Owl View," he began. "A young man died on the property. His name was Patrick Bell. He was thirteen. He was Maddie's boyfriend."

"How old was Madeline when this happened?"

"About the same, I suppose. It was one of those first summer romances. Very sweet. Nina and I used to take them into town for ice cream, and they'd hold hands in the backseat of the Jeep. That must sound quaint, coming from the city, but upstate there's more innocence to childhood. There's less of a rush. It lasts longer. Or at least it did."

"How did he die?"

"Peanuts. The boy was deathly allergic to nuts. Came in contact with them one Sunday afternoon at the house. He didn't have his EpiPen with him, and we weren't able to get him to the hospital in time."

Ernest was fighting back the emotion of the memory.

"How did he come in contact with the nuts? I'm guessing everyone was aware of such a serious allergy."

"Of course we were. Nina made sure the kitchen was swept clean of every possible offending product. She was scrupulous about it."

"Then . . ."

"Thai takeout," he said. "Brought from the city."

"The kid would have known better than to have left-over pad Thai."

"He didn't eat any of it. It was determined that he must have ingested a trace amount through Madeline. By . . . kissing his girlfriend."

"Kiss of death."

He glowered at me. "We found the boy by the side of the McKays' pool, soaking wet, in convulsions. His windpipe had closed off. His face was swollen to grotesque size. It had been a beautiful weekend. The house was full of life. Charlie was making a rare visit, and Teddy Marks was staying with them as well."

I remembered his lie about having visited the house just once over the years.

"It was late in the afternoon," he remembered. "The adults were having cocktails on the porch, and Maddie came running up the grass from the pool house, screaming in her swimming suit. They'd been playing by the pool all afternoon . . ." He wiped an eye. "We did everything we could to try to save the boy. I drove him to the Kingston ER myself . . . but it was too late."

"I'm sorry to hear. That must have been . . ."

"I'll never forget Madeline's response, after we reached him. She stopped screaming, stopped crying altogether, and entered a state of shock. She stood off to the side, her hands clasped together, watching us. Watching us try to save this boy's life. I never saw her shed another tear. Not after we returned home with the awful news, not even at the funeral. Of course, she stopped coming up to Owl View soon after . . ."

"Her room," I said. "When I searched it, it looked like it had been frozen in time—right around that age."

"Now you know why," he said.

"But why wouldn't Margaret mention any of this? How could either of them not mention it?"

"That's a very good question, Mr. Darley. But I knew they wouldn't."

"Which is why you followed me."

"Yes."

"Why didn't they tell me about it?"

"It's as though the tragedy with Patrick Bell was stricken from the record with those folks. From the moment he died, they all seemed determined to forget it. A stubborn mind can shut out anything. Maybe they thought Maddie had been through enough already, losing her father and all, but whatever it was, they dealt with it by pretending it never happened. Besides, I'm sure they would refuse to admit it has any relevance to the current circumstances."

"But you think it does."

Ernest sipped his coffee, gazed over my shoulder at a pair of bikers staring at us through the windows. Their Harleys roared with empty threat as they pulled off. Tough guy cowards. Ernest looked back to me. He had a courtly air about him, a quiet country wisdom that would stay forever baffled by the pace and madness of city folk. He worked beautiful land and had a good woman at home who could out-cook the finest Michelin-starred chef. His contact with the other side, the urban rich, had been a proud, tragic family drenched in death and success.

"I often wonder if it was an accident," he said finally.

"How so? You said the kid ingested the nuts by kissing Madeline. You think she purposely ate that stuff so she could pass it on to him?"

"No. Absolutely not. I'm not calling her a murderer, Mr. Darley. That would be . . . that would be, just, impossible."

"You're aware of what happened to Madeline's latest boyfriend last week, correct?"

"To James Fealy, yes, I'm aware. But that was not my implication."

"Then what was it?"

"I wonder if the cause of death—or should I say, the

means of death—was correct. Madeline never denied having those leftovers, but she insisted it was hours before he came over, and that she brushed her teeth and wiped away any possible remnants before she had any contact with the boy."

"But they still determined that was what did it?"

"There was no other rational explanation available. The boy's parents were not wealthy. The Bells are local folk. They did not have the means to pursue any further investigation. They were devastated, and they accepted that nothing was going to bring back their son."

"What do you think happened, Ernest?"

He sat in silence for a long while, a hint of far off fear in his eyes. "That coach," he said. "Teddy Marks. I've never trusted that man . . ."

Chapter 23

I've never been quite sure why Cass continues to work with me. Just guilt, perhaps. She is the superior investigator; we both know this to be true, yet she appears to prefer her secondary role. Perhaps it's because she must be the dominant one at all times in her other life. In this she can be the one led along, the follower. Or perhaps it is simply a matter of access. Our clients come to me. They remember my last name, remember my father, have heard the scandalous past and the unsavory present, and with those facts they feel armed with both a kinship and a certain superiority, even in their moments of greatest despair. In Cass, they would not find this. They'd find an unsmiling, disconcertingly powerful woman too able for comfort. We make a good team. I lure them in with my damaged pedigree, while she ensures that their cases actually get solved.

I was typing up my case notes, looking for some inspiration on the white screen, when she called. Elvis grumbled at the unwanted movement and climbed from my lap.

"Welcome back," she said. "How was the country?"

"Grand."

I pictured her pacing her apartment I'd never seen. A dark Victorian lair, I imagined. Thick scarlet drapes and crimson walls and black leather furniture and ancient immovable dressers covered in melted candles, wax pooled at the base in elegant dried mounds on blackened surfaces. She would have prints by Bosch framed on the walls. Or, no, Bosch would be too typical; they would be prints by Albrect Dürer. I heard Lou Reed playing in the background, and my image was complete.

"Did Marks confess?" she asked.

"To decades-old indiscretions," I said. "He was able to rationalize it quite well. Says he was just an immature twenty-something when he fell for the lusty machinations of advanced teenaged girls. Insisted he hasn't crossed that line in decades, and he denied having anything to do with Madeline."

"So he's a reformed scumbag who can't be blamed for long-ago statutory rapes? And aside from that, he's a saint in all this?"

"Something like that."

"You believe him?"

"Hell, no."

"You always had such nice things to say about him, Duck. Like he was the only adult you respected. You never suspected anything?"

"I was a dumbass kid. Clearly."

The song in her background changed to "Dirty Blvd." I heard Cass sucking on her cigarette. She exhaled and said, "You think he's been messing with our girl?"

"He claims he's never touched her. Acted shocked when I told him about Charlie's accusation. Sounded a little forced, but maybe I was just looking for some guilt. Honestly, it's hard to imagine him being attractive to eighteen-year-olds any longer."

"Can't underestimate the daddy issues," she said.

"I suppose. And Madeline certainly would seem to have her share. Then there's the blackmail."

"Marks is being blackmailed?"

I told Cass the rest of it, about the wire transfers and the attacks on his swimmers and his suspicions of John Kosta. Then I told her about my chat with Ernest and the death of young Patrick Bell at Owl View. When I finished I was more confused than when I began, and Cass was pissed.

"That fucker is dirty," she said. "No way he's being blackmailed twenty-five years after the fact just like that. There's something he's not telling us."

"As I was saying."

"What do you remember about this assistant coach, Kosta? Think it could be him?"

"He was just a likeable, unthreatening guy from what I remember. Everybody loved him. He was the good cop."

"You might want to pay him a visit."

"I intend to."

"And go see Charlie," she said. "Marks cannot be too happy with him right about now."

"He took off back to the city pretty early this morning. Called the accusation a betrayal of the worst sort."

"Not if it's true."

If it was true, then where did that place Madeline? Did she threaten to expose the secret—and tear down his entire life? That was more than enough motive for murder. And Marks had killed before, I was sure of that.

"Listen, about that party," said Cass. "The Day of the Lord thing. I found out where it is tonight."

"Oh, yeah?"

"It's out at another warehouse in Gowanus. Address is 234 Butler, near the end of the canal. Thinking we split it up in two shifts? I'm happy to go tonight, till morning."

"Cool, and we can hand off tomorrow at noon—unless you've already found her."

"Wouldn't that be nice?"

I set down the phone and returned to rubbing Elvis and

staring at my summary. I found myself thinking of Anna Lisko. The remembrance of that morning in her Soho loft sparked a sense of detached longing. Even as she was pressed against me, even inside of her, there was a distance, as if her body were conducting a physical experiment while her mind interpreted the data behind a wall of one-way glass. I decided I liked it that way. Her coldness afterward had given me a kind of comfort. There was nothing to be said until there was something to be done, again.

Now when I called her number I felt the thrill rising with each ring. She was a woman without affection, and that was not a bad thing. The sweet and the loving offered so little. On the fifth ring she picked up, and I heard her breath first, before she spoke.

"Hello, Mr. Duck. I wondered when you would call."

"You miss me?" I didn't recognize my own voice. It sounded like a faux-confident teenager batting out of his league.

She didn't answer, just breathed into the phone, waiting for my next line.

"I wondered if you might be free . . . for lunch?"

"When would you like? Next week I am very busy."

"I was thinking today, actually. This afternoon. In, like, an hour?"

"An hour?"

More breathy silence, then I heard ice falling into glass, then something being poured. I heard her take a drink. When the glass clinked back down on the counter, she said, "Okay, tell me where."

I told her of a Russian place in the East Village called Rosie's and immediately regretted the choice. She sighed like she knew it, but did not object. An hour and a half later I was sitting there sipping my third ginger-infused vodka with a soggy stack of potato pancakes sitting before me on the table. Rosie's was a small, cramped space with a farmhouse feel and dim, careless lighting. I had the room to myself, aside from the aging proprietor, presumably Rosie herself, who was acting as bartender, waitress, and chef. She had a wide, sturdy build and short gray hair around a swollen face that hadn't smiled in years. When Anna entered, the two women regarded each other across the room. Rosie's manner appeared to soften slightly, like the first thaw of March ice.

"*On s toboy?*" she asked.

"*Da.*"

Anna came over and sat without greeting. Something like amusement flickered in her icy blue eyes. "You did not have to choose this restaurant for me," she said. "They serve vodka everywhere, you know?" Her gaze was unsettling. She waited for me to break eye contact before she allowed herself to do the same.

"It was the first place to come to mind," I said.

"Men. You are so easy, so simple." She nodded once to herself, filing away more data, and tried out the cold pancakes. She frowned, set down her fork, and called over to Rosie, rattling off Russian that made her smirk, and then, improbably, let out a full belly laugh. The two women finished the inside joke and then regarded me like a new pet. Anna ordered a long string of gibberish, with Rosie taking it all in without taking notes. The only word I understood was *vodka*.

The feast that followed was served with a care reserved only for native speakers. A borscht soup, dried herring, spiced lamb kabobs, and, of course, caviar; big decadent spoonfuls of the stuff. The vodka was poured like table wine. Rosie set a chilled carafe between us, refilling our glasses at frequent intervals, before taking away the empties and returning with fresh ones. Anna appeared to be enjoying herself, and for the first hour we spoke with the loosening awkwardness of a second date. She showed no effect from the alcohol. I wondered how long I could keep pace. As Rosie cleared the last course and topped off our glasses, a wicked look came to Anna's eyes.

"So how was the country?" she asked.

"Lovely," I said. "Interesting that Teddy told you about my visit."

Anna knocked back her vodka and set the glass back down on the table with the steady-handedness of a surgeon. "Do not flatter yourself," she said. "I told him you were searching for him that morning at the pool. It was only natural for him to let me know that you had found each other."

"What else did he tell you?"

She inhaled sharply and filled our glasses. "He is my boss," she said. "Our relationship is very professional. He does not tell me so much about his private life."

"Does he ever mention a man named John Kosta?"

"His old assistant?" She thought about the name for a moment. "A few times, yes. He sounds like very good coach. I think Teddy misses him . . . although I do my best to be a satisfactory replacement."

"He's had nothing but nice things to say about you."

"Interesting that he tells you about me."

I raised my glass. She brought hers close but did not drink. The clear, cold liquid hovered just below her sharp chin. "I asked Teddy about this girl you're looking for. He says she is very talented, a big, strong girl. Beautiful strokes. But lazy, I hate lazy." She tipped back the shot and waited for me to follow suit. I hadn't been counting, but I estimated we had to be over a dozen by this point. Yet I did not feel drunk. As if reading my mind, she said, "It is the caviar. A Russian secret. If you eat plenty of caviar, it lines your stomach, and you do not feel the vodka."

Another carafe later we proved that theory wrong. The delicacy may have delayed the inevitable, but there comes a point where the booze always wins. I paid Rosie and slurred out thanks, and then we were standing, swaying, on the sidewalk, Anna's arm in mine. It was a cool night, with fall coming fast, and she pressed her body close to mine for warmth. I stepped into the street, raised my arm for a passing cab. Before I could speak, she gave the driver her address and turned on me with predatory intent. I felt her mouth on my neck, her hand between my legs.

Chapter 24

I woke just before six in Anna's bed with a dry mouth and an aching head. I slipped from bed in the lightening darkness and went in search of water and Advil. Behind me, Anna slumbered in deep sleep, a thick, smooth leg flung out on top of the sheets. I felt her scent clinging to my body as I walked, naked and chilled, down the hall to the kitchen. I poured myself tap water and went over and stood by the high loft windows looking down on Mercer Street. There was a hum of activity down the block, a few determined partiers coming out of an after-hours spot on this early Sunday morning. Above them, dawn was yawning with sobriety.

I resolved to go for a swim. There was a masters' group that would soon be gathering at a nearby pool. It was as if my body had opened my eyes and informed me of what it needed. A swim would flush away the booze haze and clear the mind for the long afternoon ahead. I gulped down the rest of my water and set the glass on the counter and swung my arms in butterfly circles, stretching out the hangover. Then I walked softly back toward Anna's room in search of my things. She was already up, dressed in short black shorts and sports bra, tying her hair back into a tight ponytail.

"You are welcome to stay and go back to sleep," she said. "I am going for run." She spoke with wide-awake clarity. The old swimmer's switch: dead asleep one minute, eyes wide and off to work out the next.

"No, I was just thinking I'd go for a swim," I told her.

She shrugged, unimpressed, bent down to tie a pair of new running shoes. Again, post-sex, the coldness had returned. We both wanted to be gone, out of each other's presence, and couldn't get out the door fast enough.

We looked at each other with nothing to say. Then she moved past me, out of the bedroom, toward the elevator. We managed a kissless good-bye out front and headed off in our separate directions.

The water did not let me down. It proved, as ever, to be an instant tonic as I entered with a shock and swam off the booze with slow, aching strokes. My masters' group is a rather pathetic collection of has-beens and never-will-be's. There's the obsessed crew of too-fit triathletes with terrible strokes, the now fat swim moms trying to swim off the pounds, and your random less-than-committed folks like me, who tend to use practices as a futile means of balancing the bodily damage. The triathlete clowns smelled the booze emanating off of me in the locker room and gave the requisite snarls of disapproval.

I swam the practice without speaking, without taking off my goggles at the wall. I stroked and flipped and thought and waited for the dread to lift. I wondered if Madeline McKay felt the same respite from her own demons the few times she still returned to the pool. I wondered if she was still alive.

No one was waiting for me this time as I climbed from the pool. I dressed without showering, relished the clinging stench of chlorine, and made my way to Joe's diner. I grabbed a *Post* on the way. It was another crisp blue September morning, low sixties, no clouds, no planes overhead. Manuel set down my beer and black coffee and I opened the paper.

There was no mention of the Fealy murder or the search for Madeline in the first few pages. Unsolved or not, it was yesterday's news. On the third and fourth pages of the paper there was a splashy report about the city's latest crime statistics. So far that year, all classified felonies were at record lows in Manhattan. Less murder, fewer muggings, fewer burglaries, fewer assaults . . . These city streets had never been safer. The island was now a playground for the rich, and it had the ubiquitous police presence to guard its loaded denizens. Every last crime was dropping, except for one: a certain specialized subset of rape. The classic stranger-in-an-alley horror, that kind of rape was becoming all but extinct in these parts. But it was the other kind of rape that they couldn't do anything about. It was termed "Non-Stranger Rape." When the evil comes from someone you know . . . what could the cops do about that? Their presence would forever be after the fact. Usually they wouldn't hear about it until much later, if at all. That particular felony was spiking. According to the report, it had never been higher.

I wondered where Marks belonged in that particular category. Where did they place decades-old statutory rape, where the victims might only now recognize the compliant scars inflicted upon them? Is it ever too late to punish? I didn't feel like helping the man with his claims of blackmail, but I knew I had to seek out his old assistant, John Kosta. They had parted ways unpleasantly, and it was about more than a power struggle on deck. Blackmailer or not, Kosta would have insight into the past lives of his old boss. He'd also remember a few things about the McKay family.

But first case first. Find the girl. So easy to become lost in the whys, when all anyone really wants to know is the what. Where was she? Who did it? Surface solutions for deeper sins . . .

I tried to imagine her movements since the moment she fled the house in Rhinebeck. She was rattled by something and headed back to the city but did not go back to her apartment. The following day she was seen on camera leaving her ex-boyfriend's place—which must have been empty, with Fealy and his roommate both remaining out east on Labor Day. She tried to reach Coach Marks but did not leave a message. She sent her mother that cryptic apology text. And then . . . where did she go? Not home. Her partner in porn, Juli, had confirmed that she'd done a bit of escorting. Was she with a john? Did she end up like Cass's doomed friend Veronica, lifeless on some hotel bed? No, she would have been found by now. Was she off somewhere on a bender, partying through sleepless days and nights with faceless disreputables? Did she finally OD, with her fellow addicts dumping her in some remote location to distance themselves from complicity? Or perhaps most likely of all, it was a simple, quiet suicide. Nothing dramatic, no note, no desire to be found, just a final decision to turn out the lights . . .

I envisioned this awful and plausible end as my eyes stared out of focus at the gossip on Page Six. Something about a troubled starlet and a threesome . . . Manuel came over and set down my western omelet next to the paper, along with a fresh Beck's. He refilled my coffee, told me I "no look so good, *señor*." I turned the page. The story wasn't dead yet.

It appeared our girl, dead or alive, was being cleared as a suspect in the Fealy murder. The cops now liked a drug dealer by the name of Peter DiCicco. They'd published his mug shot; he was already in custody. Dealer Pete, hot damn. The *Post* presented a scenario that put the rich and tragic filmmaker James Fealy in a less than flattering light. This would explain the quick demotion from the front page to a buried item after the gossip section. The shower slaying of a promising young filmmaker, the scion of a billionaire hedge fund father, killed by his nutso ex-girlfriend—now that was *Post*-style scandal. But when they couldn't find the girl or place her at the scene, and the dead turned out to be in business with a drug dealer whose principle clientele was high school and college kids, well, that's when the press and the public lost sympathy in a hurry. Good riddance would be the general sentiment. The only ones who'd care now were Fealy's parents and little brother, and even they'd feel a little less heartbroken, a little angrier, when they discovered what young James was mixed up in. That is, if the cops had the right man and motive.

Reports now claimed that James Fealy had become a sort of investor and connector for the ambitious Dealer Pete. Fealy was allegedly fronting significant sums of cash (over six figures, said the *Post*) for Dealer Pete to purchase the highest quality coke from Harlem wholesalers, plus hundreds of doses of molly. Then Fealy would help open new markets for Pete's new supply—primarily prep school kids and NYU students; kids still on their parents' dime, who could afford unhealthy amounts of good drugs.

He sounded like a dealer's dream customer turned partner. But at a certain point, the rich kid drug tourist gets spooked straight. I remembered Pete telling us that Madeline said he quit. Fealy decides he wants out, tells Dealer Pete he's done, and the dealer says no way. He's not letting his golden goose out of the noose that easily. Maybe there's even a transaction in progress, and Fealy tries to yank his investment. Dealer decides to pay him a violent visit at home. I wondered about the building's security cameras. How long were they out? Did they have any witnesses or visual evidence of Pete coming or going?

I closed the paper and finished my breakfast and fired a text to my moral-free friend Roy Perry. It wasn't his byline on the latest Fealy story, but he might have more that didn't make it to print. Then I found the number for Detective Miller and gave her a call on my way out of the diner.

"Looks like we owe you a bit of thanks," she said.

"You're welcome. What did I do?"

"Led us to Peter DiCicco. Or should I say your partner, Ms. Kimball, did. It appears she does most of your investigating."

"You were following us?"

"Of course. By the way, you didn't make a friend of Detective Sullivan last time you were here."

"Your partner's a dim prick," I said.

"Why do I suspect Ms. Kimball has heard the same thing?"

I had nothing for that. I stopped at a crosswalk, patted an empty coat pocket for sunglasses that must have been left at Anna's. The swim had cleared away the hangover and most of the dread, but now I was in dire need of a nap. I'd wake feeling refreshed and ready to start back on the search with a lucid mind, or at least as close to clearheaded as I could manage. A bus coasted to a stop in front of me, its gray diesel fumes billowing out toward a pair of young mothers pushing strollers on the sidewalk. The side of the bus ran an ad for a new David Blaine reality show called *The Sorcerer's Apprentice*. Something occurred to me, but then it was lost.

"Ah, did I hurt your feelings?" I heard her say. "Don't worry, Duck, I don't think you're dim."

"Huh?"

"Or maybe you are. But I know you're not a prick."

"Oh, right, like Sullivan. Sorry, I lost you for a second."

"You okay, Duck?"

"I'd be a lot better if people would stop asking me that," I said.

"Touchy, touchy. Haven't had your morning cocktails yet?"

"Not yet." The beers with breakfast didn't count. "So, now that we've done your work for you, does that mean you'll leave us alone?"

"Hey, you called me, cowboy. We were already leaving you alone. What did you want to talk about anyway?"

"Just read the *Post*, wanted to hear how you got to the dealer."

"All thanks to Ms. Kimball. She got that Schwartz kid talking at the club. More than we were able to do . . . So, after DiCicco left your place that night, we waited till he got a few blocks away, then stopped him for suspicious behavior. Found quite a collection in that backpack. Dozens of bags of blow, hundreds of pills, a bit of heroin. You didn't buy any of that stuff from him, did you, Duck?"

"Not me. He was only there for questioning. Ask Cass."

"Because partners never cover for each other."

"So you brought him in, started questioning, and he confessed to slashing up Fealy in the shower?"

"He's not talking, but his prints were all over the apartment, including the bathroom. And when we searched his place, we found logs of his business transactions with James Fealy. I gotta hand it to this DiCicco character, he was one ambitious dealer. He looks like he's half retarded with that giant head, but the guy knew how to run a business. He had a deep-pocketed investor and a growing young market. That is, until his benefactor tried to get out and DiCicco reacted the way dealers do."

"You sure he's your guy?" I asked. "You see him on those faulty security cameras?"

"Sure enough to get an indictment," she said, ignoring the latter question. "Why, you got any other theories you care to share?"

"I told you, I was never concerned with solving a murder. My job is to find the girl. Madeline McKay? Remember, the one who was falsely accused and splashed on the cover of every paper in town? Good luck with that lawsuit."

"The NYPD can't control what the tabloids publish. That's something the McKay family can take up with them."

"I'm sure the mother will."

"How's that coming, by the way? You any closer to finding her?"

"Getting there," I said.

"Think she's still alive?" she asked.

"What do you care?"

"Duck, Ms. McKay is no longer a suspect in a murder, as much as we would still like to speak with her. If her mother would like to file a missing persons report and ask the department for help, we will be more than happy to join your search, but she's made it quite clear she wants nothing to do with the NYPD."

"I can't imagine why."

"Don't push it. Your partner helped us with this one, and we appreciate it, but we would have tracked him down ourselves without much more effort."

"Of course you would have. By the way, I've been assaulted twice in the last week. Can you launch an investigation?"

She was silent for a moment. I could almost see her small cheeks flushing with irritation. "As soon as you come in to file a complaint," she said, "we'll get right on it."

"That's okay. I think I took care of it myself."

"I gotta go, Duck. If you find the McKay girl, we expect you to bring her in. We'll need her to make a statement in the DiCicco case, considering her likely involvement in the operation with her ex."

"I'll have to get her mother's permission first," I said. "You know how she feels about you people."

Detective Miller ended the call with an unfriendly "fuck off" that buoyed my spirits. Maybe Fealy was financing the distribution of the finest dope for every rich kid in the city. Maybe he got what was coming to him, and this town was better off without him and his knife-wielding dealer. And maybe he was dealing to poor Lucy Townes too. Maybe she tried to end it in a fit of cocaine comedown depression.

I turned the corner on 17th Street already feeling my head hitting the pillow. A nap after a good hard morning swim—more of the world's problems would be solved if we could all start our days that way. But it wasn't to be. As I approached my place, I saw Cass sitting with Elvis on the front step. She was joined by a beautiful blond girl, who was standing off to the side. The girl hugged her slim body with her chin pressed to her chest. She was wearing sweatpants and a look of vacant sedation. Elvis lunged on his leash when he saw me coming. Cass looked up; the girl hugged herself a little tighter.

"Party was busted," said Cass. "Cops raided it around seven this morning. No sign of our girl." Then she looked over at her new friend. "Duck, this is Lucy Townes."

Lucy tilted her pretty head up toward me. With her height and natural beauty, I was sure the girl could pass for an adult inside plenty of clubs and parties. But standing there in the morning light, in sweats and frowning dimples and a quivering lower lip, Lucy looked like an overgrown child. I patted her shoulder.

"How you feeling, kid?" I asked.

She shrugged, shifted a step closer toward Cass.

Cass handed me Elvis's leash and pushed herself up from the stoop. "Let's take a walk," she said.

Chapter 25

The three of us walked across to Stuyvesant Park, letting Elvis lead the way as he pissed and sniffed like a magnet drawn by unseen forces. It was a gorgeous day, the sky that special shade of New York blue that kept us voluntary captives in this mad city. A few junkies nodded on benches in the shade. Elvis howled at a passing squirrel. I noticed a blond guy with a beagle checking out Cass. He was angling to get the dogs in for a sniff. Cass pretended not to notice, looked through him with haughty indifference. She dressed to taunt, not to please. Today it was fishnets and black leather shorts over black heels; leather jacket unzipped over a faded T-Rex T-shirt.

We walked awhile in silence. Lucy and Cass hung back a few paces and spoke quietly. I waited for them to initiate. Finally, they found a bench as far from anyone as possible and sat and called me over.

"Party was quite a scene," said Cass. "Three floors of all-out decadence in a deserted factory, DJs on every level, and hundreds of party people blasted out of their minds."

Lucy nodded, smiled slightly like she'd been there before.

"Spoke to a bunch of folks: bouncers, the DJs, the roaming dealers, and plenty of wasted young kids. Madeline is definitely a part of the scene: everyone seemed to know her, or at least recognized her when I showed her picture. They all wanted to know where she was. But of course, no one has seen her, or knows her beyond the parties. Cops burst in early this morning. Then Lucy here texted me on my way home." She knocked her knee and smiled down at the teenager slouched beside her.

"I can't stay much longer," said Lucy. "I told my dad I just needed to go for a walk. When they released me, they told him I wasn't supposed to be left alone for long. I think he watched me while I slept last night."

"I know, Luce," said Cass. "We'll get you back in a few. I just wanted you to share with my partner what you told me. You can trust him. He used to swim for Marks too."

"Really?" Lucy looked over at me for the first time with anything resembling trust. "How long ago?"

"Ages," I said. "I used to swim with Madeline's brother, Charlie. We were the same age."

"Is that why her mom hired you to find her?" she asked.

"Probably. I've also done some work for some of her friends in the past." I tried to meet her eyes. She diverted them. "Lucy, do you have any idea where Madeline could be?"

"No," she said. "I don't. But I'm worried she's done something. Something . . . Her boyfriend, James . . ." She covered her face with her hands, pressed her fingertips against her eyes. Her entire body quivered and tensed as tears seeped down her cheeks.

Cass rubbed at her back. "Lucy, why don't you start by telling Duck what you told me, about Coach Marks."

The girl wiped at her eyes, breathed deeply through her nose, and let out a slow exhale. There was a toughness about her that belied her young face and her recent attempt. It's been my experience that the slow and dramatic suicide attempts are the ones that don't really mean it.

There are definitive ways to end it quickly, without question. Holding your breath at the bottom of a swimming pool is not one of them. I hoped that silent underwater cry would be the last time she considered that final solution.

"Teddy and I were having an affair," she said. "We were having . . . sex."

"You and Coach?" I asked. "When? Is this still going on?"

Cass glanced over, warning me to tread lightly. Now was not the time to overwhelm the girl with a grilling. We needed to respect the courage of this confession.

"Last year," she said quietly. "We were together . . . or whatever we were, for about six months." She wiped at her tears and let out a dark laugh. "I know how gross it sounds. He's, like, old. I don't know what I was thinking. But Teddy can be really charming and sweet. He made it seem natural. Don't ask me how."

"Lucy," said Cass. "The man is a predator. That's what they do. What Coach Marks did to you is rape."

"No, it wasn't," cried Lucy. "It wasn't like that. It's not like I said 'no.' He didn't force me to do anything."

"You're a minor, girl. What he did to you, whether you agreed or not, is illegal. It's statutory rape."

"It's also not the first time he's done this," I said.

Both women glared at me. Now was not the time.

"How did it end?" asked Cass.

"Somebody caught us," said Lucy. "Coach John. He caught us in Teddy's hotel room at a swim meet. We were kissing." The tears returned; her face dissolved into a splotchy mess of memory. "God, I was so stupid."

"What happened next?" I asked.

"I ran out of the room, and Teddy tried to talk to Coach John. Obviously, there wasn't much he could say. It was totally obvious. Then we got home from the meet and Coach

John quit like the next week. And Teddy wouldn't speak to me at practice."

"Did you ever speak to him, to Coach Kosta?" I asked.

"No. I figured he would call me or email me, or something, but he never did. I have no idea where he went or what Teddy said to him. Anyway, I couldn't bear to come to practice after that. Teddy was ignoring me. No one knew what had been going on. It was just too much. So, I said that my shoulder hurt, that I needed to take a break. I just stopped showing up to the pool, and it was like no one cared."

"When did you start hanging out with Madeline?" asked Cass. "Were you two close before all this?"

"Yeah, I mean, kind of. Madeline was always really sweet to me. She was like a big sister. She has this terrible reputation, but she's really not like that. She's like the kindest person I know. Or at least she was."

Cass nodded like she understood. Kept rubbing her back. The sisterhood of striking beauty.

"So, one of my last days at the pool, Madeline shows up for practice. She would kind of come and go whenever she felt like it. Teddy hated it, but he couldn't say anything, since she was Charlie's sister, and their mom bought him an apartment or something. Anyway, Maddie noticed I was upset, and she caught up to me as I was leaving. We started hanging out after that."

"Did you ever tell her about what Marks did to you?" I asked.

Lucy nodded. "Eventually," she said. "Not right away. At first I said I was just burnt out on swimming and that I needed a break. She understood and never pushed me to explain. She respected my privacy. But then one night at her apartment, we were doing, like, cocaine, and we were talking about all kinds of stuff, and I confessed to her."

"What did she say?" asked Cass.

"She was really quiet at first. I remember she got up and went to the bathroom, and she was in there for a long time. When she came back she was really serious, and like steaming. She held my hands and told me that she was going to get back at Teddy for me."

"Did she say how?"

"No. I begged her not to tell anyone. I said, whatever she did, please don't let it out. If my father found out . . . God, he would kill Teddy. I mean, literally. He would, I know it."

"What happened after that?" I asked. "Did you and Madeline ever speak about it again? Do you know if she ever followed through on what she said?"

"The next day she told me not to worry. She promised that my secret was safe, and that she would take care of everything. But then the next weekend she met that boy, James, and it was like she forgot about me. She started hanging out with him all the time, and partying even harder, and I figured, you know, that it was just big talk on drugs."

"Lucy, honey, what do you think happened to James Fealy?" asked Cass. "You said you were worried Madeline may have done something?"

"I don't know what to think," she said. "A few weeks ago, Maddie started texting me again, asking to hang out. She said James was this total asshole, told me all sorts of terrible things about him. I went out with her once after that, and it was like too much. I couldn't keep up with her. She's out of control now. Maddie always liked to party, but not like this. She would go for days at a time. It scared me. *She* scared me. And then, that happened with James last week. I didn't know what to think."

"And then I got in touch, wanting to ask you all sorts of questions," said Cass.

"It was too much," said Lucy. "Just too much. So, I . . . I jumped into our building's pool, and I decided that I was never coming up for air." She burst into sobs this time. She lifted her legs and hugged her knees and buried her face between them. Cass rubbed at her back as Lucy shook with terror and pain at her darkest point. I looked over at Cass. She was sharing my guilt. This girl was in no shape to relive these memories in the presence of two strangers, even if it helped us find her wayward friend. She needed professional help, not brutal, confused confessions on a park bench.

"I should go," she sobbed, looking up. "I really need to go."

"Let me help you," said Cass. "I'll walk you home, okay?"

"No," said Lucy, wiping at her tears. "Please don't. I just need to go. I'm sorry."

She avoided our eyes and stood and moved fast out of the park gates and down Second Avenue. Cass started to stand, then reconsidered and sat back down. Elvis sat panting at our feet looking up at us. He leapt up on the bench and nuzzled into Cass's lap and rested his head on her thigh. She rubbed behind his ears and stared off across the park. Neither of us spoke for a long time.

"Why did I take her to meet you?" Cass asked, finally, without looking over. "I could have just reported back. But we were nearby, at a Starbucks on Union Square, and I was so floored by what she said, I wanted you to hear it directly from her. They released her after the required seventy-two hours, and Lucy got in touch with me almost immediately, said she needed to talk. And that's how I help her, by forcing her to repeat all that stuff. Jesus."

"Even if it means her father killing Marks, we have to report this," I said. "We have to."

"Michael Townes should let me have a crack at him first," said Cass.

I shuddered at the thought. It would be worse than any orifice damage that Teddy Marks would receive in prison.

"Guess this explains who's behind the blackmail," I said. "Madeline vowed to get back at Marks for her friend. Sounds like she's been doing just that."

Cass was silent for a moment; then she shook her head. "Didn't Marks tell you his swimmers were being hurt, after he stopped paying? I can't see Madeline ever hurting her teammates to get back at him. And we're talking about a girl who's spiraled way down into addiction," she said. "You heard Lucy, Madeline's out of control, staying up for days. Does that sound like someone capable of well-plotted blackmail? Wire transfers and voice manipulators and whatever else Marks described to you?"

"So she hired someone to do it for her."

"Who?"

"John Kosta? The guy who caught Marks with Lucy, and suddenly quit a week later?"

"You mean, the coward who did nothing to help the victim? Who failed to report the crime he witnessed first-hand? Suddenly that guy's gonna blackmail his old boss for a crime he let happen? And then hurt kids he used to coach himself? No way."

"Maybe those incidents with his swimmers were unrelated, and Marks is just paranoid. Maybe Kosta is crazed with guilt for not acting," I said. "Then Madeline approaches him with a plan to make amends?" I didn't believe the words as I spoke them, but they had a certain logic.

"Bullshit," said Cass. "No fucking way."

"Only one way to find out," I said. "I'm going to talk to that fucker." I tossed the leash on Cass's lap. "Drop off the hound whenever, will you?" I left them there under the canopy of green leaves and headed for the subway.

Twenty minutes later I got off the Q train at DeKalb Avenue on the edge of downtown Brooklyn. I walked east up the hill until I reached Fort Greene Park and found a bench to get my bearings.

John Kosta wasn't too hard to find. A Google of his name plus "photographer" and "Brooklyn," and I was in business. The first hit to pop up was a site for Kosta Family Photography. The home page featured a mantel-ready pic of a smiling baby crawling on green grass. The site described a photography business devoted to capturing "*those timeless moments in the life of every family.*" In the About section, I read about Kosta's new post-coaching career. There was no mention of swimming or Marks Aquatics anywhere. Next to his bio, there was the requisite family shot, of John with his plump blond wife, named Pam, and a fat-cheeked baby named Jack on her lap. This wasn't the portrait of a black-mailer intent on revenge. In stroller-saturated Brooklyn, I guessed Kosta was carving out a nice living for himself. But as Cass reminded me countless times, you never see the truly dark ones coming. They look like the nicest, most well-adjusted . . . well, they look like a guy who owns a family photo business with his loving wife.

I called the number listed and asked to set up an appointment as soon as they could fit me in. I heard myself playing the part of fumbling husband who'd forgotten to set up a shoot as he'd promised his wife. Our son's first birthday was coming up, and we wanted to document it with some special family portraits. The woman on the line had a warm, chipper accent, with the sort of Southern drawl that disarms stressed-out Yanks. Kosta's wife, I guessed. "Sure thing, honey," she soothed. "We can fit y'all in. Not to worry, we'll make sure you stay out of the dog house at home." I stammered my thanks, almost believing my bullshit. I found myself wishing, briefly, that I led the life I was describing, but that passed like an exit half noticed on the highway.

She told me Kosta could meet for a consultation at one p.m., two hours from now. We agreed on a local coffee shop called the General's Bean, and I thanked her for fitting me in so quickly. Finding their home address was also light lifting. The business address listed on their site was on Willoughby Avenue. There was a residential listing for a J. Kosta on Adelphi Street, just three blocks over. Doesn't take much of a sleuth with a smartphone these days.

I bought a twenty-four-ounce Beck's at the first bodega I saw. I had it brown bagged and opened, swallowed down two Vicodins with my first sip, and strolled over to casa Kosta for a late morning stakeout with my beverage. It was your classic Brooklyn brownstone, divided into four two-bedroom flats. The narrow street was lined with too green trees; I counted five strollers moving up and down the block. Once upon a time, when I was a kid in the city, this neighborhood was black and cheap and less than safe—the kind of place where it would be reasonable to sit on a stoop with a brown bag bomber and sip a beer on a pleasant Sunday morning. Now the rents are almost Manhattan-high, and the demographics have paled considerably. No one has heard about a mugging in ages. Now good neighbors scowl at folks like me who need a bit of maintenance drinking to get through the day. I pretended not to notice. I found a stoop across the street from Kosta's, about five doors down. I wondered if Marks's man, Fred Wright, was somewhere on the same block, staking out the same place. I scanned both sides of the street, looking for anyone idling in his car, but noticed no one. That didn't mean much. If Fred was the SEAL-trained stealth killer that Marks described, he'd be somewhere in the shadows.

The Vicodin kicked in after forty-five minutes, as I was taking the last sips of my Beck's. I felt the warm rush of inexplicable joy as the pills worked their magic. My head began to nod in slow beats to silent music; my nose had that pleasant phantom itch; my jaw unclenched. Ah, Vicodin, hello, old friend. I considered going back to the bodega for a second bomber, but I didn't want to mess with the buzz. It was settling just right. There aren't too many times when you're not too clear and not too cloudy. You have to savor it. I was leaning back on the stoop, letting the September sun warm my face, when I spotted Kosta leaving his place.

He reached the sidewalk and looked both ways like a man expecting trouble. He took two strides in one direction, then reconsidered, and turned and walked off fast the other way. We still had an hour before our meeting. The man was heading somewhere else first, and it looked like even he wasn't quite sure where. I followed at a discreet distance. He turned left on Lafayette and moved almost at a jog down the avenue. I let him widen the gap a bit. Paranoia was emanating from the guy; he'd have noticed someone moving at the same speed behind him. Three blocks later I watched him turn into a church on the corner of Oxford. Again he looked back in all directions before pushing through the high, heavy doors of the chapel. I resisted following him inside. I've always hated the suffocating, guilt-choking air of those places, could never understand the serenity that some find inside of them. I checked around the side, and seeing no other exits, resumed my vigil on a new stoop across from the church.

An hour later, just as the bell tolled, Kosta emerged and headed toward our meeting. He was walking more slowly this time. Whatever prayers had been said inside appeared to have eased his worried mind. I walked along behind him on the other side of the street for a few blocks and watched as he entered the General's Bean with the transformed air of the pleasant neighborhood photographer. I entered ten seconds later and was greeted with his finest family-man smile. I introduced myself as Lawrence.

"Great to meet you," he said, clasping my hand in a hearty shake. "Psyched we can help you out on short notice."

He'd gained weight and facial hair since I'd last seen him. The Kosta I remembered as a kid was a slim, short man who carried himself tall. Always clean shaven, always fresh from a run, or about to go for one. This later version Kosta was about thirty pounds heavier with a paunch and a puffy face covered by a scruffy Brooklyn-issue beard. We ordered our coffees at the counter and talked about the weather and the Yankees while we waited. He looked at me with amiable warmth as he tried to place the memory of the face before him. We found a table in the back.

"You don't remember me, do you?" I asked.

"I'm sorry," he said. "I'm terrible with names, but I never forget a face. We've met before, have we?"

"It's okay, it was another lifetime," I told him. "When I was a kid I used to swim for—"

"Wait, oh man, Duck Darley?"

"Good to see you again, Coach Kosta."

"Why'd you say your name was Lawrence?"

"It is, my given name. Guess I wanted to see if you'd remember me first."

"My apologies, Duck. I see so many . . . and it's been, what twenty years?"

"Something like that."

He was relaxed now, in the presence of an old swimmer, a part of the tribe. "Well, thank you for reaching out to our little photo business. How did you hear about us? I'm afraid I stopped keeping up with any of the old crew. You were a funny bunch of kids. And so motivated ... It's amazing to think of the sets you guys used to do back then." He took a sip of his latte and let himself get lost for a moment in the nostalgia. I watched as memory lane reached its dark dead end. He chewed the beard hair beneath his lower lip. He exhaled through his nostrils like he was trying to release a sudden bout of bad energy. "Anyway," he said. "What can I do for you today? My wife mentioned a son's first birthday coming up? My congrats, dude. There's nothing more special in life, is there?"

"Not exactly," I said. "I'm not here about a photo shoot. I have no wife, no kids. I'm investigating a disappearance."

For a second I thought he was going to get up and run. He began to stand, gripped his coffee cup like he was about to toss it in my face.

"Have a seat, John," I said. "I just need to ask you a few questions."

He obeyed. "I haven't done anything," he whispered.

"That's the problem," I said.

Chapter 26

I told him I knew about Lucy and Marks, and how he'd walked in on them in a hotel room at a meet. That got his ass rooted to the chair. He didn't try denying it, didn't try explaining why he'd quit soon after and done nothing. He just sank lower in his seat in silence like his number had finally been called, and now it was time to settle an overdue debt that he'd tried to skip out on. Then I explained the situation with the missing Madeline McKay and her promise to get revenge for her friend.

"So, John," I said, "that's where you come in. Madeline approached you about helping her, didn't she?"

"No," he said without looking up. "I haven't seen that girl or anyone from the team since I left, the week after all that went down. I've had zero contact with anyone."

"How come?"

"I had no choice," he said with a mix of self-pity and loathing. I wanted to reach across and slam his sniffling face against the table until he cried for forgiveness.

"John, let me explain what you've set in motion," I said. "Since you're clearly too pussy to get it. Lucy Townes tried to kill herself last week, in part because of your failure to help her. Someone has been blackmailing Coach

Marks since soon after you left. Madeline McKay, who vowed to get back at their coach after her friend confessed the affair, is now missing and a drug addict. Oh, and her boyfriend was murdered last week. Are you hearing me?"

He finished the last of his latte and patted his jacket pocket, brought out a pack of Marlboro Lights and set them on the table between us. "I could use a smoke," he said. "You want one?"

"No."

He pushed back his chair, shuffled toward the door. I followed. His running days were long behind him. He moved with the dour air of the defeated, like a man who'd lost a battle and never regained his spirit. Out on the sidewalk he gave a furtive scan in all directions before lighting up. As he exhaled, he said: "You're right. I owe Lucy a serious apology."

"You owe her more than that, John," I told him.

"I had no choice," he said again. "I tried, I tried to address it with Teddy. I was horrified by what I saw. I knew . . . I'd heard that there had been others, through the years, but it was just rumors, and I tried not to believe them. But when I saw that, I just . . . I didn't want to believe what I was seeing."

"How did you try?" I asked. "It seems to me like you didn't do shit."

"My son had just been born," he said. "You don't understand. I kept quiet so I could keep my family. I did it for them. Teddy had . . . He has something on me. He threatened to tell my wife."

"Has what on you, John? Don't tell me you were messing with your swimmers too."

"She was in college." He sighed. "It was nothing like, nothing like what Teddy's done. A few years ago, one of our old swimmers was home from school, training with us over the holidays, and something started between us. Teddy found out about it, I didn't try to deny it. It was like he approved, even though I was married and all."

"Who was she?" I asked.

"Doesn't matter," he said. "A girl named Erica. She was twenty-one, a junior at Cal. The fling, or whatever it was, lasted through that summer, at meets or whenever, and then she went back for her senior year, got a boyfriend, and that was that. I got my shit together, and Pam and I decided to start a family. Marks made it very clear: if I said anything about Lucy, then he would pick up the phone and call my wife. She'd leave me, no question about it. She and my boy mean everything to me. I'm sorry about everything I've set in motion, but I'll do anything to keep my family together."

Kosta paused long enough to tap out another cigarette, slipped it between bearded lips, and shook his head as he sparked the flame. "I'll never forget the way he smiled when I confronted him about Lucy. It was like he'd been waiting for that moment for a long time—for someone to dare to call him out. The day we got back from the meet, I asked to talk to him after practice. We were sitting in his office next to the pool. I'd waited for the kids to clear out of the lockers, and I remember listening to their laughter as they left. Then it was silent, just Marks and me sitting there looking at each other, next to that still water. I told him how I knew there'd been others through the years, but I hadn't believed the rumors. But now I knew they were true. I told him it needed to end."

We came to a crosswalk two blocks from his home. He took self-pitying pulls at his cigarette and stared at the sidewalk. His shoulders slumped forward. The man had fallen far, his defeat made all the more poignant by his externally decent life. Wife, child, business: a man who should be grateful for his lot, but had sold too much to maintain it.

"Did you ever threaten to report him?" I asked.

"Of course." Kosta coughed out a cloud of smoke. "I said, if he didn't end it with Lucy, I would have no choice but . . ."

"*If* he didn't end it," I said. "How courageous of you, John."

"Fine, call me a coward. I know I deserve it. But I knew he was going to bring up Erica. I was just looking for a way out, where I could do the right thing, but still keep my job and my family together."

"You failed," I told him. Then I took his cigarette from his bearded lips—I couldn't resist—and I ground it out at his feet. "You failed in more ways than one, you fucker."

Kosta recoiled, braced for a blow. Somehow I held back.

"I know," he said. "He fired me a week later. Then he had me blackballed from the entire sport. The bastard called up anywhere I might have had a chance to get hired, and told other coaches, in all confidence, that there were 'rumors' about me. Like he was doing it for the good of the sport. The balls on that man . . ."

An impressive set indeed. In hearts, they call that shooting the moon; in poker, it was like a pairless bluff on Fifth Street. Somehow no one had called, and Marks had played his assistant coach right out of the game. Others must have heard the rumors about him, even if he'd contained his affair with Lucy. Yet no one had the courage to call.

We walked the next half block in silence before I asked, "John, do you think Coach could have had something with Madeline as well?"

He considered it for a few steps, shook his head. "It doesn't fit," he said. "Sure, she's beautiful, but she's the exact opposite of the girls Teddy likes. He likes the ambitious ones, without the talent to match, like Lucy. Maddie had all the talent in the world, and couldn't be bothered with it. He gave her special treatment, yeah, because of her brother. But she's not his type. Besides, the McKays were like his benefactors. Didn't the mother buy him that fancy apartment on the Upper East Side as a 'thank you' for Charlie's success? Teddy may be a predator that's preyed on plenty of young girls, but he's a calculating son of a bitch, and he's not stupid. I can't see him ever messing with Madeline."

"Her brother disagrees with you," I told him.

"Charlie? He told you Teddy was messing with his sister?"

"He did. He was pretty convinced about it."

"Huh. Well, I guess it could be possible. I suppose the opportunity would have been there, with him spending so much time with the family. But I don't know, I just can't see it . . . and I've seen plenty from that man."

We turned onto Kosta's block. I sensed him stiffen next to me, the previous paranoia returning. "You think someone's been following you, don't you?" I asked.

He stopped, gazed up at me with eyes dipped in fear.

"Don't worry, you're not paranoid. You're right. Someone has been on your tail."

"I know." His eyes were trained up the street on a black Tahoe with tinted windows parked across from his house, not unlike the one that had pulled up behind me on that Williamsburg street days ago. "I know someone's been in our home, going through our things. It's not obvious, but you know when your stuff is just a bit off, little things that are slightly out of place? And I keep sensing someone behind me every time I'm walking down the street. I turn and look, but . . . I don't know, I feel like I'm losing my mind sometimes."

He didn't take his eyes off the SUV.

"You recognize that Tahoe, don't you, John?"

As he nodded we watched a big man dressed in black emerge from Kosta's building. He was wearing sunglasses and a Yankees hat pulled low, but I recognized his bulk. Fred Wright, Marks's muscle, on the job, investigating this sad sack next to me. I was about to call out when I saw his eyes fix on the Tahoe across the way. His huge mass seemed to expand at the threat; his hand dipped into his jacket pocket. We watched as Fred crossed the street and rapped on the tinted passenger-side window. It slid down, and then Fred staggered back a step, his arms drifting up. Two shots rang out, and blood burst from Fred's chest. He collapsed in the street as the Tahoe peeled away.

While Kosta stood there paralyzed, I gave futile chase. There was no hope of catching him, but I did manage a good look at his plates. I scribbled down the digits on the palm of my hand and went back to Kosta. He was starting to unravel, the blood drained from his face. I thought he might faint at my feet. He tried to speak but failed to form words.

We ran over to Fred, on his back in a widening pool of dark blood. His big mass heaved and twitched in its final throes. His eyes were wide and scared as we watched him take his last, blood-choked breath.

Chapter 27

Kosta went for his phone to stammer out a call to 911. I put a hand on his arm and told him to wait a minute. The sight of this body did not leave me with the bilious dread that the Fealy murder had provoked. Maybe it was the nature of the crime scene: a knifed naked corpse in a shower versus a fully clothed hit in broad daylight. Instead I was left with a calm detachment and a clear sense of what needed to happen next, before the cops showed up and Kosta started vomiting out his fulfilled paranoid fears. I told him who lay dead before us, explained his connection to Marks. The blood was spreading across the street. It followed the uneven slope of the pavement and began to drip down into a gutter.

He gripped his phone and absorbed what he could. I told him that, if the cops asked, I was unable to get the plates off the Tahoe as it sped off. He looked at the hand in my pocket but didn't question it. Then we heard the sirens. We weren't the only ones on the block to respond to shots fired.

The cops came roaring up like too-late cavalry. They searched the area, sealed the crime scene, and treated us like their top suspects. We described what we witnessed. No, officers, we were too far away to get a good read on the license plate. They went inside Kosta's apartment and searched it for a long time. We stood outside between squad cars and waited for more questions. Kosta chain-smoked until his pack was empty. I texted Cass, gave her the basics and the plate numbers. I wanted her to run them first; I wanted a crack at him before the cops took their turn.

The case kept unraveling with more violence to hide new layers of secrets. I felt like I was walking underwater, with slow, breathless steps, fighting to stay down and not float up and away. I watched with a sense of unreality as a heavy blond woman came hurrying down the sidewalk pushing a stroller. Kosta rushed to her. He hugged his wife in a teary embrace, then bent down and managed a smile as he kissed his young son in the stroller. His wife surveyed the scene in front of her home with a trembling chin. She looked like the fragile type. I went over and joined the family and reintroduced myself to her.

"You're the man who called earlier," she said. "About the portraits for your baby's first birthday. I'm so sorry you had to witness this."

"It's okay," I said. "Your husband already got the job."

She looked up at Kosta. He gave her a reassuring squeeze on a fat forearm, avoided eye contact with me. I suggested maybe she go to a nearby playground with the baby while the police finished up. She didn't want the little guy to see any of this, even if he'd never remember. She was quick to agree. I stood back a few steps as Kosta whispered his shaken good-byes, then she wheeled the stroller around and we watched as mother and child retreated from the scene. The sky was still a stunning blue, not a cloud in sight, a beautiful day they'd remember.

This was my second murder scene this week. The second time in seven days that I'd come upon the dead. And they say death always comes in threes. When I related this to the Brooklyn homicide detective, he didn't like it much either. This one's name was Fanelli, a helmet-haired Italian from the neighborhood who'd only ever wanted to protect and serve his beloved borough. He was built like a Golden Gloves boxer gone to seed. Big, firm belly, nose flattened, meaty arms that probably still hit the heavy bag a few nights a week. He asked me for ID.

"You've got some bad luck, Mr. Darley," he said, handing it back. "Why don't you start by telling me how these two bodies are connected?"

"They're not," I told him. "Didn't you hear? NYPD already has the first murder suspect in custody. Couldn't have been the same guy."

"But the same guy—you—was the first one on the scene at both murders. So, again, why don't you tell me how these two are connected?"

"By a girl," I said. "A missing eighteen-year-old girl that I was hired to find."

"Her name?"

"Madeline McKay."

"Where is she?"

I gave him a look like I was restraining myself from breaking his nose. He returned it. It would have been a fair fight. Aikido can hold its own in most any attack, but no one wants to mess with a well-trained boxer. I'll bet on a tough middleweight over an MMA badass any day. We had our manly standoff, and I told him I didn't know.

"The first dead guy was her ex-boyfriend," I said.

"Right, they liked her for the murder last week," he said, remembering the headlines. "And the second?"

"The second was just killed in front of the home of one of her old swim coaches. John Kosta. He lives there with his wife and kid." I motioned over to him, sitting on a bumper. Someone had given him another cigarette. He sucked at it greedily.

"How'd he know the dead guy?"

"He didn't."

Fanelli gave me another boring look of keep-talking menace.

"The guy's name was Fred Wright, an ex–Navy SEAL. He was hired by an old colleague to look into John Kosta. His friend had reason to believe he was being black-mailed."

"Who's the friend?"

"A swim coach named Teddy Marks."

I could see the hamsters spinning their wheels inside Fanelli's head. He'd get there soon enough. I crossed my arms and waited. It didn't take him long; maybe he was brighter than he looked.

"What'd you say the missing girl's name is? McKay?"

"Madeline McKay, yes."

"She related to that Charlie McKay, that Olympic champ from a while back?"

"Her older brother."

He nodded, impressed by his memory. "I remember that kid, I always follow the Olympics and shit. Tried out my-self back in '88, as a welterweight." He gave a little jab to prove it. "That kid McKay was a stud, I remember. How many golds did he win?"

"Four."

He seemed disappointed. "You sure? Thought it was more. Didn't Phelps win like twenty or something?"

"Twenty-three, actually," I said.

"Ah well, four's still pretty good."

"Not bad."

"So, his sister, she some kind of fuck-up?"

"Appears that way."

"And how does their coach fit into all this? You said he's being blackmailed? For what?"

"Got me. Like I said, I was hired to find the girl, not to solve murders or uncover blackmails."

"Sounds like you're doing a hell of a job."

I held my tongue and managed to get through the rest of Fanelli's questions without incident. I told him some of what I knew, but not much. I'd be hearing from Detective Miller soon enough. I'd share the rest with her. Maybe she had the right man in the Fealy murder, maybe Dealer Pete acted alone in a drug deal gone wrong, and this murder had nothing at all to do with the first. Maybe I was the only connective tissue, a roving bad luck cloud of death that cursed those in my path.

I was starting to believe it as I waited for the subway hours later, after Fred had been wheeled away in a black bag and Kosta and family had been put up at the local Sheraton. I stood on the platform feeling too sober and too agitated to think. I needed strong drink and a fistful of pills, and I intended to pour both down my throat as soon as I was released back into Manhattan. As I leaned against a tiled pillar under the DeKalb Avenue sign, I watched a couple of wasted college girls come tripping and laughing onto the platform. The lights of the next train appeared at the end of the dark tunnel. They were looking at pictures on one girl's phone, lost in their private hilarity. The other girl leaned in to get a closer look. A heel buckled under her and she lurched forward. The subway lights were brighter now; the roar of the coming train filled the station. The girl went down and skidded across the platform until half her body was hanging over the edge. I felt someone rush past me. He dove for her, grabbed her by the calves, and pulled her back to safety just as the train rushed before us.

The whole incident took maybe three seconds. The someone who saved her turned out to be a young resident at Beth Israel, on his way to the hospital for his graveyard shift. On the train, the girls wept and gushed their thanks and gave him their phone numbers, swearing if there was ever anything either could do . . . I thought the friend was about to drop to her knees and thank the guy right there. The one who'd been saved, the less cute of the two, was too shaken to take it all in. It was just dawning on her how close she'd come to being decapitated. I sat across from them, and she kept looking over at me with blame in her eyes. *You were closer than the hero doctor*, the look seemed to say, *you were closer and you didn't move.* And I didn't. I could give her many distracted reasons why, but the fact is if I had been the only other person on that platform, the girl would have been dead. The young doctor slipped me a smug look on his way off.

My phone was dead by the time I reached the top of the subway steps coming out of Union Square. It was a warm, still Sunday night, the square deserted save for a few skaters practicing their tricks on the tarmac. I walked east toward Irving, already tasting the whiskey sitting in wait on my kitchen counter. I thought of the window coming down, the look on Fred's face before the shots tore through him. I thought of the killer fleeing the scene in the same car as my attacker from the other night. It couldn't be the same guy; I'd hurt him too bad. There was the nagging worry that I might have killed him as I pounded the back of his skull against the curb, but he was probably just suffering from a top-shelf concussion. Or perhaps he was lying somewhere in a coma, brain injuries still uncertain. Best to try to forget the damage left in your wake. I reminded myself it was self-defense. Besides, there were lots of black Tahoes out there on the city streets. It was probably just a case of vehicular coincidence.

The stories we tell ourselves just so we can turn the page.

I returned to my subterranean flat and took the necessary steps for personal sanity. I fed the hound, let him out in the garden. I swallowed down a triple helping of pain-killers. I poured myself five fingers of Bulleit. Then I called Elvis back inside and together we fell into the couch and turned on *SNL*, recorded from the night before. The host was a blond starlet I didn't recognize, delivering an un-funny opening monologue. I refilled my glass with another hand of the amber before she wrapped it up to forced laughter. The haze, all I wanted was the haze. I needed to fill my mind with a fog so thick I could forget all the death and the dying around me. It would all still be there in the morning, along with the throbbing head, but I didn't care. I just needed a brief respite of annihilation, followed by a few unconscious hours on the couch.

My buzzer sounded before I could get all the way there. Cass, I thought, of course. I hadn't bothered to recharge the phone. She'd be worried, she'd have the details on those plates, she'd be pissed I hadn't gotten back to her. Fuck it, she could let herself in, but the buzzer kept buzzing and Elvis started whimpering, and finally I set down my glass and staggered to the door.

"Cass?" I called. "You forget your keys?"

"Mister Duck," said another woman's voice. It took a moment to place it. "It's Anna. Please let me in," she said. "It's important."

I unbolted the door and turned the knob.

I saw her unsmiling face first. Then I saw the man next to her. Then I felt his fist in my face.

Chapter 28

They say the drinking will catch up with you. I didn't believe it. In my years fresh out of prison, I'd known self-discipline like any Olympian. I willed myself into a dangerous black-belted badass each day at the dojo. I swore off the booze, didn't touch a drug. I was rehabilitated. Learned my lessons in those thirteen months behind bars, bet your ass. I wasn't going to let a felony record or a disgraced family name hold me back. I was ineligible for a private investigator's license? Fine, who needed one? It was time to live my life on the other side. I would help those in need and find the things they'd lost. And I would be able to defend myself against anyone who stood in my way.

Sooner or later, the true nature reemerges, doesn't it? I could blame it on that bullet I took for Cass. Blame it on the painkillers I needed, really needed back then, to cloud the pain of my torn-up insides. I could blame it on bad genes and a need for drink that stretched back generations. I could blame it on my father. They would all be fair reasons, all with a different shade of truth, but the fact was I got sick of sobriety, of being the clear-headed wannabe superhero. I liked my gig as a finder, or pseudo PI, or whatever it was I wanted to call myself. But I found I could function just fine on the sauce. Made me more fearless. I even remembered the aikido from time to time, in moments of sudden violence.

But not this time.

This time I came to with a broken nose and a revolver pointed at my chest. Anna held it in her sturdy hands in the chair next to the couch. It did not shake. Standing above her was a man who appeared to be a carbon copy of the man I'd beaten, without the injuries. He was a big, ugly beast with features in grotesque proportions. He had the mangled cauliflower ears of a wrestler, a nose with the nostrils of a racehorse, and a wide mouth turned down over a heavy jaw. His fists were clenched at his sides. He raised them as I blinked open my eyes.

"Greetings, Mister Duck," said Anna. "Did we disturb you?"

"Anna, what are you . . ."

"This is my brother, Ivan," she said. "I believe you crossed paths earlier today, yes? Outside the home of this Mr. Kosta?"

"We never got a chance to chat," I said.

"Your timing was not so good, I'm afraid." She looked down at the gun in her hand. "I did not expect to have to kill you," she said. "But after what you did to Denis, you leave us with no choice."

"Is that your other brother?" I asked. "How's the back of his head doing?"

She translated this for Ivan. He responded by stepping past her and delivering a left hook to the side of my head. My ears rang out as I fell to my side and then slid off of the couch. I curled into a fetal position with my arms wrapped around my head. Ivan began kicking in my kidneys. Anna called him off before I could lose consciousness again.

"*Dostatochno!*" she cried.

Ivan's assault stopped, and he leaned down and picked me up by the neck and tossed me back on the couch. He slapped me once across the face with a meaty open hand before he stepped away and resumed his position behind his sister.

"We must kill you," said Anna. "But first we must make you suffer for what you did to poor Denis. This will take time, my lover. By morning you will be begging for death."

"Anna, why? Last night . . ."

"Why, why, why? What is this American obsession with why? You are all so desperate for answers. We were hired to look after you. That is all."

"By who?"

"It does not matter," she said. "We are paid to perform a service for someone, the same as you. As for our time together, you must understand that there are many means of distraction—through pleasure and pain, yes? Your lovely partner, I know she understands this, with her cute dungeon games? When you did not respond to pain, after that first beating, I tried pleasure. It was not bad, was it, the time we spent? But if I had known last night about Denis?" Now she stood from the chair, took one step, and towered over me. "I promise you, you American bastard, I would have killed you in your sleep." She spat down at me and swiped the butt of the gun against the side of my head.

Elvis howled out in protest from across the room. Ivan turned and rushed toward him and kicked my hound hard in the ribs. Elvis crashed against the wall, then tried to scamper away down the hall as Ivan stalked after him.

"*Eno!*" called Anna.

I heard more pained howling before Ivan returned to the living room with a smirk on his ugly face.

"Fucking cunt," I said. "You don't fuck with a man's dog."

Both laughed, exchanged some amused mocking in Russian. Ivan went to the kitchen and began opening drawers until he found what he needed. He emerged with two steak knives, one in each hand.

I considered my options. I could rush Ivan, maybe slow or stop his progress enough so that Anna was left with no choice but to shoot me. End it quick. Or I could dive at Anna, take a bullet, hope it missed the important parts, turn the gun on her, and then hope I had time to take on Ivan with his knives. The fact that I had a liter of whiskey and a few thousand milligrams of Vicodin in my belly did not better my odds.

Ivan raised both knives and scraped the blades together as he approached. He inhaled and exhaled through those gaping nostrils. His black eyes were dull and devoid of doubt.

"Back in Ukraine," said Anna, "Ivan studied to be doctor. He is very good with the knife, very skilled. You will see, Mister Duck."

I remembered James Fealy's sliced and severed body in the shower. Very skilled indeed. Anna leaned back in the chair, not lowering the gun, and settled in for a sadistic performance by her brother.

"Who hired you?" I asked again.

It was met with a grunt and another laugh, then the sound of a key turning in my lock. All heads turned toward the front door as Cass crossed the threshold. In that moment of distraction I dove toward Anna and caught one hand on her wrist and another on her throat. But not before she squeezed the trigger. The sound of a gunshot exploded through the room, and Cass's eyes went wide in pain and understanding. She dropped to her knees as a circle of blood spread across the stomach of her T. Rex T-shirt.

Ivan was on me with knives raised as I rolled beneath his sister and wrested the gun from her. I fired once point blank at him. The bullet ripped through his face with a spray of red mist. Down went Ivan, crashing through my coffee table as he fell for the final time.

Anna was writhing and hissing above me like a cornered cobra. She was a powerful woman. She flipped over and drove a knee into my crotch. In the same motion, she knocked the hot gun from my hand and lunged down and bit into my cheek. I tried to throw her off but failed. There was too much raging survival fight in this savage woman. I tried to reach up and hit her back, but couldn't get any momentum behind my blows. She opened her mouth and spit a chunk of my cheek from her bloody lips, then dove at me again for another bite. I might have taken care of her brothers, but I was losing this one. I was pinned down and being eaten alive, and I was running out of fight.

A third gunshot ended all that. Anna's body went limp above me, and she crumpled off onto her side.

I looked over to find Cass on her knees, bleeding from her stomach, holding the steaming gun.

Chapter 29

She was unconscious in my arms by the time the cops arrived. Gunshots are a rare sound in these parts. Once again I was sure there was no shortage of neighbors dialing 911 and reporting the danger that followed me. Police came pouring in with lots of bad noise, slipping through the blood. They spread out and addressed the bodies splayed around them on my floor. They confirmed the deaths of Anna and Ivan and found some life left in my partner. A faint pulse, no breath, their looks confirmed that her survival was doubtful. Ambulances roared down my block to join the brigade of NYPD. EMTs pushed past the officers and kneeled before Cass, strapped her to a gurney, placed the breathing mask over her pale face.

I looked in worse shape than I was. A ravaged face, ringing in the ears, half my ribs probably broken, but I had enough adrenaline pumping through me to feel sober and alert. I refused to leave the apartment until an emergency vet had been called for Elvis. His prognosis was not much better than Cass's.

On the way to the hospital, Cass flatlined. They zapped her three times, each more resigned than the last until her heart kick-started enough to offer some last strands of hope. We were separated as they wheeled us into the ER, memories no more than a blinding white light and voices, hurried, serious voices, all around us. I remember ranting, screaming about killing those evil bastards, begging them to save Cass, asking about Elvis: *"Is my dog okay? Somebody fucking talk to me!"*

I must have been sedated, because my next memory was waking in a hospital bed with my face swollen and stitched, my sides and stomach aching, and a needle plunged into the top of my hand. I hoped it was more than saline in that dripping bag above my head. Detective Lea Miller sat at my bedside, grim-faced and impatient.

"You're up," she said.

"Cass . . . is she . . . how is she?" I asked.

Miller looked down at her sensible shoes. "Still too early to tell," she said. "She's in surgery It's not looking good, Duck."

I stared up at the cracked ceiling, wanting more than anything to trade places with her.

"We need to talk," said Miller.

"Not now."

"Yes, now. You've had a hell of a week, Darley. Your body count is getting rather disturbing."

One week, four murders in my immediate presence. Killed one myself. Cass another, before Anna could kill me. Disturbing indeed.

"Elvis?" I asked. "Is he okay?"

"Looks like the King is gonna be fine," she said. "Some internal injuries, I'm told, but he'll live."

"Thanks for checking."

"Fellow dog lover," she said. "Have a mastiff at home. Name's Freddy."

"Guessing Freddy's had a better week than my guy."

She shrugged, managed a smile, and looked me in the eyes with something that looked like real warmth. Then the cop persona returned.

"Duck, the man you killed was on FBI watch lists. Ivan Lisko, and his brother Denis, entered the country illegally. They were known radicals back in Ukraine. Ivan had a long list of bad associations to his name. His younger brother Denis once beat a man to death with a tire iron outside a bar in Kiev. A few nights ago, Denis was beaten into a coma on a Williamsburg street. You know anything about that?"

"Nope."

"About the sister, Anna . . ."

"That bitch," I said. "If she killed Cass . . ."

"Your partner killed her, correct? Duck, I'm going to need you to walk me through what happened in your apartment."

I did the best I could. No sense holding back at this point. I took her through the last twenty-four hours of my cursed life. I told her about Kosta and the alleged black-mail; Fred Wright coming out of Kosta's place and being shot down in the street; asking Cass to run the plates and keeping that knowledge from the Brooklyn cops on the scene; returning home and getting aggressively shit-faced and unprepared for what was about to invade my home. I even told her about those girls on the subway. At the end of my recap, Miller continued taking notes as her hand caught up with my words. I rested my head back against the thin pillow and pressed the call button for a nurse. I intended to ask for more meds, the heaviest shit they had. A male nurse appeared in short order. He was a tall, thin black guy with a face of resigned realism.

"What's your name, buddy?" I asked.

He told me it was Clancy.

"Two questions for you, Clancy," I said. "When can I get out of here? And how much drugs can you give me to go? I'm thinking those super-sized Percs. I'm in a hell of a lot of pain, man."

"I'll have to check with the doctor," he said. "But I think we can get you out as soon as the officer here has finished questioning you, if that's all right with her."

Detective Miller looked up from her note pad, gave a quick nod, and continued her note taking.

"Not the first time you've had your nose broken, is it, Mr. Darley?" asked Clancy.

"Not the first or the last."

"That bite on your cheek is gonna take a while to heal. We had to put in twenty stitches. Gave you a tetanus shot. It was a hell of a gash, probably gonna leave a scar."

"Not my first one of those either," I said. "What do you think about those Percocet, Clancy? Maybe a few for the road before I get the script?"

"You need to be careful with those things," he said. "Has anyone discussed the dangers of painkillers with you?"

I thought all three of us were going to start laughing, thought someone must have put up good old Clancy to this gag. Turned out I was the only one laughing. Clancy shook his weary head and walked off. Miller set down her pen and looked up at me.

"This should be a wake-up call," she said. "It doesn't get much lower than this."

"There's always another circle," I said.

"Poor Duck," she said softly.

I didn't like the pity or the judgment, and I told her as much. I added that she must be one clueless cop if she thought this was as bad as it got. I asked her about Dealer Pete. Had he confessed to the murder of James Fealy yet? She absorbed my abuse until Clancy returned with some of those magic pink pills in a little cup. While I swallowed them down, Miller stood from my bedside and left without a word.

I knew no charges would be forthcoming. I'd killed a dangerous foreign national, on FBI watch lists, for Christ's sake. Don't they give out medals when you kill one of those fuckers? Besides, it was all in self-defense. My wounds were proof.

And Cass . . . Jesus, if I lost her. I couldn't bear the thought. I'm not a religious man. Got no time for that fear-mongering garbage. But this time I prayed. Don't know who I was praying to exactly, but I closed my eyes and prayed to whomever or whatever it is that decides such things. I prayed for Cass to pull through, and I offered myself in return. There for the taking, Big Man, feel free to cut me off whenever you see fit. Just allow Cass to walk out of this hospital and heal.

When a doctor finally appeared, he couldn't tell me much more about her condition. I should be prepared for the worst. Thanks, doc, I'll keep that in mind. After a lecture about the pills, he handed over my coveted script for Percocet and told me I was free to go after my IV was unplugged and I was all signed out. If Cass made it out of surgery, I could visit the ICU later in the day.

It was another gorgeous September afternoon as I left the hospital. Deep blue skies, and that special crisp scent of fall on the horizon, the city may feel unbearable at either extreme for most of the year, but there's that six-week window where New York City holds its own with the best weather on earth. We're the best at everything, at least some of the time. I breathed it in, paused for a moment of gratitude, then remembered Cass upstairs and cursed those too blue skies. The survivors of September 11th must feel the same way. God, what a beautiful day that was . . .

Miller was waiting in her unmarked black Crown Vic out front. Her partner, the sloppy, strap-on-loving Detective Sullivan, was in the driver's seat. She waved me over.

"Give you a lift?" she asked.

"No, thanks, I'll walk."

"Get in," growled Sullivan.

"Well, if Sully insists," I said.

I climbed in the back like a perp without handcuffs and winced as pain stabbed through my wounded parts. Those Percocet could kick in anytime they pleased. "Going to Seventeenth and Second, driver," I said.

"Your apartment's a crime scene, dumb fuck," said Sullivan. "We're taking you to a hotel."

"The Plaza? Thanks, Sully, that'd be great."

"Try the Holiday Inn," he said. "Twenty-sixth and Sixth."

Detective Miller turned in her seat to face me. "The Lisko brothers were on watch lists for a reason," she said. "They're dangerous. Do you have any idea who could have hired them?"

"*Were* dangerous," I said. "Past tense. And no. Isn't that your job?"

The partners ignored me as we swept past a row of greens down Second Avenue. Sullivan turned on his blinker as we approached 17th Street.

"I thought . . ."

"We need to stop by your place to pick up your passport," said Miller. "You're not to leave the city, understood?"

"I'm a flight risk?"

"You're an unstable man, witness to multiple murders, one by your own hand. Yes, you are a flight risk."

"Don't forget, I'm still on a job. I still haven't found the girl."

"You're advised to stay at the hotel until our investigation concludes and you're permitted to return home," said Miller. "We'll have officers downstairs in the lobby."

"We'll see where things take me," I said.

I watched the back of Sullivan's neck redden. His fat

hands gripped the steering wheel a little tighter. He turned on 17th and pulled to a stop in front of the Hotel Seventeen next door to my place.

"Why can't I just stay there?" I asked.

Sullivan turned off the ignition, rolled down his window, and lit a cigarette. Miller glanced back at me. "C'mon, Duck," she said. "You're allowed to stand in the doorway, but you are not to touch anything. Just tell me where to find your passport, and I'll navigate your apartment without upsetting the crime scene."

"Bedroom," I said. "In the nightstand, next to the condoms. You mind grabbing me a change of clothes and my wallet too? Oh, and my phone and charger? Should be on the kitchen counter."

She sighed and got out and I followed. Familiar nameless neighbors looked back at me with revulsion. I'd avoided mirrors and forgotten how I must appear, with both eyes bruised and a reset nose and a large bandage covering the bite out of my cheek. I wondered which one had called 911 first. I wondered if I was going to be evicted when I was finally allowed to move back in.

Miller nodded to a uniform standing watch and ducked under the yellow crime scene tape across my front stoop. Inside, my living room looked like a still from a horror movie set. The thick smell of death made my eyes tear. It's a hard scent to describe, but once it hits your nostrils, the sense memory places it forever. I'd become fast accustomed to it. It reminds one of old Parmesan cheese, with a choking pungency. Dried puddles of blood were all over the floor. My coffee table had been crushed by the weight of Ivan's falling bulk. The police outlines of Anna's and Ivan's dead bodies were traced in the floor. Miller slipped into a pair of latex shoe covers and moved carefully back to my bedroom. My passport was next to the condoms, as

I'd described. She carried a pair of my jeans, a black sweat-shirt, and my phone and wallet in her other hand.

On the way across town to the Chelsea Holiday Inn, she convinced Sullivan to let us stop at the vet on 19th and Park so I could check on my ailing hound.

"Thanks, Lea," I said from the backseat. "Appreciate it."

She stiffened at my use of her first name, but let it pass.

The attendant at the front desk had a lazy eye and a thick Queens accent. She took one look at me and knew whom I was there to see. "Come on back, sugar," she said. "Your boy's going to be okay."

I found Elvis asleep in a crate with his midsection wrapped in white bandages. The vet, a stooped and kindly old guy named Coleman, explained his internal injuries and stressed how lucky he was to be alive. He and his attendant stood behind me as I leaned down and opened the crate and reached in to rub my hound. He whimpered in reply and picked up his head in thanks. The vet assured me that they'd keep him safe and on the mend until everything was sorted out.

As I closed the crate, the attendant looked down at Elvis and said, "Whoever did that to your boy ought to be shot."

"Not to worry," I said. "I shot him in the face."

Chapter 30

My room at the Holiday Inn was bright and small and tacky, with a cheap orange headboard and matching orange side tables. The walls were an institutional beige, the curtains a styleless pattern of brown and blue and orange. It was a soulless room made for a suicide. Not for the first time, the notion had a certain appeal. But not for long.

I pulled the curtains, plugged in my phone. Then I turned off the lights and lay on the king-size bed without pulling back the covers. I hadn't eaten anything since yesterday's lunch, and the Percocet fog was settling thick. I closed my eyes and let it swallow me up.

When I woke, the darkness felt like dead of night, but the clock on the nightstand read 9:14 p.m. I called the hospital with doom in my gut, inquired about the status of Cassandra Kimball. Out of surgery, I was told, visiting hours were over, but she was still on this side of life. I exhaled and thanked whatever or whoever it is that decides such things. Skilled doctors or higher powers or just random goddamn life luck . . . Didn't care. I just looked forward to seeing her again.

I checked my messages, another mountain of voice mails from various media, desperate to talk to the city's walking messenger of death. Roy Perry had sent fourteen texts since he'd learned of the "Massacre on 17th Street," as the *Post* appeared to be calling it. There were messages from Margaret McKay, full of concern and sedatives, asking me to call her at the Rhinebeck number as soon as I was able. I pictured her searching the big house for signs of her daughter, tiptoeing into her girl's frozen bedroom and pondering the lost, forgotten years since.

Of note, there were no messages from Charlie. I wondered if he'd spoken to Marks and how that conversation had ended. But most of all, I wondered who in this ugly affair had hired Anna and her brothers to look after me.

I climbed from bed and limped to the bathroom, avoiding mirrors as much as possible. I popped a few more Percs and took a scalding shower, absorbed the pain as I considered the various players in this madness. Coach Marks and his sniveling former assistant, John Kosta; Anna Lisko and her thug brothers; poor Lucy Townes, still reeling from her attempt and her abusive relationship with Marks; I considered Margaret McKay, the mother superior at the center of it all. And then there was the protective big brother, convinced that his old coach, his father figure, his mother's lover, was screwing around with his sister. This was a man with the resources and the wherewithal to execute an airtight blackmail. And he would be a logical outlet for a damaged sister needing help with revenge.

When I was dry and dressed, I tried his cell, but it went straight to voice mail. I texted, asked when he'd like to meet and talk, tossed my phone on the mattress, and went to the small fridge beneath the television. Some minibar raiding was in order before any further steps could be contemplated. But when I opened its door all I found was an empty expanse of chilled white shelves. No bottles in this cheap room, nothing. Made for a suicide indeed.

Downstairs, an earnest young uniformed cop stood from a lobby chair as I walked from the elevator. He was blond and chubby, with a suspicious look in his watery blue eyes. I walked straight over. "I'm going to get a drink," I told him.

"You're not supposed to leave the hotel," he said. "If you'd like a bite to eat or something to drink, there's a restaurant right here." He motioned to the back of the lobby where a sign advertised an awful looking trap called the Prime Café.

"Am I under arrest?" I asked.

"No, but . . ."

"Then let me explain something: If I stay up in that room, I will kill myself. You'll find me hanging from the closet. If you try to prevent me from leaving this place, I will resist, with extreme force, and you'll either have to arrest me then or kill me in the struggle, probably the latter. Or you are welcome to tag along. How does that sound?"

I didn't wait for a reply, just walked out into a warm night and a crowded sidewalk full of blithe pedestrians enjoying the safe surfaces of a pleasant September evening. There was a stylish dark bar called the Black Door next to the hotel courtyard. I pushed inside and waved down a cute bartender. She recoiled at the sight of me. I glanced across at the high mirror above the bottles and forgave her. Not even the flattering flicker of the votive candles and the low-watt wall sconces could save me. I was a mangled mess of black eyes and misshapen features, a figure not fit for public display. I ordered a double Bulleit and a bottle of Stella, drained both in less time than it took her to make change.

There was a light crowd of locals, a drunken group of after-workers long past happy hour. I heard the whispers, noticed the troubled glances cast my way. I was given a wide berth. I couldn't imagine the vicious vibe I must have been giving off. The blonde on the bar stool next to me slid off and turned her back. When I called for refills, the bartender poured the whiskey from a long arm and a careful remove. The cop lingering outside the front door did not improve my game. I didn't care. I was in foul spirits, devolving with each sip of the amber.

As the whiskey went to work, I reflected on my murderous lover Anna and her twin brothers. One dead by my hand, the other beaten close to it. They'd been hired to look after me, to give me some warnings, to slow my pace. The assignment had turned to something more after I won that round with the bat-wielding brother Denis on that Williamsburg sidewalk. But who had employed them to begin with? *We are paid to perform a service*, Anna had told me. Her cavernous loft apartment, with its sparse personal belongings, indicated that she was being paid well. Only one guy came to mind.

Charlie had seen Marks make a pass at his sister. He'd seen something that convinced him of his coach's unseemly motives. He'd stood by as his mother lavished his family's fortune upon him, buying him that apartment, falling for him and taking him in as a replacement father. He knew what Marks was capable of. Like everyone in his orbit, he'd heard the rumors, seen the way he was with the girls on his team. I considered the resentment that must have built, bubbling in him for years. Marks may have coached him to gold, but at some point Charlie must have turned on his old master. The man had invaded his family from all fronts. The pass at Madeline would be too much to abide. Then, let's say his sister had approached her big rich brother and told him about Lucy. Demanded revenge. Charlie would act.

Had he hired Anna and her brothers to do his dirty work? Were they the inside muscle for Charlie's systematic destruction of his coach's sordid life? But then his sister disappeared. What had really happened between them when he saw her at the house in Rhinebeck? Something more than he was saying. I remembered the USB cable found discarded beneath her bedroom dresser. So Charlie had diverted his muscle in my direction, to keep an eye on me, to slow my search, but why? Did he know where she was?

I gulped at my whiskey, waved my empty glass in the bartender's direction. I was growing more surly with every sip. I'd be cut off soon, asked with all delicate discretion to take my business elsewhere. I tried to be polite as I ordered more refills. Another double Bulleit, another Stella, please, thanks so much. Yes, I had a bit of an accident, my apologies for my rather fearsome appearance. I don't mean to scare your customers. She served me, warily, and didn't respond. I drained it down, got my Irish up.

I was going to see that fucker, and he was going to start explaining. And I didn't want any cops trailing behind me. I pounded back my beer, fumbled for my wallet, waved my hand for the check. The bartender was quick to lay it out. I thought I felt the entire bar exhale at my pending departure. I'd rung up a hefty tab, quick. Seventy-five dollars in less than a half hour's drinking. They may not have liked my presence, but they should appreciate that kind of business. I laid a hundred-dollar bill on the bar, for their trouble, and lurched off in search of the bathrooms and another form of egress.

In the back, past the men's room, there was a private party room with another full bar. It was empty, aside from a young Mexican bar-back sweeping the floors. He was the first person to eye me with something like compassion.

"*Salida*?" I asked him.

He pointed toward the front door.

"No, *back salida*?" I asked again.

He stopped sweeping, gripped his broom for a moment. Then he pointed to the corner of the private room and stepped aside. I slammed through the back emergency exit and came out in a narrow alley. I turned left and stumbled west until I came to a sealed-off construction site a few doors down. I squeezed through the covered gates and raced past a crater in the earth a hundred feet wide. More progress ahead, more condos would rise up from this site in no time. I came out on West 27th, raced over to the corner of Seventh Avenue, and started waving. I got lucky. A lighted cab was just pulling through a green. It slid before me and I dove in, keeping my head low. Gave him the West Village address, didn't hazard a look back until we crossed 14th Street. No sign of NYPD behind us.

I had the cab let me off at the corner of Bedford and Seventh and walked the short block down to Leroy. It occurred to me for the first time that Madeline lived right around the corner, just a few blocks up on Barrow. Charlie's street was a short diagonal stretch of the Village with little foot traffic. I found 13 Leroy halfway down on the north side.

I was wrong about his house. Shouldering in alongside those classic Village homes, there are a few modern monstrosities, the ones with the sleek clean lines and tinted windows and a look-at-me pretension that now passed for "design." Charlie lived in one of those. It was a wide former carriage house covered in bright ivy across the front. No stoop or parlor windows, only a modern cedar door and a matching one-car garage wedged between the ivy. Above it was two more floors of oversize double-glazed windows and a roof garden visible on top. I pressed his buzzer passing judgment, outrage rising.

Charlie answered the door with a grand, phony smile. He wore khakis, an untucked blue button-down rolled up past thick forearms. His wide feet were bare. His thinning blond hair was combed straight back, frozen in place with plenty of product. He extended a big hand.

"Duck, Jesus, what's going on? I saw the news. You okay?"

"I look okay?" I asked.

"You look like shit," he said.

I shouldered inside, almost retched at his offensive taste. He shut the door without taking his eyes off me. The inside was worse than the exterior. I saw a floating staircase and modern art and no crown molding in sight.

"Can I get you a drink?" he asked. "Smells like you've already had a few."

"You're not checking your phone, are you? I called and texted."

"It died," he said. "Been charging. Sorry, man, what's up?"

"Bullshit," I said. "Finance tools like you check their phones every thirty seconds. Now why haven't I heard from you?"

I could feel my heart hammering in my throat, adrenaline pumping hard enough to break through the whiskey. More than any hit of cocaine ever could.

"I've been wanting to talk," he said.

That did it.

I stepped forward and shoved him hard in the chest. He staggered back a few steps, caught his balance against a banister. I kept coming, shoved him again, down onto the stairs, raised my fist.

"Duck! Wait!" he cried. "Wait!"

I took a step back, fist stayed cocked, every fiber on fire, ready for him to fight back. "Start talking, motherfucker," I said. "Start talking."

He pushed himself up, wiped a strand of frosted hair back into place. He pulled at his shirt, tried to gather his pride. Charlie was a large man, powerfully built in mind and body. He wasn't used to being pushed around. His ears grew hot as he considered his next move.

"What would you like to know?" he asked.

"Anna, her brothers, the blackmail," I said. "That was you, behind it all."

"I didn't ask for that," he pleaded. "Not what happened to you and your partner."

"You fuck," I said. I pushed him again. This time he was braced for it. He stiffened and absorbed my aggression, didn't budge.

"I was behind the blackmail," he said. "Okay? I admit that. Fucking Marks, the son of a bitch, he tried . . . He thought he could take anything he wanted. My mother, my money, my *sister*." His voice went up a hysterical octave as he said this last word. That was the straw.

"And Anna, her brothers?" I asked.

"Working for me," he said. "But I swear, I did not ask them to go that far. After what you did to their brother, they wouldn't listen. I tried to call them off. Anna and Ivan, they saw red, they said they were going to kill you."

"They failed," I said.

"They underestimated you," he said. "We all did."

"Why send them my way at all, Charlie? I was looking for your fucking sister. Why didn't you want me to find her?"

"Duck, there are things . . . If you'd just listen for a second, there are things I can explain."

"Try," I said.

As he sought the words, I heard the first faint thump. Then another, a little louder this time, coming from up the stairs. Charlie pretended not to hear it. His face fell for an instant. Then he turned and tried to lead me to the living room.

"Let me get you that drink," he said. "I swear everything will make sense."

Again, a thump, thump. Something upstairs, hitting a wall.

I stopped by the foot of the stairs. Charlie turned to face me, unable to deny the sound. Thump, thump . . . *Marks*, I thought. He has the fucker captive up there. Our eyes met, and Charlie came at me. Again, the aikido instinct returned, somehow. I caught him with a hip throw defense and brought him down to his polished hardwood floor, released his wrist, then drove my elbow down hard into his nose. Blood splashed, and Charlie cried out. I leapt over him as his hands went to his face and then charged up the stairs to find Marks. The thumping was harder now, louder as I got closer. It was a head banging against a headboard . . . behind the door at the end of the hall.

I raced toward the sound, flung open the bedroom door, and flipped on the lights. It wasn't Marks.

Madeline McKay was bound to a king-size bed. She wore a men's white oxford shirt that hung to her upper thighs. Her legs were bare and spread, tied to the bedposts by her ankles. Her wrists were fastened over her head and knotted to a brass bedframe. A red necktie was stretched in her mouth and tied around her head. She looked at me with wide-eyed terror, writhed against her captivity. I rushed to her. A hypodermic needle and several small vials rested on the nightstand. I pulled at her ties, yanked at the knots. Her eyes grew wider, pleading. Then she blinked rapidly and stared in horror over my shoulder.

I turned in time to see her brother rushing at me. I readied for his onslaught. Charlie stopped, raised a small black device in his right hand, and fired. Two electrical probes caught me in the neck. Fifty thousand volts coursed through me.

Down I went.

Chapter 31

I was wading in warm, waist-deep surf. Something big and dark brushed past my thigh. A fin broke the surface and disappeared again. A girl paddled by on a surfboard. I tried to call out to her but couldn't form words. She looked back at me, and she had the face of Madeline. A hard look was broken by an innocent smile. She turned back to the surf and started paddling and pushed her board down and dove under a rising wave. I tried to swim after her, but the wave broke, and I was swallowed by the churning white water.

When I surfaced, I gasped for air, sure that if I went under again I'd never come up. But I was somewhere else now, in a rain forest with steam rising from the green forest floor. Thick snakes dipped down from low branches, eyeing me, wondering if I was worth the struggle. Monkeys swooped and cackled above my head. Piercing calls of tropical birds filled the suffocating air. Again I saw Madeline up ahead. She was hiking fast through the bush, waving a machete to clear a path. I tried calling out again, and nothing came out. She did not turn around.

As I ran after her, the rain forest began to fall away until I found myself on a dark city street. I raced through the center, past honking cabs and swerving bikes, ignored the angry calls in my wake. I saw her up ahead, entering a courtyard of projects somewhere down by the East River. I looked down to find myself running over syringes and used condoms and broken vials and shattered bottles. Neglected babies wailed overhead. Madeline turned and waited and waved me inside a building.

The inside was lit only by the red glow of the emergency exit sign. There were bodies strewn across the floor, propped half up against the walls. Lighters sparked in the darkness, and the room filled with the sickly sweet smell of burning crack. Then coughing turned to laughter turned to silent bliss in the filth. I felt Madeline grab my hand. She pulled me into an elevator, and the doors closed and it began to descend. I felt us sinking, clinging to her damp hand, until a stinging splash of cold water brought me back.

I blinked back to reality to find myself strapped to a chair in another dark bedroom. I'd been stripped down to my boxers, my arms tied behind my back, my ankles fastened to the legs of the chair by surgical tubing. The room was lit only by streetlight, filtering through cracks in the blinds. Charlie stood before me holding a steel bucket at his side. His nose was swollen, misshapen. Blood crusted around the nostrils where I'd elbowed him. A large leather bag sat by his feet. He slapped me hard against my wet bandaged cheek.

"Wake up," he said. "Time to talk."

I felt a trickle down the inside of my arm and looked to see a thin rivulet of blood running from a puncture wound, where Charlie had injected me.

"Morphine," he said. "You needed to settle down."

"Nice dreams."

"You were far too worked up earlier. That was no way to behave in someone's home."

Across the dark room there was a mattress on the floor;

a body lay lifeless across it. Charlie followed my eyes. He went to a standing lamp by the bed and turned it on.

"That better?" he asked.

I wished he'd left it off. The room glowed with sick bright death. Marks was on the mattress. A gash had opened up his skull. His head rested in a halo of red.

"He came in here much like you," said Charlie. "Full of bluster, making demands, trying to push me around." He laughed at the dual memories. "Did you two really think you could push me around?" He came to me again and gave me another slap against the cheek. I felt Anna's bite wound open and begin to seep through the stitches. "Those were some fancy moves you pulled on me. What was that, judo? I do admit you're not as useless as I thought."

"You throw a hell of a party, Charlie," I said. "No one here gets out alive, is that it?"

He glanced over at Marks. "You should know me better than that by now. You know partying's never been my thing. I'm all about getting shit done, always have been."

"Is that what you've been doing here? Taking care of shit? What have you done to your sister, Charlie?"

He didn't reply. He turned off the light and strolled to the window. He opened a Venetian blind and peered out. He put his hands on his hips, chin held high, the same way he'd posed so many times atop so many podiums. Through the windows, the sounds of the city filtered up from the street: traffic and sidewalk voices, the faint sounds of someone playing "Gimme Shelter." Eight million lives out there in this naked city, and eight million ways to die. A line I'd always loved and now remembered like last words. And somewhere, in an expensive and tasteless home, there were two bound prisoners and one dead man, part of a horror I had failed to fully contemplate. I wondered how I had missed his madness.

Charlie stood before the window for some time, perhaps formulating his next move, some way to dispose of the mess he'd created. Finally he shook his head and walked back toward me. I watched as he knelt before his leather bag, unzipped it, and removed a slim laptop. He laid it aside with great care, then began to remove instruments of violence, one after the next. Blades and metals gleamed through the darkness. When the bag was emptied, he tossed it aside and stood and examined his collection with satisfaction.

"Cops know you're here?" he asked.

"Maybe."

"Maybe," he repeated. "Or maybe you lost them on the way over. You've never been too keen on the boys in blue, have you, buddy?" He glanced over his shoulder, back at the window. "I guess we'll see. Shouldn't be a big deal either way. I'll tell them you came by, drunk, which is true, and that you left sometime later. You're probably suffering from PTSD, your head's all messed up, especially with all that booze. Who knows where you might have staggered off to?"

"And Coach? Your sister? What are you going to say about them?"

He smiled, a cocky smile of complete confidence. "All in good time, my man. First, we should chat," he said. "I need to find out exactly how much you know or, more to the point, how much you've told anyone else." He looked down at his weapons. "These should help you tell the truth."

"I've got no reason to lie," I told him.

"We'll see," he said. "I would recommend against it. So, tell me, Duck, what do you think is going on here? I'd love to hear your thoughts."

"I thought Marks was the sick one," I said. "But turns out he's got nothing on you."

"You're partly right," he said. "The old man was a sick

bastard, and he got what was coming to him. It was long overdue, really. The blackmail was just the first step. I never expected . . ." He paused at a memory too painful to consider.

"She's your sister, Charlie."

"Oh Duck, she's much more than that."

"I can see that," I said.

"She is my love, the only thing in my life that has ever mattered to me. My gold medals, my millions, all meaningless. It's Madeline who moves my world. I would do anything for her."

"Is that why you have her strapped to your bed down the hall?"

"Exactly where she must be," he said. "She needed to slow down, she was out of control. She's always been so reckless, but she always comes around. She'll understand."

"Help me understand," I said.

His face darkened. He stepped forward and hit me with an open hand upside the head. "Don't patronize me, Duck. You can't understand. No one can. We've long since made our peace with that."

"We?"

"Madeline and I." He sighed. "Star-crossed as it comes, I'm afraid."

"Your sister is not at peace, Charlie. She's an addict, a broken soul. It was you that made her that way."

Charlie leaned back down and scanned his instruments. He chose an X-Acto knife, examined it; touched the sharp blade with the tip of his finger. Then he straightened up and stepped toward me with it hanging loose by his side.

"You know, I used to think I wanted to be a doctor," he said. "Before I found out that they didn't make shit. Ha. But the work always did fascinate me. Opening a body, administering drugs and cuts that can determine life or death. It really is like playing God. If there was one, that is. I guess doctors, some of them anyway, are about as close as it comes. But the lifestyle, alas, it wasn't for me. I needed to make real money. I always have been obsessed by the gold." He smiled at his own cleverness, his self-evident success. "But I never lost my fascination with medicine. I suppose I became a bit of a hobbyist."

"That how you won all those gold medals?" I asked. "Shooting yourself with dope?"

He smiled. A quick twitch of the head, a few rapid blinks of the eye—he lacked his mother's lifted poker face. He glanced over at Marks. "It would kill Coach if he ever found out," he said.

"No more secrets in this room," I said.

Charlie raised the knife and pointed the sharp tip a centimeter from my left eye. He turned his wrist, considered the angle of entry. One thrust forward and my eyeball would be a blinded exploded membrane. After a long, sick moment he lowered it an inch. Before I could exhale, he pressed forward with the blade. It broke skin high on my cheek. He traced a path down the right side of my face to the corner of my mouth. Now both sides were disfigured—one by bites, the other more surgically. He examined his incision, the blood clinging to the razor.

"Not bad," he said. "Not bad at all. I could have been a plastic surgeon. Would have saved Mom a bunch of money." He laughed, reached out and carved another quick parallel line down my face.

I felt little pain. The morphine must have still been working its magic. I tasted blood seeping into the corner of my mouth, a metallic, almost comforting taste. Charlie watched it drip with a detached excitement like a boy in the woods happening upon an animal carcass. It seemed to thrill him. He turned and set down the X-Acto precisely where he'd found it. Then he selected a new toy, this time a telescoping black baton. With a flick of his wrist the baton shot out to full size. He waved it in slow crosses like a blunt sword between us.

"I suppose there is a certain kismet to your presence here in the end," he said. "My first rival, and my last, in a sense. I'll admit, Duck, as difficult as you've been, I do admire your hardheadedness. You're tougher than I imagined, maybe a bit smarter too." He tapped the baton in the palm of his hand, nodded with a certain demented respect. "Those barbarian Lisko brothers certainly underestimated you, didn't they? Ha. Well played there, Darley, I must say. As for Anna, she was the brains of that clan, wasn't she? And a hell of a lay, wouldn't you agree?"

He strolled toward me like a ballplayer approaching the batter's box, all swagger and big stick confidence. "Just think," he said. "If you'd been a little softer, you might have survived all this."

He stiffened in his stance, eyed my knee like a fat hanging curveball.

"Duck, are you aware of my sister's performances online?"

"Fallen Angels," I said. "Cass found them."

With a quick step forward, he unleashed a home run swing that connected with a bone-crunching crack. I cried out, tried to stifle the pain. The morphine couldn't help much with that.

"I don't believe you," he said. "Are you sure you didn't find them some other way?"

"You mean jerking off? No, Charlie. How about you, is that how you discovered your sister doing porn?"

Charlie resumed his baseball stance, this time in front of the other knee.

"It is, isn't it?" I asked.

He replied with a wild swing of the baton. It missed the knee mark, but connected with my left shin. There was the sharp sound of bone breaking. I gasped, felt the tears intermingling with the blood on my face. He leaned in close. "You have no idea how that felt," he said. "No idea. To find your own sister, like that, at that moment."

"Bet it happens all the time," I wheezed. "To plenty of guys, all worked up, and then there's sis or mom."

I was beginning to wish for quick death, wondered how much I needed to provoke him for Charlie to finish me off. "I'll bet it turned you on even more," I said.

"You want me to kill you right now?" he shouted. "Is that what you'd like?"

"Yes," I answered truthfully.

He jabbed me in the stomach with the baton, then flung it across the room. "Oh, you'll get your wish," he said. "When I'm through with you."

Charlie went to the laptop lying next to his instruments. He raised the screen and sat before it and typed with concentration. What he saw seemed to bring physical pain. His jaw clenched, his hands shook over the keyboard. Then he stood and presented me with the screen.

"I want you to watch something," he said. "Please tell me what you see. And do not spare details. I would like to hear them."

He clicked the play button on a video and maximized the window. An image of Marks's poolside office glowed on the full screen. Marks sat at his desk, facing out, with an excited, smug smile spread beneath his mustache. His legs were open in a wide stance; there was a visible bulge beneath his khaki shorts. Madeline walked into the frame wearing only a racing suit. Her legs were long and toned, and she stood with the posture of a woman in touch with her carnal side. She turned and glanced at the camera, a wicked smile playing on her lips. Her lips, those wide, fishy lips . . . I remembered her previous videos. Madeline turned back to her coach and positioned his chair to face her. She peeled her suit slowly off of her shoulders and down her body. Then she sank to her knees before Marks.

"Duck," said Charlie. "I asked you to describe what you see. Please don't be shy."

I shook my head, watched as Marks's shorts were undone and dropped to his ankles. Watched as Madeline stroked him. The laptop shook in Charlie's hands as he looked down and watched her inhale. Her head began to move up and down between his legs.

"What is she doing, Duck?" asked Charlie, trembling. "I can't hear you."

"She's blowing him," I said. "You were right, Charlie."

"No!" he shouted suddenly. He slammed the laptop shut and flung it like a titanium Frisbee in Marks's direction. It struck his lifeless body and crashed to the floor. "No. What she is doing is killing him. She is guaranteeing his death."

"Where did you find that?" I asked.

He pointed toward the offending laptop, shouted, "That was *her* computer! She filmed it—in secret. She wanted me to see it. The slut, how could she do this to me?"

I thought he was going to break down, but he channeled his anguish back to anger in a hurry. "She said it was for revenge," he seethed.

"For Lucy."

Charlie glared at me. "How did you know that?"

"She told us," I said. "After she was released from the hospital, Lucy sought out my partner. She said your sister promised her that she'd get revenge for what Marks did to her."

"Did to Lucy?"

"That's who he was screwing, Charlie. Not your sister. Not until she decided to make that thing. My guess is, she was planning to ruin him with it."

For once it appeared I had the upper hand on the intel. I

decided to push it. "You poor fuck, you thought she did that to hurt you, didn't you?"

The comment seemed to deflate him. "That's why Lucy tried to kill herself last week, isn't it?" he asked.

"What do you think?"

He looked over at Marks, gave a sudden mad laugh. "I think I helped her out on that score. Ruined, he is!"

"It was at the house in Rhinebeck, wasn't it, Charlie?" I asked. "That's where you saw it. She showed it to you, didn't she? I found the cord."

He gave a slight nod, lost as he pieced together his sister's motives. He returned to the window, stared out, and began to speak in a quieter voice.

"She was up in her bedroom," he said. "I didn't knock. I was thrilled to see my girl. I'll never forget the look she gave me. That sick smile. She was so high, so far gone. It looked like she hadn't slept in days. She was sitting cross-legged on her bed in front of her laptop. It was attached to a camera, like a Go Pro but smaller, some kind of spy gear. I heard moans coming from it, in a familiar voice. She turned it around for me to see. I thought it was more of her porn videos, more of that Fallen Angels filth. Then I saw who it was. I tried to grab it from her. We fought. I managed to steal the computer and camera away from her. The cord must have been flung away in the struggle. I wondered where it went. She ran off, laughing like a crazy person. I didn't go after her; I couldn't move. When I heard the front door open and shut, I reopened the laptop and took a closer look. I wanted to die. I swear, I almost killed myself right there."

"You should have," I said.

He was past the point of provocation. He ignored the bait.

"The camera had a sticker on the side—it read 'property of Scion Productions.' "

"Fealy."

"That little fuck must have helped her with it. Who knows what else she told him."

"Which meant he had to die," I said.

Charlie nodded like I was a co-conspirator, finally getting on the same page. "Had to," he said. "I had no choice, right?"

"They were broken up," I told him. "He probably had no idea she took it. She had keys to his place. She must have grabbed it when he was out east."

Charlie shrugged. "It doesn't matter," he said. "It was just a matter of time before I had to kill that punk. Madeline must have known it too. I don't know what she expected me to do."

The righteous ravings of the mad; what can one say? He was looking for communion, some understanding for his hand being forced to inevitable evil. I couldn't play along.

"So," I said, "what's next? How are you gonna dispose of Marks and me? What do you plan on doing with your sister in there?"

Charlie exhaled heavily. "I'll figure it out," he muttered. "I always do."

He returned to his collection of toys and knelt down before them, rummaging through the blades and the hard metals, searching for something specific. "Here we are," he said, holding up a pair of bolt cutters. Then he felt around inside his bag and pulled out a red ball gag. "Can't have you crying too loud about the pain, can we?" he asked.

I realized with an awful clarity what the bolt cutters were for. He stepped toward me with the smirk of a serial killer. He was almost giddy with anticipation. First he fastened the leather straps of the gag around the back of my head and forced the red ball between my lips. He pulled it tight and slapped the back of my head. I sucked in air through my nose, panicking with the loss of oral freedom. "I always wanted to try this," he said. "I hear it's insanely painful." Charlie got down on one knee in front of me. I shut my eyes, waited for the worst. I felt the blades of the bolt cutters latch around my Achilles. Then, with a grunt, Charlie pressed them together and snapped the tendon in two.

I was screaming into the gag as he gathered the rest of his gear and left the room.

Chapter 32

He left me there the rest of the night. The pain came from a circle of hell beyond Dante. At some point my mind became detached from my body, and I began to regard the scene from a distance. It was as if I was watching the horror from above, already dead and hovering in a disturbed purgatory. My mind zoomed down and peered over the carnage like a Google Map's satellite image.

I shut my eyes. Sleep was an impossible notion. I longed for rivers of whiskey and fountains of pills, anything to sink me into a state of bearable oblivion. Time began to pass. The darkness began to lighten. First blue light fell through the blinds. Outside, the sound of sirens gave me a jolt of false hope. They faded fast.

I looked down at my stripped and shattered body and considered how many bones had been broken. I tried to shift my chair toward the window. The pain from my severed Achilles shot up my leg into my gut like fire. I bit down on the gag, dragged myself another inch. I thought I would pass out from the pain. Kept going. When I reached the window I pressed my forehead against the edge of the blind and pushed it aside until I could see through the glass. Slow moving men and women walked their dogs on the sidewalks below. A garbage truck crept down the block as disinterested garbagemen tossed bag after bag into the back. Across the way I could see lights coming on in adjacent apartments, but no one near the windows. I reared my head back and began slamming it into the glass.

As if he'd been waiting for that cue all along, Charlie opened the door and stepped into the room. He set down his bag and leaned easily against the far wall. His blond hair glistened with new product; he looked rested and freshly showered, in another pair of pressed khakis, a starched white oxford shirt. "You're up," he said pleasantly. "Have a nice rest?"

I searched out the window but no one looked up. He came to me and grabbed the back of the chair and flipped it over. I went down. Hit the back of my head against the floor. Looked up at him. He glowered down at me, eyes ablaze, kicked me in the stomach with a leather loafer. Then he reached down and dragged the chair across the room. He propped it back up next to the mattress. Marks stared back at me with dead, bloodless eyes as Charlie undid the leather straps behind my head and freed me of the gag. I gasped, sucked in air. My jaw ached; my mouth was dry as a desert.

"What am I gonna do with you two?" he asked. "What am I supposed to tell my mother? I suppose with Marks here, once that video gets out, everyone will think he took off and tried to escape the scandal. It's gonna break her heart." He knelt before him and looked into his face. Charlie sighed. "It didn't have to be like this," he said. "Not for either of you."

He walked over to the window, drew up the blinds, and stared down onto the Village streets. The morning light brightened the room, filled it with dark truth. "This used to be a carriage house," he said. "Back in the nineteenth century, built around the time of the Civil War. This neighborhood has seen every level of New Yorker since then, from poor-ass immigrants to worthless junkies to middle class families, and now, filled with folks like me—ones with real money. Back in the seventies, you could have gotten this place for fifty grand. I bought it for fourteen million—and now that's a steal. I could unload it tomorrow for twenty." He glanced back at me, then over to Marks. "After all this is over, I probably will. There's an old boiler in the basement, thought I'd feed you two in there. Your ghosts can haunt the next owners."

"What about Madeline?" I asked.

"Glad you asked," he said. "Why don't we ask her?"

He came to me, tilted the chair forward, and I went back down to the hardwood floor. I felt the cuts in my face open, tasted more blood in my mouth. "Sit tight," he growled. "Be back in a sec."

Lying on my side, I watched him leave the room, saw a light turn on down the hall, heard another door open. There were grunts and unintelligible curses as Charlie retrieved his sister. I searched the room with bleary eyes, thought about crying out, if only to provoke faster death. I don't know why, but I kept quiet. It wasn't survival instinct. I think I just wanted to hear what he planned to do next, with Madeline.

She was pushed into the room soon enough. Charlie had wrapped her in a plush white robe. Her arms were tied behind her back, and he guided her by the wrists with an impatient hand. Her eyelids fluttered heavily, drugged. She staggered, shuffled her feet, perhaps the first time she'd been upright in days. She looked to me in confusion, then over to Marks. Her body tensed; she stopped moving. Charlie pulled her close against him.

"More blood on your hands, sis," he said.

Madeline didn't react. Maybe she had lost the capacity,

or maybe she was doped to the gills, too high to register reality over nightmare. He pushed her down at the foot of the mattress. She sat, looked over at me.

"Who's that?" she slurred.

Charlie came over and straightened up my chair once again. My broken bones burned and cried out at the rough movement. He slapped the back of my head. "Lady asked you a question," he said.

"My name is Duck," I told her. "Your mom asked me to find you."

"My mom?" she asked.

"She's worried about you."

Madeline made a face, looked up at her brother looming by her side. "Don't worry," he said. "She doesn't know."

"Yes, she does," I said.

The siblings looked to me together, rage in one set of eyes, shame in the other.

"He's lying," said Charlie. "I spoke to her last night. She's as clueless as ever."

Madeline sagged. I couldn't be sure how much she was registering. Her eyes were more shut than open, and she swayed on the edge of consciousness. Something was getting through, but it wasn't much.

"Tell me about James Fealy," I said to her brother. "Tell me how you killed him."

She blinked, eyelids raised as she fought for more clarity. Charlie took the bait.

"With a knife." He smirked. "In the shower. Would you like to share the rest, Duck? You witnessed my handiwork, after all."

"When was it? The day your sister disappeared? After she went to his place and tried to warn him?"

He glanced at Madeline. "Ah, Duck, are we really going to do this? My sister is in a fragile mental state at the moment. Do we really want to subject her to such dirty details?"

"You tell me," I said.

He gave it a second's thought. "Very well, I suppose you're right. Time for our girl to hear the naked truth, isn't it?" He rubbed at Madeline's back. She gave a shuddered reply, tried to inch away from him. He wrapped an arm around her shoulder, pulled her back close. "It had to be done. You know that, right?" he asked her. "I'm sure you told him things you shouldn't have. And he helped you make that fateful video, after all. Of you and this sick bastard." Charlie motioned to Marks, then spat over his body. He turned to me.

"She came to me," he said. "The night after our altercation upstate. She had sobered up a bit, and she begged me to have mercy. She knew what I needed to do. Didn't you, sis?" Madeline tensed in his grasp; Charlie squeezed her tighter. "I couldn't grant her request, of course. That Fealy boy had to go. I paid him a visit the next day, after Madeline here became my guest at the house." He turned and gave her a lingering, nauseating kiss on the cheek. "Tied up and good drugs—a few of her favorite things. I do hope you've enjoyed your stay."

I averted my eyes, felt a sickness in my stomach worse than the physical pain. "The cameras," I said. "In the lobby of his building. How did you manage to turn them off?"

Charlie beamed, proud of himself. "Nice of you to notice," he said. "I am a man of many talents, aren't I? Programming and hacking, it's what got me into trading in the first place. It comes down to the same thing—how to stay a step ahead of everyone else. While my brain-dead teammates were playing video games between practices, I was teaching myself to code, learning how to break into systems. This was nothing. For a nice building, you'd think they'd try a little harder with their security, but everyone's still so clueless. I just used this program, Metasploit. It was simple. I scrambled their CCTV systems for a few hours while I went by and waited for Fealy. When he arrived home, I followed him inside and let myself in with Madeline's set of keys. It was just an extra treat that I found him in the shower. It was even easier than I expected. Then I went home and restarted their cameras, and then I got lucky again when they found that dealer's prints all over the place. I do believe they have him in custody, isn't that right? It's true what they say: the harder you work, the luckier you get. I've proven that my whole life."

I remembered coming upon Fealy's naked, slashed corpse in the pool of blood in the shower. Charlie had enjoyed himself. It had been a sort of peak performance, akin in his mind to his gold medal swims or his big days in the markets.

"You're a sick fuck," I said.

My father had once been fond of the old maxim that you should never trust a man who doesn't drink. The man knew how to bend an elbow and had contempt for anyone who didn't. I hadn't learned much from him, and clearly I had failed to heed this lesson. A man afraid of alcohol is a man afraid of himself. Afraid of losing control of the demons that lurk, bubbling barely contained, beneath the surface. Even now, with his madness exposed without apology, Charlie possessed the air of clear-headed control. Another challenge faced and overcome with a bloodless resolve.

"Hardly," he said. "Do you remember what my boss, Danny Soto, told you? You're just not cut from our cloth." He looked back to Marks on the mattress. "Coach may have dug his own grave, but the man does deserve some credit. He taught me what a champion truly was. What were you, like thirteen when you left the team?"

I nodded.

"Yeah, so you quit before things even got started. All that age group stuff—that was just pussy shit. Anybody can be fast at ten or twelve, just takes some size and a bit of ability. But then the real athletes start coming on around high school, and we just trash by all those pretenders who used to beat us when we were kids." He smiled at the memory, the tables-turned triumph. "I always hated you, Duck. We were friends, but I fucking hated you. You and your dad, a couple of big-talking frauds; even as a kid, I noticed that much. And I was right, you know? That's the nice thing about sports and money, the thing I love about both pursuits: sooner or later, the champions emerge, the ones who want it most. The ones who are willing to do whatever it takes."

"Whatever it takes," I repeated. "You've got that part down."

"Damn right," he said. "Anyway, as for Fealy, that kid's death led to getting a dealer off the streets, a dealer who dealt to high school and college kids. Happy ending there— two bad birds with one sharp stone. Net net, the world is a better place without them."

"How about Patrick Bell?" I asked. "Is the world a better place without him too?"

The sound of the name gave a jolt of clarity to Madeline. She glared at her brother with confusion and hate in her hazy eyes. She opened her mouth to speak; no words came out. Charlie gave a sick smile.

"Poor boy." He sighed. "He had a deathly allergy to nuts, right, sis?"

She looked back to him, trembling at the scarred memory.

"You always thought it was your little kiss that did it, didn't you?" he asked her. "No, it wasn't that. I suppose it's time you heard the truth. It wasn't you. I had to take care of that boy. It was so simple, just a few drops of peanut oil in his smoothie. Do you remember those smoothies I brought out to you by the pool? To the cute young couple?" Charlie seized at the memory. The murderous instinct seemed to rush up through his body, darkening his skin with coursing black blood. "How could you blame me?" he asked her. "We had only just begun. And then you betrayed me. With that, that little boy?"

He released his grip and shoved Madeline away. She tensed, refused to go down. She stared up at him with a purity of hate. The drug clouds behind her eyes seemed to clear like a passing storm. Her face looked worn and aged, the youth shed too soon, left only with the disregarded pieces of beauty. The high cheekbones, the heavy lidded eyes, those wide, fishy lips—accessories ready to be stripped and sold for parts. Silent tears slid down that beautiful, wrecked face. She tried to blink them away, didn't take her eyes off of her brother.

He did not appreciate the sight of her tears. "Now you're crying?" he shouted. "Don't tell me you're surprised! After the ways you've betrayed me? Tortured me by acting like a whore, on camera, for the world to see? What did you expect?"

She opened her mouth. Again, no words could rise.

"What now, Charlie?" I asked.

He swung around to me, eyes burning beyond rage. He moved to his bag, knelt and reached in, and brought out a butcher's knife. Charlie waved it before me. "Now, how about I cut your throat?" he asked.

"And Madeline, you plan on cutting hers too?" I asked. "The love of your life, the one who means more than all your medals and millions? The one you've killed for?"

"That's up to her," he said. "That will be up to my sister."

He walked to her now, stood over her with shoulders shaking. "What do you say, sis? Are we even?" I thought he might even reach out a hand in reconciliation. Instead I watched as Charlie pressed the sharp edge of the knife into the palm of his hand. He looked down at it until it broke skin, flinched slightly, and raised the blade. He wiped his bleeding palm against his face, leaving a red streak from his ear to his jaw. Madness had overtaken him completely. For so long he had held it at bay. Through Olympic triumphs and financial fortunes, through a public life as a shining example of our success-worshipping city: a place where anything was possible, if you had the will and the talent and maybe a few bucks behind you. But now the waters had parted to reveal the abyss below.

Madeline looked up at him. Her face may even have softened. She tried to smile.

"I knew you'd understand," he said. "I knew you'd come around. Sometimes it takes a while, doesn't it?" He reached out and petted her cheek with his bleeding palm. She started to recoil, then forced herself to lean into it.

"Last night, before I came to bed, I realized we couldn't continue here in this city. Too much has happened, there is just too much that puts us at risk." He motioned toward Marks, then back at me. "I'm sure we could dispose of these gentlemen without much trouble, but we don't need more questions, do we? It pains me to leave, but there comes a point where we must move on. I suppose we always knew this day would come, didn't we?"

Madeline nodded, her expression unchanged.

"That's my girl," he said. "Don't worry, I've taken care of everything. This evening, I've booked us a flight to Caracas, first class out of JFK. I have our passports packed, a few bags ready to go. We won't need much; we'll buy whatever we need when we get there."

"Inspired choice," I said. "Hard to extradite murderers from Venezuela."

"Just a starting point," he said. "Thought we'd make our way down through South America."

"You've got it all figured out. Suppose you've got a load of cash stashed there too?"

"Of course, Duck. One of the first things Danny Soto taught us: the minute you make real money, move some of it somewhere safe, somewhere untouchable. You never know. Danny owns like half of New Zealand, says it's the only piece of his fortune that he trusts. I moved some of mine to the Caribbean, where it's anonymous and will be easy to access, especially from down there. Time you saw more of the world, sis. I know how you feel about travel, but I'm confident you'll overcome your fears in time."

"You'll protect her, won't you, Charlie?"

He stepped toward me in a flash of anger, the bloody knife pointed at my neck. "Watch your tone," he said. "That's exactly what I'll do." The knife tip pressed into my neck until I felt the skin opening. Convinced it was my last moment, I thought of my father seated in his prison cell, thought of my mother drowned in the bathtub, thought of Cass, and hoped to see her on the other side.

"No," she said.

Charlie released the pressure and lowered the blade. "Excuse me?" he asked, turning.

"I'm not going with you," said Madeline.

Her brother pressed the blade of the knife once again into his palm. He trembled before her. Blood dripped at his feet. "I would consider very carefully what you are saying," he told her.

"I'm not coming with you, Charlie," she said, cold and calm. "I understand what that means. You can kill me. I should have done it myself years ago."

"Madeline," I said. "Wait."

For what? Hell, I don't know. For her brother to kill me first, so I didn't have to witness that final horror.

"Do me first," I heard myself say.

Charlie turned and raised the knife. His eyes had that hollow look of a man programmed to execute on command, a look devoid of self-doubt. I recognized that look. It was the same impenetrable mask that he wore behind the starting blocks of all his races. He drew the blade back, his eyes alight. I closed mine and accepted my fate.

I opened them to a wail of hate that will forever scar the memory. Madeline launched herself at her brother, head down, arms bound behind her back. The crown of her head connected with Charlie's chest and sent him falling backward into me. He thrashed at the air with the knife as the three of us went sprawling to the floor.

Madeline was on top of him, and without the use of her arms, she fought with the only weapons at her disposal. She kneed him in fury between the legs, flung her head back and brought it down in a driving head butt. Their foreheads connected with a loud crack. As Madeline raised her head once more, Charlie managed to lift his arm.

The knife hovered above them, the metal shining in the new morning light. As Charlie drove it down, I threw my body into its path. The blade broke flesh just below my shoulder. He brought it out and stabbed down again as his sister continued her frenzied assault. I felt a cold sensation rushing through me, blood flowing from my body from multiple points.

Madeline let out another wail and delivered another strike of her head. The fight went out of Charlie, and his body went limp, the knife still embedded in my body.

Chapter 33

Madeline rolled onto her back and lay panting beside her brother for some time. I felt myself drifting toward death, knew that a loss of consciousness meant end of life. I forced my eyes to stay open. I called over to her. She looked at me in a daze.

"The knife," I gasped. "Help."

She managed to sit up, scooted toward me, her wrists still bound. She pressed her back against my chest and felt around blind for the blade. Her hands finally found it. I cried out as she yanked it up, felt more blood burst through the wound. Then she maneuvered it upside down and tried to cut herself free. She missed, slashed herself across the hands, her forearms. She never flinched. Continued pressing herself against the blade until it found her ties and sliced through the binds. Madeline slumped forward, picked up the knife.

She looked at her brother knocked out beside her, looked at Marks dead across the room. She held the knife before her eyes; then turned it with the tip facing her heart.

"Madeline," I whispered. "Don't. You're free."

She glanced at me, knife still positioned one thrust from suicide. It stayed there as she considered my words. Then, slowly, it began to lower. The body between us began to stir. I was too weakened to react. I didn't think Madeline registered the movement. I tried to warn her, felt consciousness slipping away.

Charlie gave a roar and leapt at her, alive and murderous. Madeline turned to him, and their eyes met. The years of abuse and unholy union passed between them. Then she drove the knife into Charlie's throat. Blood sprayed from his neck across her face as his jugular was severed. She kept pressing it in until his eyes went wide in final truth.

I passed out soon after. I wish I could say I saw my entire troubled life flash before my eyes. I wish I could report that I saw some kind of light. No such luck. All I felt was relief.

When I woke, under too-bright hospital lights, in a full house of pain, I can't say I felt lucky to be alive. I hated that cliché as much as Lucy must have, as much as any damaged soul who's felt the pull toward the final silence. A small army of cops and docs soon surrounded my bedside, asking too many questions, delivering the litany of injuries. More scars, more stitches, more reasons for nice, fat pills that killed the pain. I was told to expect a limp for life, or at least a few years if I took my rehab seriously.

I was swooning in an opiate haze, trying to white-out memory, when I had a visitor. I thought I must be dreaming. There she was, seated in a wheelchair before my bed. A young nurse averted her eyes and left us in private.

"You look like shit, cowboy," Cass said.

"She's alive."

Cass nodded, wheeled closer to my bedside. She leaned forward and touched my cheek. "Poor Duck," she said. "How bad was it?"

I didn't have to answer, just looked back into her bottomless black eyes and held her gaze. She nodded, understanding. "I'm sorry," she whispered.

"Guess we're even," I said.

She glanced down at her wounds, covered by the flimsy hospital gown. Somehow she pulled it off, still looked gorgeous. Cass shook her head.

"It was never about that," she said.

"Sure, it was. And now the debt has been cleared."

"I'm too selfish for it to be that simple," she said. "I never felt like I owed you anything."

"Then why . . ."

"Same reason I go to the dungeon. I was drawn to the darkness."

"Careful what you wish for," I said, waving an IV'd hand around the small room. "What else would you like to know?"

"Charlie and Madeline?"

"He'd been abusing her since she was twelve years old. Killed anyone who got in the way. Starting with her first boyfriend, six years ago."

"His own sister."

"Sick as they come."

"Jesus," whispered Cass.

"Madeline got her revenge, as she promised Lucy. She filmed herself blowing Marks. Charlie saw the video—at their last meeting upstate. Turned out he'd been blackmailing him already, for sins real and imagined. The video just guaranteed his death."

"And Anna, her brothers?"

"Enlisted to help in the cause," I said. "They didn't like what I did to brother Denis on that Williamsburg sidewalk."

"I knew you went too far," she said.

"I always do."

We let that linger between us. Then I asked, "When do you think they'll let us out of here? I gotta see how Elvis is doing."

Cass looked out the window, avoided my eyes. She tilted her head in sorrow as a bright glow of sunlight shined against her high cheeks. "I can't do this anymore," she said. "I think I'm done."

"With what?"

"All of this: the city, the dungeon, playing the sidekick detective, everything. I need to go away for a while. I need to find some balance, some light against the darkness. There's a Buddhist retreat, upstate near Woodstock, I think I need . . ."

"Marry me."

She smiled. A little. "Don't ask for things you can't take," she said.

"I can take it. Look at me. Is this not a guy who can take a beating?" I motioned to the masochistic evidence across my body.

"Poor Duck," she said. She reached out and touched my temple, let it linger, traced a finger down my face. She removed it before it could reach my lips, before my heart could beat any harder. "You'll never understand, will you?"

"I understand that the facts never make sense."

"Sense is another universe," she said.

"Don't leave."

She squeezed my hand. "Please try to take better care of yourself," she said. Then she turned the wheelchair and rolled herself away.

Detectives Miller and Sullivan stopped by and questioned me sometime later. Sully managed to treat me without contempt. Over an eight-day span, I had been directly linked to six deaths, witnessed every body up close. Now that they were able to identify the killer in each one, they'd lost that cop edge. They seemed almost human. Miller and I even made a tentative playdate for our dogs to meet in the Union Square dog run.

I'd made another appearance on the cover of the *Post*. They were calling me "Death Darley" now. I sent a text to Roy Perry, telling him that his exclusive would have to wait.

While the slow healing process began, they went to work on my broken mind. I was diagnosed with post-traumatic stress disorder by a well-meaning shrink who treated me like an Iraq war veteran past the point of redemption. I was informed that my apartment was no longer a crime scene. A company called Gotham Trauma Services had been hired to scrub the floors clean of blood, brain tissue, and assorted human debris. I'd need a new couch, rug, and coffee table. I was told that the city's Office of Victim Services covered $2,500 of the cleanup cost, but that Gotham had charged $7,500 for a particularly messy job. The other five grand was on me. Maybe I'd pass the bill on to Margaret McKay.

Eventually they let me out of there. On my way home, I picked up Elvis at the vet's and limped by the liquor store without looking. I wasn't sure how long I'd manage. There were no grand resolutions haunting my battered head. I didn't believe in "rock bottom" or any of the wake-up call platitudes served up by the suffering souls in AA. I'd gone deep enough to know that there was no such thing as the bottom. But I also knew it was time I took a look at my passions for dissipation.

When I reached my place, I intended to hunker in, order delivery for every meal, deny my thirst, and avoid the world for as long as possible. But home had lost its charm. The living room reeked of disinfectant. Every dish and glass was sitting out on the kitchen counter, scrubbed clean of blood splatters. The only unsoiled piece of furniture was the club chair that was always reserved for Cass. It didn't feel right to sit in it.

So Elvis and I settled out in the garden with a stack of books full of blood and suffering. The September sun was a lost memory, and the city was showing its true cold colors. Heavy clouds gathered overhead, and the last leaves blew from the trees. The garden was nothing but shadows, with no false hope. I opened a book by James Ellroy. He seemed to know a bit about dark places. I sipped at tasteless seltzer water and waited to hear from Margaret McKay.

I sat out there each day until I could no longer stand the chill. Then I'd stumble inside for a few hours of fitful sleep before returning to my silent page-turning vigil out back.

Finally, I woke one morning and gave Elvis a long proper walk around the neighborhood. Then I showered and stepped into a clean pair of clothes. I found myself limping the three blocks north to Gramercy Park.

She wasn't too happy to see me. There was the threat of a scene when Raymond the doorman refused to let me up. When I offered to call the cops for them, they reconsidered, and I was permitted to board the elevator. Now Margaret McKay stood in her doorway like a mummified Cleopatra. All the work she'd had done stood out in relief against a suddenly elderly face. Her dark eyes looked out at me from some lost place beyond the living. She steadied herself with an aged hand against the doorframe. The other clutched at a large emerald stone hanging from her neck. She wore a simple black dress that hung over a skeletal frame. Her feet were bare, her toes unpainted.

"May I come in?" I asked.

"If you must," said Margaret. She turned and walked back down the hall of the darkened apartment. I followed.

The place held its breath in mourning. The curtains were drawn. The only light in the room came from an antique lamp on a small table beside a leather club chair. A Durrell novel was folded open under the light, next to a half-empty glass of white wine. Margaret lifted the glass, drained it, and moved deeper into the shadows of the living room.

I heard her sigh out of the darkness. "Would you like a drink?" she asked.

"No, thanks."

She raised an eyebrow and padded off toward the kitchen. I heard the refrigerator door open, a bottle being removed, a glass refilled. I sat down in her chair and examined her reading material. It was Durrell's *Clea*, the last of the Alexandria Quartet. I turned to the beginning and found a quote from the Marquis de Sade. Something about "the perpetual consequence of crimes." She returned with her wine before I could turn to the first page.

"I hope you didn't lose my place," she said.

I had. I closed the book and set it back down under the light. "Sorry about that."

"No, you're not."

I watched her drink. I considered ending my experiment with abstinence. It would be a fitting setting to return to the sauce. No higher power could deny that.

"I'm sorry," I said. "About how everything . . ."

"She's missing," said Margaret. "Again."

"Madeline?"

She nodded, her grip tight around the slim glass. "She left her room at New York Presbyterian, where she was undergoing psychiatric care."

"How long ago?"

"A few weeks. It seemed she was making progress."

"And no word from her since?"

"None," she said. "She emptied her account this time."

"Jesus."

"Lawrence, I hope you won't be offended if I don't enlist your services once more."

"Don't think I'd be up to the challenge even if you asked."

Margaret took a long drink. I watched the wine slide down her slim, creased throat. Then she brought it down and frowned into the remains. Her body was dying before me, her spirit dead already. She straightened her spine, rolled back her shoulders, but it was no use. Despite the continued beating of her heart, she had already crossed over. I wanted to go to her and wrap her lifeless figure in my arms. She was a wealthy woman with an Olympic champion for a son and a talented, beautiful daughter. Where had it all gone wrong? From the beginning, I supposed. She'd married the wrong man. Then he died young, and she sent her children to another wrong man, one who couldn't keep his hands off of the not-yet-women he coached. And she had produced the smartest and most talented man of all. A force of nature that took what he wanted, set monstrous goals, and achieved them all. A monster he was, a sick man beneath the surface. A man who'd turned his sickness on the closest innocent he could find. Poor Madeline, she never had a chance.

"Charlie," I said. "Did you ever suspect?"

Her body didn't react. She sipped at her glass.

"Lawrence, I have been blind to many things in my life. Perhaps it is my greatest strength, the ability to ignore the darkness in men and continue living. I knew about Teddy's history, as I told you. And I knew about my late husband's activities, before him. But there is some darkness that is impossible to see through."

Margaret turned her back to me and returned to the shadows of the dark room. A thin streak of light snuck through the high curtains and caught her pale skin as she moved past.

"I think you should go," she said.

I turned to leave. Down the hall, framed photos of Charlie in Olympic triumph still hung on the walls. I stopped in front of one; he stood on top of a podium, hand over his heart, eyes damp. I could almost hear the national anthem as it played in his honor. The peak of any life. Before it all started, when his sister was still an innocent little girl, their father newly dead. The resemblance to Madeline leapt out at me, in their wide mouths and high, sculpted cheeks. I had to look away.

Epilogue

In the months that followed, the media requests poured in, as did the job offers. My well-publicized dealings with death shot me to the top of the Google results anytime someone searched for "private investigator NYC." I guess they equated front-page experience with competence. Never mind the PTSD or my tenuous sobriety. Never mind that I wasn't even licensed. I turned them all down, every job, every eager news outlet desperate to hear my story.

Instead I took Elvis on long, limping walks and read book after book, the bleaker the better. I grew out a beard to cover the scars. Cass called to say she'd decided to extend her stay at the Buddhist retreat upstate. She suggested I join her. I told her that wasn't happening. Like Madeline, I seemed to have developed a phobia of travel, of leaving the unsafe confines of the city. I needed the people and the perpetual light around me at all times. The thought of a dark, empty night in the country filled me with a dread I was in no rush to address.

I stayed out of work through the new year, living off credit cards, until a case arrived that suited my comfort zone. It was a painless gig covering a painful divorce. My specialty. There were no personal ties to complicate matters, no reminders of a past I'd rather forget. Just a rich cheating husband and a sad-eyed wife named Jamie who'd had enough. I followed him for a few days. It didn't take long. His wife really could have done it herself. Every Tuesday and Thursday he would go to the Standard for lunch, and after his Cobb salad he would walk a few blocks west to the Liberty Motel. A few minutes later, the cocktail waitress from the hotel bar would take her lunch break and meet him there. She was a leggy young blonde who was clearly in thrall with the illicit thrill. He was a swarthy, sporty Italian who didn't take much precaution, the sort who could compartmentalize and shrug off the simple sins. I took the necessary pictures and brought them to Jamie with all due sympathy. Then I succumbed to a revenge romp with her in their marital bed. It didn't make either of us feel much better, but her payment helped me replace the furniture in my empty living room.

The winter was a brutal one in the city, crushing the spirits of its citizens with stretches of single-digit temperatures and heavy wet snow. I found myself hibernating inside my lightless apartment. Elvis and I began to grow fat together, thickening with our sedentary lifestyle.

One blue Tuesday morning, on a rare excursion outdoors, I resolved to go for a swim. Somehow I'd managed to stay sober for months, but I could feel my body decaying from lack of movement and constant food delivery. A hard wind was blowing down Third Avenue in mean gusts. I leaned in and let it bite my face. As I turned onto 14th Street and approached the Palladium, I could smell the chlorine wafting up from the basement pool. The scent filled me with an unexpected joy. I felt myself smiling as I pushed through the doors and flashed my ID and went down into the hot chemical air.

I found an empty lane and relished the shock as my body broke the surface. Then I swam without stopping for an hour or so. Flipping at every wall, making slow, unhurried progress up and back, lap after lap. I thought of Madeline McKay, I thought of her brother, of our coach, of our parents. All of us united by this isolated movement through the clear waters of a swimming pool.

When I returned home with wet hair frosted, brittle from the wind, I collected the mail and began to sift through the junk. I almost missed it. It was a small postcard with a photo of a bronze statue, a melancholy woman seated on a bench in some seaside town. It was postmarked from Brazil. On the back of the card, there were two words scribbled in red ink. It read: "Thank you." It was signed "MM."

I looked at her writing for a long time. Then I turned over the postcard and looked at that bronze woman for even longer. I wondered if her mother had heard from her, wondered if I had some responsibility to pass along her whereabouts. I decided I didn't. She'd overcome her fear of leaving this urban prison, and at some point she'd boarded a plane for a place of endless sun and no memory.

I tore the card into tiny pieces, and then I went to the bathroom and dropped the remnants into the bowl and watched the ink and the image dissolve in the water. Then I flushed it all away.

She knew the way home.

ACKNOWLEDGMENTS

Some thank yous are in order . . . There are too many to list, so we'll leave it to the essentials, along with some collective bows. You know who you are.

First, the man who said *yes, this is worthy*, but only after requesting four or five rewrites before he officially agreed to be my Agent. (This might have been annoying if not for the fact that his insights were always right.) Alec Shane, of Writers House: Thank you. My debt is immense.

Next, to my first Editor, Peter Senftleben–the one who said: *Yes, I want to publish this*. The day before Thanksgiving, 2015, in Venice Beach, CA, when the email arrived . . . I won't forget that moment.

To my Editor, Esi Sogah, who inherited my manuscript, and to everyone at Kensington Books: From the moment I met Esi, and from the first drinks I raised with the Kensington crew in New Orleans at Bouchercon, I've felt at home and grateful to be a part of a publishing team that truly treats their writers as family.

To my parents and sisters, to bruder Lars and all of Imagine, to my friends and first readers: Thank you. Writing fiction seems to be a form of socially accepted insanity. Being close to the mad folk who need to do this is not always pleasant. My love and gratitude for putting up with me . . .

And finally, to my wife Teri and my daughter Eva – you are everything. I love you.

Keep an eye out
For
More Duck Darley mysteries
Coming soon from
Casey Barrett
and
Kensington Books